sMOTHERING

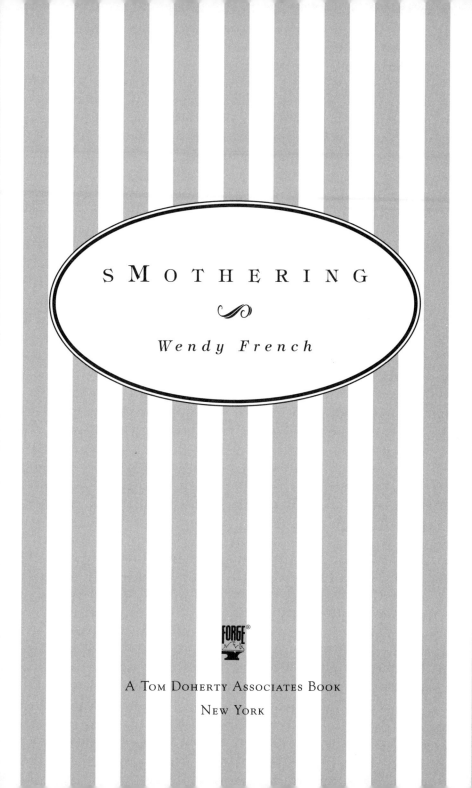

sMOTHERING

Wendy French

FORGE®

A TOM DOHERTY ASSOCIATES BOOK

NEW YORK

SMOTHERING

Copyright © 2003 by Wendy French

Book design by Michael Collica

A Forge Book
Published by Tom Doherty Associates, LLC
175 Fifth Avenue
New York, NY 10010

www.tor.com

Forge® is a registered trademark of Tom Doherty Associates, LLC.

Library of Congress Cataloging-in-Publication Data

French, Wendy.
    sMothering / Wendy French.— 1st ed.
        p.   cm.
    "A Tom Doherty Associates book."
    ISBN 0-765-30793-6 (acid-free paper)
        1. Parent and adult child—Fiction.   2. Mothers and daughters—Fiction.
    3. Portland (Or.)—Fiction.   4. Young women—Fiction.   I. Title.

PS3606.R468S66   2003
813'.6—dc21
                                                              2003046857

First Edition: November 2003

Printed in the United States of America

0   9   8   7   6   5   4   3   2   1

❧

For my parents, Stuart and Sally McDonald. Dad, the funniest person I know, and Mum, who laughs until she cries.

And for my husband, Dave "Shouldn't you be writing?" French, who suggested I try and kept cheering me on.

ACKNOWLEDGMENTS

I am tremendously grateful to my agent and Kiwi confidante, Sally Harding, who always knows just what to say, and Robert Mackwood for taking a chance on me. Also, to Megan Abbott for pointing me in the right direction.

I'd like to express my gratitude to my editor, Natalia Aponte, and her assistant, Paul Stevens, who pulled me from the pile and got the ball rolling. Also to Karen Richardson, and all of the kind folks at Tor/Forge.

Special thanks to Jack Hodgins and Lorna Crozier, wonderful professors at the University of Victoria. And to the ladies of Mt. Hood: Linda Kearney, Deanie Barbour, Kelly Hale, Anne Schmidt, and Diane Terhune.

Huge thanks to Mike Hipple for being so generous with his time and his camera and Ryan Griffiths for his super-tech Web wizardry and years of friendship.

For ongoing support and encouragement, I'd like to thank dear friends and family members: Kate Rappe, Tamarah Robinson, Lisa Haas, Ian McDonald, Katja Solomon, Rosemary and John Tincombe, Sandy French, Peggy Campbell, Nick Thomas, Megan Olesky, Dave Sorley, Emily Tubb, Fran Hodgkins, Cheryl Warwick, and the CAS department at NW Natural for the cube-farm camaraderie.

sMOTHERING

ONE

My mother sang the national anthem like she really meant it, but her voice was the only thing she didn't try to save. Margarine containers and twist ties filled her kitchen drawers, while collections of elastic bands on every doorknob were dangling testaments to her recycling abilities. Her used tissues, crumpled and shoved into pockets and sweater sleeves, multiplied almost as quickly as the number of artificial sweetener packets she stole from restaurants and deposited in her purse, awaiting the great saccharine shortage of the new millennium.

She used color-coded, dated labels on the mountains of leftovers crammed into her deep freeze: a quarter cup grated carrots. Two cups split-pea soup. One piece lasagna. The only tag-free item was a tier of her wedding cake. It was wrapped in foil and tucked in the bottom left corner, awaiting what opportune moment and which unfortunate guests? Did she think antique carrot cake would come in handy? Would she serve twenty-six-year-old marzipan in a pinch?

I could only hope that other mothers were like her, a combination of idiosyncrasies and careful manners, wrapped in a department store wardrobe of navy, black, and gray. Sensible shoes and pearl earrings. Restless hands and perennial hiccups.

I hoped that every mother was a knit-purl-knit-purl kind of woman, producing countless stitches of tiny sweater sleeves and collars for her nonexistent grandchildren, *just in case.*

I looked past her annoying habits with the practiced disdain of a twenty-three-year-old daughter; a roll of the eyes or an ambivalent shrug performed on cue. I looked past the feminine hygiene products cushioning the cardboard walls of her care packages, and the spontaneous long-distance etiquette lessons, which usually took place on my dime. I could even look past her cheerful insistence that anything could be fixed with a strand of dental floss or a piece of slightly chewed gum and a little ingenuity.

What I couldn't look past was her presence in my doorway at seven-thirty on a Thursday morning, suitcase in hand.

"Mom, what are you doing here?" I asked, aiming for a tone of pleasant surprise and missing the mark entirely.

"Claire," she murmured, dropping her Samsonite on the hallway floor with the unmistakable thud of impending doom.

She reached for me and I entered her embrace, immediately enveloped by the faint scent of rose water, which she'd worn since my memories began. Her familiar blue raincoat pressed against my T-shirt and flannel pajama bottoms, soaking me with the realization that she was no hallucination. She was bulkier than she'd been when I visited Omaha the previous spring, no surprise, considering recent letters had revolved around middle-age spread and varicose veins, rather than who was marrying, divorcing, and cheating on whom in my hometown.

"Aren't you going to invite me in?" she asked, releasing her grip and peering past me into the sloppy center of the one-bedroom apartment she'd never seen.

"Oh, right. Of course. Come on in," I said, glancing expectantly down the hallway and seeing only mottled beige carpeting and a shiny piece of what I hoped was a Top Ramen seasoning pouch. Painfully aware of apartment forty-one's active social life, however, I could almost guarantee it was a hastily discarded condom wrapper, a fitting welcome mat for his ever-revolving front door, but a definite turnoff for a sudden parental visit.

"Where's Dad?" I asked.

"At home." Her tone was matter-of-fact, as though the news weren't enough to bring me to my knees. "This is much smaller than I expected." She stepped across the threshold of number forty-three and onto my unswept, uneven wood floors. "Not that it's too small," she quickly added. "It's very compact. Very *cozy*."

Dad was still in Omaha? Who would protect me?

"Why didn't he come?" I rubbed my arms as a shiver that had nothing to do with my dampened clothing ran through me.

"He's working on some house projects. He couldn't get away."

What kind of projects would prevent a trip to his favorite city?

I glanced at Mom's solitary bag and was almost swept away by a sudden wave of giddiness. One bag wouldn't hold much more than two Weekender outfits. Maybe she'd only be in town for a couple of days!

Before my racing heart had a chance to sprint, a grim reality sunk in. Omaha to Portland was no weekend jaunt, and though her luggage normally traveled in packs, one bag of her mix-and-match wardrobe could stretch beyond ordinary limits to a week's worth of clothing. *Minimum.*

"How long are you in town for?" My voice was surprisingly even.

"I'm not sure." She lifted her shoulders in an absent shrug.

Her hair was more gray than chestnut, and her trademark braid was coming undone. The flush of her cheeks highlighted her girlish freckles, while dark brown eyes gazed past me as she looked directly into my bedroom.

Dear God, no.

"Where are you, uh, staying?" I stammered, crossing suddenly shaking fingers behind my back.

"If it's all right with you, I thought I'd camp out here." She gave me a sorely misplaced smile of camaraderie. "Just us girls."

If it was all right with me? How was I supposed to say no? To hear her tell it, delivering me into the world had taken more time than most people spend on postgraduate degrees, and the reward of a screaming blue infant hadn't been quite substantial enough to warrant the effort. As far as she was concerned, I *owed* her. Of course, I wasn't her only offspring, and buried in that fact was a small seed of hope. There was an opportunity to unload her on an unsuspecting sibling, and I wasn't about to pass it up.

"What about Stephanie?" I asked. "She's dying for you to see her new place."

It wasn't entirely true, but my sister did have ample room to spare for matronly nesting. Never mind that she had always been the preferred child of the McLeod family, living up to her girlish and glittery name in every possible way while I mastered the supporting role of "disappointment." Only a year separated us, but that year might as well have been a decade.

Steph was tall and slender from day one, with a sunny disposition balanced by rather stunning intelligence. Her strawberry blonde hair was a gift from our dad's end of the gene pool and it had been her crowning glory for her turns as cheerleader, debate team captain, and star of ambitiously overacted high school music theater productions.

While Stephanie basked in her polysyllables and soft consonants, I consistently managed to fulfill all of the duties and obligations of a name like Claire. I was Claire of the nondescript brown ponytail and combination skin. Claire of second-to-last chosen for any and every recess game. A nose-picking, scabby-kneed, reigning queen of anonymity, if anyone had taken the time to notice. Those six fateful letters on my birth certificate condemned me to a life of plantar warts and lackluster grades, wide hips and the inevitable dowager's hump I was certain would spring overnight from a suspicious mole at the center of my back.

Steph was the star while I played a pale and featureless moon in the McLeod family, and I'd thought it would stay that way forever. Of course, that was before my beloved sister dropped the bomb.

"She's not still living with that woman, is she?" Mom asked, her lower lip drawn almost magnetically toward her chin in an abrupt frown.

"Alison?" I prompted. "Yes, she is. They've been together two years, Mom."

My sister's girlfriend had taken a little getting used to. Physically, she was about as different from Steph as, well, as *I* was. After one brief encounter, a coworker of mine dubbed her the ugly dyke-ling, which I resented but never corrected. At times, it seemed weakness was my strongest trait.

I'd known Alison and I weren't on the same page the first time we spoke on the phone (I'd told her I was Steph's sister and she said, "So am I," unaware that I was a blood relative and not a fellow club member), but I'd eventually fallen in like with her. Steph had never been happier and, regrettably, I'd never noticed anything missing from her seemingly stellar life until Alison filled what must have been a substantial void. For that, I could only support their relationship.

"You know, I still hear from Marco," Mom said quietly.

I always had to bite back a "polo" when I heard my former brother-in-law's name.

"How is he?"

"Lonely. He wants her back." She smiled sadly.

Researching methods to increase his low sperm count had been a pet project of Mom's during the fourteen-month marriage, not that she was one to butt in or anything.

"I heard he got married again."

"Rebound," she snapped. "I don't give it a year."

"So, are you going to see Steph or not?"

"I don't think so," she said, biting her bottom lip.

"She's your daughter, Mom. Who cares if she's gay?"

"She isn't gay." Her gaze left mine as she crossed the room to brush dust from the coffee table with her fingertips.

"Uh, yes, she is."

Mom had been horrified when Steph came out of the closet, and was apparently willing to wait as long as necessary for her to crawl back in. I even imagined her straightening coat hangers and donating outdated clothing to Goodwill in an effort to create a more spacious and welcoming environment for her errant daughter.

"You tell your sister that when she snaps out of this nonsense I'll come see her house."

"Snaps out of it? Mom, it's *genetic*."

"Don't be ridiculous." Her hands swept the tabletop erratically. "It's a phase she's going through. She's having a hard time right now, but it will pass. *Genetic*." She shook her head in disbelief. "Your father and I aren't lesbians, are we? Are you trying to tell me the whole McLeod family is just a big bunch of gays?"

"Maybe we should drop it," I suggested, knowing from vast experience and multiple migraines that we wouldn't get anywhere.

"Maybe we should," Mom murmured as she took off her raincoat and hung it on my brass coatrack, a seven-dollar bargain from an east-side garage sale. It rocked back and forth precariously for a moment, apparently as uncertain about welcoming her as I was, before settling on all four legs.

I watched Mom absorb the details of her surroundings; the bent slats of the venetian blinds covering my only window and saving me from a peeling-billboard view. The wilting fern on the sill, under- or over-watered, I was never quite sure. The small dining table, covered with old magazines and ringed stains, a cracked sugar bowl and a collection of unpaid bills. Discarded sweaters, jackets, and miscellaneous tote bags hanging on the backs of my mismatched chairs. I'd been planning to sand and paint them for almost two years, a project I could still get excited about for six to seven minutes at a time before abandoning it in favor of a *Full House* rerun or an undeserved nap.

I could almost feel her cringe at the cobwebs in the corners of the ceiling and wished I'd had the foresight to knock them down with a broom. As I glanced past her and into the kitchen, I noted dirty dishes filling the sink and countertops piled with fast food wrappers before quickly turning away. I tried to look through her eyes at the crushed throw pillows on my brand-new, yet terminally used, couch and the overpopulated ashtray next to the remote control. I'd quit smoking three months earlier and somehow forgotten to empty it.

"If I'd known you were coming . . ." I began.

"It would have looked very much the same," Mom finished with a short laugh. "I know what your bedroom used to look like, dear. Now you just have more room to spread it around."

Dad probably wouldn't have noticed the faint odor of cat urine I'd inherited from the previous tenants, but Mom's nose wrinkled with distaste.

"I like your, er . . . display," she offered, pointing toward my metal lunch box collection.

"Uh, thanks." I scratched my lower back and tried another approach to a prickly topic. "So, you don't know how long you're staying?"

"I've got all the time in the world." She perched uneasily on a corner of the couch, as though it were the lap of a perverted uncle.

"Great," I managed, through gritted teeth. I didn't want to panic, but if we were going to spend any length of time together, with no supervision, it was quite likely that one or both of us would require medication.

"Do you have any juice?" Mom asked.

"Sorry, no." Hell, I didn't even have toilet paper.

"What about tea?"

"I haven't been to the grocery store lately." I smiled wanly.

"What on earth do you drink around here?" she asked, toying with her watch strap.

"I usually grab a coffee on the way. . . ."

"It would be cheaper to make it here, Claire."

"Thanks for the tip."

"You don't have to take that tone with me."

"I'm sorry, you've just caught me kind of off-guard this morning." The understatement Olympics were beckoning.

"Why don't we have some breakfast? The food on my flight was horrid, and you look like you could use a good meal."

She squinted at me. "Has your skin always looked this sallow? I know you were a rather yellow child, but . . . well, never mind that now." She stood and dusted off her backside, making no attempt to disguise the effort. "What shall I make for breakfast?"

"Oh, God. What time is it?"

"Seven thirty-five."

"Shit! I've got to get ready for work!"

"Language, Claire," she warned, as I turned away.

I ran into my bedroom, cursing her under my breath. What kind of lunatic would "drop in" from halfway across the country? What kind of imbecile was I to let her in the front door?

Shaking my head, I pulled a pair of dirty jeans from the laundry hamper, relieved that, for once, I didn't have to worry about my wardrobe.

Casual Day was supposed to be the great equalizer at Alta Media, and while I wasn't sure how Neal came to the conclusion that denim was the key to a united staff, he'd had enough stupid ideas in the past two months to stop me from asking questions. Like the stained Levi's I slipped on to show I was a team player, Neal's master plan was bound to be full of wrinkles.

I found a reasonably clean red and white gingham blouse and a pair of oxfords, not exactly high fashion, but undeniably casual. I brushed my hair with a few savage strokes and briefly wondered why Dad hadn't joined Mom on her trip. Of course, it was possible that he'd suggested she take a vacation without him, but he loved Portland and made wistful plans to visit every time we spoke. He could have spent hours in Powell's Books, walked the riverfront, or saved his youngest daughter from a spiraling descent into hell.

Where was he?

Maybe Mom had literally nagged him to death and left him in his recliner with the hope that the paperboy or mailman would stumble across him and notify the authorities. Maybe the last words he heard were "Are you listening to me, Robert?" It was an unlikely scenario, but I couldn't rule it out entirely.

I checked my image in the mirror and smeared a perfumed magazine insert across my neck and wrists before applying eyeliner above and below my not-quite-hazel-but-a-far-cry-from-green eyes. Good enough.

I glanced at my watch and groaned.

"You're not wearing *that* to work, are you?" Mom asked when I met up with her in the kitchen. A grungy dish towel was tucked into the waistband of her pants and she was already busy unloading dead perishables from my refrigerator and stacking them in a pile on the counter.

"It's Casual Day." I shrugged.

"Apparently."

"Listen, Mom. Could you try *not* to clean while I'm gone?" I asked. Less than fifteen minutes with her and I was ready to scream.

"I'm just getting rid of some of this rotten stuff." She paused before continuing, "Or did you want to keep it?"

"No." I bit my tongue. Barely.

"If you'd just put an open box of baking soda in here . . ." she murmured, digging further into the depths of the crisper for surprisingly limp produce. "You've got some eggs. Do you want me to make you an omelet?"

"No, thanks. I don't have time." Considering how long they'd been in there, I was surprised I didn't have chickens.

"Well, what are you going to eat?"

"I'll pick up a bagel on my way to work."

"Pick up a bagel," she scoffed. "You have time for breakfast. Now sit down and I'll whip something up."

"I can't. I'll be late."

"So, be late. I'll call them, or write you a note."

"This isn't junior high, Mom. Besides, I'm on probation."

She lost her grip on a mushy tomato, which splattered on the floor in a pulpy mess. "Probation?" she gasped, reaching for the general area of her heart.

For crying out loud.

"No, no. Not that kind. Probation at work. I've been late too many times."

"Don't you use an alarm clock?"

"What kind of a question is that?" Did she think I relied on some kind of internal, biological timepiece?

"You should set it at least half an hour earlier. Then you'd have time for breakfast and . . . er, *personal grooming.*"

"Thank you."

"So, you're on probation." She planted her hands on her hips. "And if you're late again, what would they do?"

"Geez, I don't know. Neal might throw a temper tantrum, maybe lie down and beat his little fists and feet against the floor." I wouldn't put it past him.

"Who's Neal?"

"That miniature Mussolini Gord hired to take over the office."

"Short men have tall problems." Mom shook her head. "So, you can't even stay for a piece of toast?"

"No bread, no toaster, no time."

"If you say so."

Her trademark sigh sparked an almost allergic reaction and I took a deep breath before speaking.

"When I get home, we'll have some dinner and you can fill

me in on all the gossip from home. Like why Dad was willing to let you run footloose and fancy-free across the country."

"What time will you be back?"

Suddenly, I was fourteen years old again. I half expected a reminder to wear my retainer.

"Just after five. There's a grocery store about two blocks from here if you need anything. Just make yourself at home."

"I have some knitting to do." She pointed at the needles sticking out of her purse.

I'll bet. Since Steph was out of the heterosexual loop, the weight of prospective grandchildren lay on my rounded shoulders. No pressure, of course.

I grabbed my bag and walked toward the door.

"Claire?" Her voice was tentative and I turned toward her, hoping she wasn't going to open some menopausal floodgate. I didn't have time to deal with it.

"Yes?" I asked.

"Have you considered a perm?"

"No." So much for emotional breakthroughs.

"It might give your hair a touch more body. Not that it looks bad, but . . ." Her hands gestured vaguely around her head.

I took the high road and ignored her.

"So, I'll see you around five. Like I said, just make yourself at home. There's a spare key in the freezer." The same place she hid her own.

She offered me a little wave. "Have a nice day, dear."

I stepped out of the apartment and breathed a sigh of despair before heading for the stairs.

That was when it hit me.

Had I just given my mother license to rifle through my belongings? What if she found the petrified condoms in my underwear drawer? Of course, her visit wouldn't affect my sex

life, which had been flatlining for half a year; but she didn't
need to *know* that. What if she came across the satin leopard-
print G-string I'd "won" at a bachelorette party, or stumbled
upon my bank statement? Privacy was officially beyond my
control. By five o'clock she would have inspected, perused,
and peeled away the layers of my life like an onion; no detail
too personal, no observation too humiliating. In mere hours I
would be as emotionally naked and vulnerable as the day I
was born.

Casual Day, my ass.

TWO

Before my feet even hit the pavement in front of my building, I knew I had no time to spare for a mocha latte or cheese bagel.

It was barely sprinkling, the air misted with the kind of rain I would have considered refreshing had I remembered my umbrella or coat. I ran toward the bus stop, a threadbare satchel slapping against my thigh with every step.

The flaming hues of autumn leaves were a blur as I dodged past strolling businessmen, who sidestepped puddles with annoying efficiency, and thick clusters of schoolchildren, bogged down by backpacks and bag lunches. No one moved quickly enough for my liking, and by the time I reached the peeling paint of my bus stop bench, a cloud of noxious fumes was all that remained of my ride.

Damn.

My next bus wasn't due for half an hour, so I opted for an alternate route. After only three transfers and six additional blocks of speed-walking, I made it to work, breathless and agitated.

All things considered, half an hour late wasn't as bad as it could have been. Hell, losing and finally locating my keys in the depths of my couch had cost me nearly an hour in the past.

I waited impatiently for an elevator, wishing I had the energy or inclination to climb eleven flights of stairs, and, once I'd climbed aboard, checked my watch three more times on the way up.

"You're late," Carol, our resident vegan sang from behind her desk as I crossed the reception area.

The thick-framed, nonprescription glasses perched on her nose were only slightly less pretentious than her vast collection of faux fur vests and pleather jackets, ultrasuede shoes and vinyl pants. Only the bitchiness was bonafide.

"Half an hour late," she said, eyeing her chunky metallic watch and reaching past the bowl of diced tofu on the corner of her desk to grab a roll of Lifesavers.

She'd patronized me since my first day on the job and, two years later, showed no sign of letting up.

"I'm aware," I told her.

"So's Neal," she smirked, slipping a butter-rum candy past crimson lips.

"What did he say?"

"Nothing. He left a memo on your desk." She turned up her radio in an obvious effort to tune me out, as though the pitter-pat of a drum machine and muted synthesizer chords would do the trick.

"Fine," I snapped. "Thanks for your help." I spun on one heel and headed into the main office.

"Oh, Claire?" She called after me. "I forgot to mention, your mother phoned."

Already?

"She wanted to know where you keep the vacuum." Carol tapped one acrylic fingernail against the base of her memo holder, slightly off the beat. After four years in a marching band, it was enough to make me twitch. I reached for the note, groaning inwardly. Hadn't I specifically told her *not* to clean?

"Thank"—

"Then she called to tell you not to worry, she found a broom and could probably make do." She smiled sadistically and lifted another pink slip from her pile.

"Great, now I've got to—" I began, backing toward the door.

"Five minutes later she wanted to know where the laundry room was and whether the machines were coin operated, because she wanted to take care of, and I quote, 'that mound of dirty clothes' behind your bedroom door."

"Thank you." I gritted my teeth.

"Have you considered a laundry hamper? I hear they're the latest rage."

"I appreciate the tip."

"No problem." She paused. "Oh, here's another one . . ."

My mother, my nightmare.

"Thanks, Carol." I snatched the last memo before she could broadcast it and stalked into the office.

The majority of Alta Media's staff worked in a warehouse setting of cubicles and fake plants, fluorescent lighting and cheaply framed art prints that would be raffled off at the annual Christmas party to make room for new cheaply framed art prints. Our carpeted cube walls were set in a mazelike configuration that I could probably walk blindfolded without faltering, and housed the standard corporate fare of ergonomic chairs, telephones, headsets, computer terminals, and a population of disenchanted employees who had somehow been sucked into the telemarketing vortex.

As I waded through the sounds of rustling papers and

revoltingly cheerful voices surrounding my desk, I considered, for the umpteenth time, that I wasn't sure how I'd ended up there.

Telemarketing, for crying out loud. I was a telephone marketing representative.

A theory I'd developed in recent years noted the correlation between job satisfaction and the number of words in a title. One-word careers like lawyer, doctor, and actor were obviously desirable, whereas customer service representatives, insurance claims processors, and short-order cooks were living in their own private yet very public hells. I knew exactly where I fit into the spectrum, and was justifiably disappointed. (Of course, proctologist was a one-word title, but no theory was foolproof.)

"Floor meeting in five minutes," Jason, one third of my cube cluster, murmured as he brushed past me in a pair of faded Levi's and a flannel shirt.

I tucked my satchel in the bottom drawer of my desk, rather than hanging it on the back of my perfectly adjusted chair. Glancing around the bustling office, I saw almost enough denim to convince me I was either at a rodeo or back in high school.

It was immediately apparent that casual attire did not suit everyone.

I compared the snug fit of Anna's symmetrically torn jeans to Rob's baggy, barely-hanging-on-to-the-curve-of-his-ass dungarees, Jen's asexual overalls, and Daniel's pathetic acid-wash flashback. My coworkers looked like an entirely different staff, far from the tucked, pressed, and polished crowd I was accustomed to. It kind of gave me the creeps.

I peered from one end of the room to the other in search

of the one body I wanted to view dressed down, or undressed, for that matter, but Adam Carello was nowhere to be seen.

"Neal scheduled a meeting for nine-thirty." Heather, the final third of my cluster, handed me a steaming cup of coffee clouded with cream.

"So I heard." I stirred the liquid with the tail end of a ball-point pen and groaned at the thought of a Neal-a-thon.

"Rough morning?" she asked, scratching a patch of eczema on the back of her hand. If she'd left it alone, it would have disappeared months earlier.

"Beyond rough," I nodded, rolling my eyes. "My mother's in town."

"You didn't tell me she was visiting," Heather whined.

She seemed to think that because we shared the occasional lunch break, she was privy to everything that went on in my life. She was fine to work with, and I didn't dislike her as intensely as most of the staff did, but sometimes she was as irritating as her skin problem.

"I didn't know she was coming," I explained. "It's a surprise, like a swarm of locusts." Locusts with phone privileges. "I'll see you in there, Heather. I've got to make a call."

Hopefully Dad would know how long she planned to stay in town. Surely, in his new supertech state, he'd planned the trip online for her.

"See you in the conference room," Heather called after me as I raced toward the reception area. "I'll save you a seat."

"Whatever," I muttered, checking my watch. I had only a minute or two to call home before the meeting, and while I could have waited until it was over, I couldn't handle another batch of Mom's phone messages. I'd deal with her as soon as I had a clearer idea of what was going on in Omaha.

"Carol, to make a long-distance call from here, do I have to dial a special prefix or anything?"

The grand dame of reception dusted face powder across her forehead and closed her compact, before glaring at me. "Who are you calling?"

"My dad." Not that it was any of her business.

"Is it a personal call?"

"No. I'm going to run him through the toothpaste survey." I let the sarcasm fill the air between us.

"No need to get frosty," she sniffed.

"Is there a prefix?"

"No, just dial straight out." She paused. "Neal won't like it."

"He doesn't need to know." I hoped my words came across as the thinly veiled threat they were.

I raced back to my desk as the denim horde filed into the conference room. The phone in Omaha rang eleven times with no answer and I slammed the receiver down, annoyed that my parents weren't using the answering machine I gave them for Christmas.

Glancing back at the pile of papers filling my In box, I sighed when I saw a familiar gray sheet. Neal Godd, my nine-to-five nemesis, had left me a tardiness memo, written on his personal stationary. It was bad enough that his long-winded e-mails flooded the office with unnecessary or redundant information on a daily basis, but the handwritten messages were even worse. Memos like "thumbs-up on the airline survey" or "let's get rolling on that chocolate campaign" were not only patronizing, but juvenile.

Unfortunately, the most annoying aspect of Neal Godd's memos wasn't their vapid content or punchy lingo, but the paper they were written on, or more specifically, the silver embossed heading on each page that read "The Word Of Godd."

In addition to being a thorn in the side of every employee on the floor, he also held a master's in arrogance.

"Claire!" His nasal voice called from the doorway of the conference room. "We're trying to start a meeting here." He tapped the face of his watch with a stubby fingertip I was sure spent more time up his right nostril than anywhere else.

I grabbed a notepad and entered the crowded room, spotting Heather, who shrugged apologetically at her failure to save me a seat. I leaned against the back wall and prayed Neal would be faster than usual.

As always, our fearless leader had placed several pie charts and bar graphs against the chalkboard at the front of the room, the point of which would never be addressed. He stood in front of the assembled group of about forty and began a lecture on guerrilla phone tactics.

I hit my internal mute button and ignored his point-by-point delivery in favor of admiring his outfit. I hadn't expected Neal to participate in Casual Day, and by the look of his starched golf shirt and the department store creases in his brand-new jeans, I wasn't sure he should have. He was the type of man who tried to overcome his short stature with a combination of loud speech and louder clothing. He looked more natural in the flashy ties and excessive gold jewelry he usually sported, rather than the beige checked shirt he was wearing in an effort to be one of the gang. I supposed he wanted to look like a golf pro, but the result was closer to a club-dragging caddy.

"And your main goal right out of the gate is what, Kevin?" he barked.

"Politeness," Neal's favorite mouthpiece answered.

"No." Neal made a loud buzzing noise in the back of his throat, like some kind of no-budget game show host. "Anyone else?"

"Efficiency." Adam Carello's voice came from the far corner of the room. From what I could see, the object of my long-distance desire was looking delicious in a red hooded sweatshirt. There was nothing like a goody in a hoody. I'd have to wait until after the meeting to see how he filled out the rest of his casual wear, and I looked forward to the opportunity.

"Exactly," Neal nodded. "Efficiency. Thank you, Adam. We want that first few minutes to be a meet-and-greet, like old friends at the country club or cousins at a family reunion. We're talking instant bond here, people."

If I'd ever dared to approach family or friends with the kind of cheesy familiarity Neal was suggesting, they'd have told me to fuck off. To think that a smarmy tone was going to work on complete strangers over the phone was downright delusional.

"Should we ask them how they're doing?" one of the new trainees asked.

"Do we *care* how they're doing?" Neal snapped. "No. Time is money, folks." He rubbed his palms together like the greedy little bastard he was. Where on earth had Gord found him, and why was he being inflicted on us? "We have to handle the warm-up in under twenty seconds, then it's on to the task at hand. Keep it friendly, of course, like you're talking to your grandmother. But fast, like Grandma's terminally ill and a quick run through our survey will score her a spot in heaven or wherever. Now, we've only got one more week on this toothpaste project—"

"Toothpaste seems too personal," Courtney whined.

"Nothing is too personal." Neal punctuated his words with

a sharp, karate-chop movement. "You just tell those clowns on the other end of the line that manufacturers are counting on them, their fellow consumers are counting on them. Hell, you might as well let them think the whole country is hanging on their every word. Their opinions are going to change the faces of toilet paper, fast food, and bank loans."

I'd heard it all before. Weekly.

As he lectured and interrogated my coworkers like an overzealous evangelist trying to convert the reluctant masses, I imagined the havoc Mom was wreaking on my apartment. She was probably herding the dust bunnies out from under my, well, *everything,* and I suspected my fridge would contain nothing more than the suggested open box of baking soda by the time I got home. I hoped she wouldn't read the personal mail I'd stacked on my bedside table, or rifle through my unpaid bills, but I wouldn't put it past her.

Shivering at the thought, I tried to concentrate on the meeting.

"What if we can't get through to the person on our list?" the new trainee asked. Someone was going to have to tell her to put a sock in it.

"I always ask for them by their first name only," Courtney said. "That way whoever answers thinks it's a personal call."

"Good point." Neal nodded. "Don't ask for Mr. or Mrs. So-and-so or you'll never get through. You've got to come off like a family friend. Same point I made earlier."

He nattered on for another forty-five minutes, belaboring the point until I thought I'd collapse on the neutral, high-traffic carpet. When he finally wrapped up, we'd all been bored into walking comas.

"Claire, I'd like a word," he called to me as the staff filed out of the meeting.

"How about *jackass?*" I muttered, provoking a quiet ripple of laughter in my immediate area.

I knew from experience that all ears had probably perked up when Neal ordered the tête-à-tête, but I followed him into his office anyway, wincing as he backtracked and closed the door behind me. He obviously wanted a very *private* word. His internal blinds were closed, so I could only imagine the raised eyebrows and increased volume in the cube farm.

Neal's corner office was inhabited by half a dozen dying plants, very much like my own, a virtual library of leadership books, and a set of unused golf clubs, purely for show. It overlooked the city, an urban landscape of shimmering, tinted glass and a handful of bridges. The stagnant room smelled like cough syrup and vinyl furniture.

"Wow," he said, resting his hip against the desk and motioning for me to be seated. "It feels great to be in regular clothes for a change, doesn't it?" He glanced toward his jeans. "I haven't worn these babies since—"

"The fitting room?" I asked, pointing at the *30"×30"* sticker on his thigh.

To his credit, Neal blushed before changing the subject.

"Claire?" he asked, as though there were someone else in the room.

"Neal?" I responded, wondering how he kept his dark hair slicked back so securely.

"I was hoping to schedule a lunch meeting with you."

"With me?" Lunch meeting? My small intestine started playing Cat's Cradle.

"With you." He smiled.

I had to think fast, since he'd taken me by surprise. We weren't exactly a "lunch meeting" company. "I, uh, can't today, if that's what you were thinking," I stammered. "I've got some, uh, personal stuff to take care of." Vague, yet off-limits to probing due to my careful choice of the word *personal*.

"I'm not *asking* you, Claire."

"But—"

"I'm *telling* you, employer to employee, that we need to have a meeting. Don't worry, it's nothing bad." He winked and offered another smile.

How could it be anything but bad? What kind of employee enjoyed spending her free time watching her table manners in front of her boss?

He stared at me, apparently waiting for a response.

"I guess that would be okay," I mumbled, hoping a lunch meeting wasn't geek-speak for a date. I'd heard something about him having a girlfriend, but suspected he was creating his own hype.

"Terrific. We'll go to Morrison's."

"Oh," I nearly choked. Not a real restaurant! "Why don't we just hit the sandwich stand in the lobby?"

Morrison's was supposed to be fabulous, but what would I tell Heather and Jason? News like that would fly around the office in two seconds flat. Would Adam Carello give me a second glance, or a horrified double-take, if I strolled to the elevator with Neal?

"The sandwich stand," Neal chuckled, tracing the crease of his pant leg. "I could hardly have a private conversation with you down there. Morrison's it is. We'll leave at noon."

My heart sank as he nodded briskly to indicate our meeting was adjourned.

Casual Day was shaping up to be a real bitch.

I stepped out of the office and into a beehive of artificial activity that came to a sudden and complete halt the second I shut the door behind me. I'd been on the outside of a closed door often enough to know how ticklish unsatisfied curiosity could be, but there was no way on earth I'd spill the beans to my fellow peons. I offered a tight-lipped smile to the expectant faces around me and quickly walked to my desk, noting the whispered hum of speculation that followed me like a wedding train.

"What was that all about?" Heather asked, peering over our shared cubicle wall.

"Nothing, really." I shrugged, untangling the wires of my headset.

"Did he go off about you being late again?" Jason's voice floated over the barrier.

"Pretty much," I lied.

The three of us may have worked as a unit, but when it came to holding things in, Heather's lips were about as effective as a cotton ball in a drainpipe. And Jason? He traded gossip like stock on the Internet. It was definitely in my best interest to keep the lunch plans to myself.

"Well, what did he say, exactly?" Heather asked, still hanging over the wall.

"I don't know, *exactly*." I grasped for a threatening Nealism. " 'Don't be late again, or else.' "

"Or else what?" she asked.

"That was it." I shrugged and plugged my headset into my phone jack.

"What do you think he means?" She bit her puffy lower lip, the victim of a mail-order collagen injection kit.

"Look, Heather, I've already missed an hour and a half of production time, so I really need to get to work."

"Gotcha." She nodded and ducked back into her own workspace. "We'll talk about it at lunch."

Guess again.

Although it didn't bother me all the time, every now and then I felt a little saddened by my lack of friends in the city. Back in Omaha there were countless people I'd known for my entire life. People who remembered my birthday parties and the orange cast I'd worn when I broke my wrist one Halloween. They knew my story and I knew theirs. But when I moved to Portland, I didn't know where to meet people, other than the workplace. There were no groups for twenty-somethings without social lives, and the club scene seemed to be overrun by the mission to mate.

I had Stephanie, of course, and I'd been thrilled when she followed me out West, but she was busy with Alison most of the time. Never mind the fact that there was something rather pathetic about depending on my sister for a social life.

The hard part was, as much as I wanted secure friendships, I dreaded the prospect of creating them. The two-minute rundown of my life over a cup of coffee. The three or four hand-picked anecdotes, which conveyed different aspects of my personality for a stranger to absorb. The self-effacing tale of the Roller Blades, the disastrous consequences of a neighborhood prank gone wrong, and the sentimental moment with Mr. Knuckles, an ill-fated angora bunny, were supposed to make me seem well-rounded and interesting. Of course I, in turn, had to listen to similar anecdotes from everyone I met and try my best to create a whole person from a number of equally random and misshapen pieces. There was too much effort involved. Too much work.

All of the friends I'd made in Portland had been on the job, and there were limits to how far the relationships could go. Soon after I vacated my last position, a couple of the girls and I met for lunch a few times to talk about who'd been fired or promoted after I left and tear apart whatever nightmarish plans the boss had for the business. We reminisced, but the hilarity of supply room gossip was uninspired, at best, a mere week after I'd moved on. The people who used to know every detail of my life from lengthy chatter at the watercooler didn't know about my new job and didn't care to. It turned out that all we'd had in common was a nine-to-five shift and a generic resentment of middle management. Inevitably, they would talk among themselves about people who joined the company after I'd left. They tried to include me, offering thumbnail sketches of who was who while I smiled and nodded, not giving a damn and waiting for an opportune moment to pay for my calamari and get back to real life.

Before I left Omaha, I'd imagined the group of friends I'd find in Portland, a crowd that was part sitcom, part therapy group. We'd go on road trips together, or sit around a coffee shop after work, sharing opinions and cracking jokes. I wanted the friends with cool jobs and cooler haircuts, but ended up with the losers who collected late fines at the local video store and suffered from chronic transmission problems. My friends had inconvenient allergies and paid their whopping telephone bills in ten-dollar increments. They had shallow savings accounts and limited imaginations, and I was always left wishing I was with someone more interesting, someone successful and entertaining.

I switched on my computer and let out a long breath, embarrassed by the glaring truth that the someone more interesting I craved was really just someone a little less like . . . me.

THREE

Waiting for my computer to grind into action, I groaned at the thought of another day attached to my job by a phone cord that was borderline umbilical. Another day blurring the already indistinguishable lines between home and work and home again.

At times it seemed I'd spent the first three years of my twenties counting the minutes until morning coffee breaks, lunch hours, and afternoon breaks, urging myself not to look at the face of my watch until I was absolutely certain at least ten minutes had passed since the last time I'd checked. I counted the waltzing minutes then hours of my days, anxiously anticipating something I couldn't quite define.

To make matters worse, my free time was no picnic, either. Since my ex-boyfriend Paul and I'd parted ways, loneliness and boredom had a tendency to gang up on me. Instead of looking forward to romantic evenings with the man I adored, my post-work afternoons were suddenly clogged with the sort of tedious tasks I'd never imagined when dreaming of the freedom of adulthood. And while I searched for some fragment of reckless abandon in the act of balancing my checkbook, or finding the partners of dryer-warmed socks in a mountainous pile of laundry, reckless abandon was an elusive beast.

Inevitably, weeknights found me glassy-eyed in front of the TV, stuck between a *Murphy Brown* rerun and the mating rituals of anything from pygmy goats to sea urchins on the Nature Channel, stale popcorn kernels jammed between my teeth and the low hum of dread reminding me of the workday to follow. When I returned to my desk in the morning, I'd resume counting the minutes, hours, and days until a lackluster weekend would begin. I never had to live with any kind of uncertainty because the whole damn cycle would start again every Monday.

Naturally, I worried that some day in the distant future, when I reached the decrepit age of thirty, I'd look back on an entire decade of wishing time away and curse my stupidity, desperate to have even a single day to spend again. In the meantime, enjoying every minute of my life was simply out of the question.

I entered my trio of computer passwords, *"this, place, sucks"*, and hoped Neal had no way to access my personal sign-on. In all honesty, I probably would have loathed any job with the same vigor and sincerity I awarded Alta Media, but I was too settled in my cube to look for anything else. Another job could turn out to be even worse, after all.

Lukewarm coffee soothed my mother-worn nerves as I waited for the computer to run through a series of virus scans before my work screen appeared. Scrolling through several pages of highlighted telephone contacts, I reached the plain text where I'd left off the day before.

Dear God, was it only Thursday?

The system dialed a number for me and I waited through four rings.

"Hello?" a male voice barked.

"Hello, Mr. McArthur?"

"Who's this?"

It was probably as close as I would get to a positive ID, so I forged ahead.

"Mr. McArthur, my name is Claire, and I'm calling to—"

"Interrupt my wife's nap?" He sounded like he'd been hoarding his hostility like empty pop cans, waiting for the day he could cash it all in.

"No," I stammered, "I'm sorry if I—"

"Why do you people keep harassing me?"

"I don't think—"

"Damn straight, you don't. I get calls at all hours, people trying to sell me crap I don't need."

"Sir, I'm not trying to sell anything. I'd just like to ask you a few questions."

"Let me ask you some first. How do I get off your goddamned list, and why don't you give me your home number so I can call *you* tonight and interrupt your bloody dinner?"

"Mr. McArthur, if you could just—"

"Go to hell," he snapped, as though I weren't already there, and the line went dead.

One down, seventy-five to go.

The way the company worked, reps didn't get credit for hang-ups or anything short of a completed survey. If a victim started out enthusiastically, became bored, and abandoned the call before I'd asked all seventeen questions, the call was voided as incomplete and I got nothing. Because of this asinine rule, I liked people to hang up on me in the first few seconds, rather than waiting politely until I'd finished my opening blurb. Efforts to save my feelings only cost me money.

I typed an *x* next to Mr. McArthur's name and sighed as the system dialed another number.

"Hello?" a familiar voice answered.

I scanned the screen and saw that Mr. McArthur was highlighted again. *Piece of shit computer!*

"Hello?" he repeated. "Godammit, I know it's you again. I can hear the rest of the drones yacking in the background. If I could reach through this blasted phone, I'd wring your neck in two seconds flat. And another thing—"

I pressed the "end call" button, wincing as I cut him off in midrant. Before I could take a breath, the computer was dialing again.

"Hello?" a little girl answered.

Why any right-minded parents let their children handle the phone was beyond me. Because I spent no time around kids, it took me forever to come up with the magical combination of words that would convince them to hand the receiver to an adult.

"Hi," I said sweetly. "Is your mom home?"

"No, she's in Peoria, but my husband's here if you'd like to speak to him."

I felt the blood rush to my cheeks. Smooth one, Claire. Turning the call around would be a major feat on a good day.

"Mrs. Goldstein?"

"Obviously."

"Mrs. Goldstein," I repeated after clearing my throat. "My name is Claire and—"

"I don't need any." Her tone was as firm as my abs would have been if I hadn't quit the gym after two visits.

"We're conducting a survey, and—"

"I'm not interested."

"If you could just spare a couple of minutes . . ."

"Look, the baby's crying," she said wearily. "I gotta go."

I decided to use a new tact on the next call, formulating a

plan as the computer dialed. I would force whatever unfortunate soul answered the phone through the survey if it killed me.

"Whitley residence," an ancient female voice croaked. I
couldn't tell whether the rattle in her throat was phlegm or
dust.

"Hello, Mrs. Whitley. I was hoping you could spare a few
moments for some questions about toothpaste." My indifference masquerading as enthusiasm was a better performance
than I'd thought possible.

"What?" she asked.

"My name is Claire," I said, slowly and loudly. I usually did
pretty well with elderly women. "I was hoping to ask you a few
questions about toothpaste for some market research."

"Gladys?"

"No, my name is Claire and—"

"Did Gladys put you up to this?"

"No, I'm trying to conduct a survey, Mrs. Whitley, and—"

"Is this a prank call?"

"No." It was already taking far too long.

"Gladys has nothing to do with it?"

"No, ma'am."

"It would be just like her, you know," she insisted.

"Could I ask you a couple of questions, Mrs. Whitley?"

Just seventeen fucking questions, please.

"I don't know what good it will do. . . ." She hesitated, giving me the opening I'd hoped for.

"Your opinions are very important to us." I glanced at the
"Sarcasm, just one more service I offer" bumper sticker tacked
to my cube wall as I spoke.

"I suppose I could spare the time," she said.

Judging by our lengthy opening, it seemed she had time
to burn.

"Great," I chirped, pulling my questionnaire into view.

"But I don't have any teeth."

I gritted my own. "Pardon me?"

"I said I don't have any teeth. That's why I thought Gladys put you up to this. I beat her at bridge yesterday, and she's just fuming about it."

"I'm sorry, I didn't realize—"

"The worst thing about these dentures is they don't fit quite right. They were fine when I got them, but now I think my head must be shrinking. The ones on top rattle around something terrible. I suppose I could make another appointment with Dr. Guest, but—"

"I'm afraid I've wasted your time, Mrs. Whitley," I interrupted, attempting to terminate the call before I heard her entire dental background, a true oral history.

"You need folks with teeth, I suppose." She sighed.

How was I supposed to answer? "Yes," I said solemnly, "I need folks with teeth."

"Couldn't I answer the questions based on past experience?"

"Excuse me?"

"Well, I had teeth, once. It was years ago, but I remember them well. I'm sure I could answer your questions, dear."

"I, uh . . ." I checked my watch. It was already ten-thirty and I had no call credits. "That would be great."

Forty-five minutes later, Mrs. Whitley and I had successfully completed a survey that should have taken less than ten.

"Give me strength." I hit the pause button on my keyboard and lay my forehead on my desk.

All around me I could hear the rapid-fire buzz of questions asked and the frantic clickety-clacking of responses entered into the system.

"Sorry to interrupt your, uh, *production*," Carol snarled, "but I've got some Mommy messages to deliver."

I reluctantly lifted my head from the cool surface of the desk. "When did she call?"

"When *didn't* she call?" Carol spread several pink slips between her fingers like a hand of cards, but stepped out of reach when I tried to grab them.

"Can you just give them to me?"

"I can do better than that," she smirked. "I'll *read* them to you."

"This isn't funny."

"Guess again, Claire." She cleared her throat. "Message number one reads, 'What would you like for dinner? It's your choice.'"

I grunted and reached for the stack, but she dodged me again.

"Message two was from five minutes later. 'I feel like Italian. Is that okay?'"

"Back off, Carol."

"Cotton panties might help you with those yeast infections," she sneered.

"What?"

"Mommy said your medicine cabinet was full of Monistat." She smiled as her volume increased. "I'm suggesting an underwear alternative. Cotton *breathes*, you know."

"They were samples," I loudly explained, knowing my cubemates could hear everything. "They came in the mail and it seemed pointless to throw them away." It was true, but even I didn't believe it under the circumstances.

"Whatever you say, Claire."

"Can you just give me the stupid messages?"

"Fine, take them." She dropped the papers onto my desk and stalked away.

I leaned back in my seat, flushed with humiliation. Forgiving my mother for blabbing personal details to the biggest bitch on staff was about as likely as me winning the Nobel Peace Prize for beating the crap out of Carol with a side of beef. I had to put a stop to the calls. Immediately.

I stood up to take stock of the damage Carol had done in a few short seconds. Luckily, Jason was on the phone, but Heather smiled weakly at me and broke eye contact, which meant at least one good thing had come from the Monistat revelation. Maybe Sister Eczema would keep to herself in the future.

Mom picked up on the second ring, and I could barely contain my anger.

"What the hell are you doing?"

"Claire?"

"Yes!" I hissed. "What are you trying to do to me?"

"I haven't the foggiest idea what you're talking about."

"The goddamn phone messages!"

"Claire, calm down."

"What are you thinking? I mean, what in the *hell* possessed you to discuss the contents of my medicine cabinet with the company receptionist?"

"Carol?"

"Yes, Carol!"

"There's nothing wrong with making polite conversation with—"

"Satan?"

"Honey, I just called to see what you'd like for dinner, and ask about the—"

"Monistat?" I growled. "Jesus Christ!"

"A yeast infection is nothing to be ashamed of, Claire. It doesn't mean that you're dirty, or—"

"First of all, I don't *have* a yeast infection. Secondly, why would you share that kind of information with someone you don't even know?"

"Well, *you* never tell me what's going on in your life, and when I saw all of those pharmaceuticals . . ."

"They were free samples," I snarled.

"Yes, well, I was concerned, so I asked your friend if you'd mentioned any female troubles and—"

"She's not my *friend,* Mom. She's a bitch on wheels."

"Oh." She sounded surprised. "She said she was a very close friend of yours, and I don't keep medical secrets from *my* friends. Granted, we were all in nursing together, but I don't think there's anything wrong with discussing this sort of thing with your girlfriends. We're all women, after all."

Why was I surprised that she would discuss her discovery with Carol? Her medical background obliterated her common sense when it came to personal issues. The woman told my prom date to make sure I had plenty of fluids at the dance, as I'd been suffering from diarrhea earlier in the day. She wanted to throw a party when Steph and I began menstruating. She could expound on the life cycle of scabies for hours on end.

"Once again, Carol is *not* a friend, and I'm now going to spend the rest of my life trying to make her forget you even mentioned any of this."

"That's a bit melodramatic, don't you think?"

"Half of the office heard about it!"

"Well, I'm sorry, honey. I was just trying to help."

"Please don't."

"I was worried about your health, darling. If you'd only *talk* to me, I wouldn't have to pry information from strangers."

Suddenly this was *my* fault?

"Mom . . ."

"And I don't like the vulgar language I've been hearing from you. You're father and I didn't raise you to—"

"I think it would be best if you didn't call me here, Mom."

"Not even for—"

"I have to go. I need to get back to work."

I tapped the release button on my phone and dialed Dad's number with shaking fingers.

"Thank God, you're there," I blurted at the gravelly sound of his voice.

"Claire? What's wrong?"

I could almost see him, standing in the kitchen, surrounded by mauve walls and pansy-sprinkled valances. He was probably wearing a ragged pair of Levi's and a plaid flannel shirt, softened by thousands of cycles in Mom's trusty Kenmore. He would smell like coffee, as he did at any hour, and his graying hair would be parted as carefully as the curtains of the Sunset Theater at the beginning of a show.

Had I interrupted him reading the paper, or was he trying to decide what to make for his lunch? I couldn't remember a time I'd seen him cook more than a grilled cheese sandwich and tomato soup. Had Mom left prepared meals for him to eat in her absence, or had he already received an avalanche of invitations from curious neighbors, dying to know why Mom had left town and willing to sacrifice a few slices of roast beef or a seasoned chicken breast to find out?

"What's wrong?" I repeated. We had always communicated well, even during my teen years of misguided angst and half-baked rebellion. Dad and I could talk about anything, or nothing at all, depending on what we needed at the time. "Well, I'm trying to get through my workday and I keep getting phone messages from Naggedy Ann."

"So, she arrived okay." He chuckled.

He was probably standing at the sink, looking out at the back lane, where he'd taught me to ride a two-wheeler. Every other kid in the neighborhood had training wheels, but Dad felt that was cheating. Over the course of two weeks, I'd become intimately acquainted with every blackberry bush lining our property. Every painted mailbox and fencepost for two blocks in either direction had been struck by my flailing limbs. Every kid in the neighborhood had giggled as I crashed into hedges and toppled to the ground.

Mom had watched me practice from that same window, her eyes darting between the soapy dishes passing under a steady stream of water and the not-so-valiant efforts of her youngest child.

"What is she doing here?" I asked.

"Visiting." I heard him slurp his coffee.

"So I gathered. She's already planning tonight's dinner. It's Italian." I couldn't bring myself to detail her other messages.

"That'll be nice."

Was that all he could say? "What prompted her to make the trip, Dad?"

"She needed a little break from home. You know how she gets, honey." Another slurp. "Anyway, she's been talking about coming to see you for months."

"And you couldn't have warned me?"

"She wanted to surprise you, I guess. How's work going?"

Nice transition.

"Fine. Why didn't *you* come?"

"I wish I could have. I've got a lot on my plate right now."

"Dad, you're *retired*. Other than a couple of weekly golf games, your plate's been scraped clean for months."

"She wanted to spend some time alone with you, Claire. I'm not going to fault her for that. You and I have always been close and I guess she feels she's missed out. Not to mention the fact that she's having a bit of trouble adjusting to retirement. Couldn't you try to humor her?"

"How long will she be here?"

"That's entirely up to her. She found a deal on an open-ended ticket. Two hundred and sixty-five dollars."

"Jesus Christ!"

"I know. It's usually more than double that."

"That's not what I'm reacting to."

He laughed. "Do you think I don't know that? Listen, Claire, your mother loves you very much."

"She has an odd way of showing it."

"She has an odd way of showing a lot of things, but that doesn't mean she doesn't care." His voice had an almost wistful quality to it, and I wondered if he missed her already.

Before I could ask him, I heard the high-pitched squawk of Mom's cuckoo striking the hour. I'd lain in wait to snap the wooden bird's head off in grade five, and received the spanking of my life, then refastened it with Elmer's glue, backward.

"Listen, honey, I've got to go. The Cochranes have invited me for a late lunch."

"I'll talk to you later, I guess. Say hi to them for me."

"Will do. And Claire?"

"Yeah?"

"Be kind to your mother."

"Uh . . . sure."

I hung up the phone, a little wounded that Dad thought I

needed the instruction. *Of course* I would be kind to my mother. Even if it killed me, which was entirely possible.

"What's your count?" Jason asked, suddenly appearing over the cube wall.

"You don't want to know," I warned, afraid to utter the number *one*.

"I've only got thirty-three," he confided, knowing perfectly well that he was way above the quota.

"Ha!" I barked. "Then you *really* don't want to know."

"It'll be better after lunch. Want to hit the food court with me?"

"Not today, thanks."

I crossed my fingers with the hope he wouldn't question me further. If word that Neal and I were dining together got out, I'd be doomed, so I had to do my best to ensure that the meeting remained a dirty little secret, like voting Republican or watching *The Real World*.

Unfortunately, adhering to the theme of the day, my best would probably fall short of the mark.

FOUR

As the dreaded noon hour approached, I planned to feign interest in stale paperwork, production sheets, or, if necessary, my cuticles until my nosy coworkers left for their lunch breaks. My hope was that Neal and I could sneak out when the office was empty, return separately, and no one would ever know about our meeting.

Unfortunately, Neal was a little too prompt for my strategy.

"Ready to roll?" he asked at five minutes to the hour, buttoning his ankle-length wool coat and smiling, totally oblivious to the sudden silence around us.

Five minutes to twelve. No one else was even digging for their wallets and takeout menus at that point, which made our early departure about as tempting as an impromptu topless dance on my desktop.

"Claire, are you ready?" His volume actually *increased*, as though he couldn't see Heather peering around the side of my cubicle wall, or the frantic elbowing and head tilting taking place at our illustrious watercooler.

All eyes were upon us, and in the space of seconds, I felt

like the reluctant half of a wildly successful freak show. If only we'd had the foresight to charge admission.

"Yes, I'm ready." My whisper emerged as a hiss while I scrambled for my coat, then remembered I'd left it at home. Exasperated by the raised eyebrows and quiet snickering coming from all corners, I yanked my satchel out of the bottom drawer and slung it over my shoulder.

"Let's go," I muttered, hurrying toward the exit, hoping I'd catch a bit of good luck and the people on the far side of the office wouldn't realize that Neal and I were together.

Of course, I couldn't outrun the ripple effect of mass speculation and by the time I reached Carol's reception desk, her twisted smirk was the perfect punctuation to my humiliating departure.

The elevator took a lifetime to reach the eleventh floor and, thanks to a muted instrumental version of Loverboy's "Working for the Weekend," it seemed to take even longer to drop us in the lobby.

"Are we taking a cab?" I asked, noting the misty rain outside and shivering.

"Nah, let's walk."

I felt the unwelcome sensation of Neal's hand pressing against the small of my back, propelling me into an open segment of the revolving door. Before I could put one foot in front of the other, he stepped in, directly behind me.

For crying out loud.

When I moved forward, the back side of the door pushed his body against me in a crush of thick shoulders and sour breath.

"We're supposed to go one at a time," I grunted, as he nailed my Achilles tendon with the toe of his pointy Italian shoe.

"We'll make it," he said, shuffling his feet in time with mine, and we lurched toward daylight like a geriatric River-dance. "All it takes is a little teamwork."

I prayed that "teamwork" wasn't the theme of our lunch.

We emerged on the sidewalk and untangled our limbs before I strode away from my host and toward Morrison's. I side-stepped a cluster of window-shoppers and was nearly T-boned by an electric wheelchair before Neal appeared at my side.

"Hey, slow down," he gasped, stubby legs working overtime to keep up with me.

I cut my pace in half, hating the fact that the courtesy would only prolong our time together.

"We've only got an hour," I reminded Alta Media's resi-dent time-card freak.

"It's a business lunch," he assured me. "We don't have to watch the clock."

"*Great.*"

As we walked, I envied the groups of people around us, talking and laughing as they made their way to small cafes or noisy restaurants, ducking into doorways steamed by hot food and jovial conversation. No one else looked as reluctant as I felt, hustling through the crowd with unwanted company.

We managed the ten-block walk to the restaurant in eight minutes, no thanks to Neal's constant reflection checks in department store windows. He didn't make a single adjustment to his hair or clothing, which led me to the unfortunate con-clusion that he *wanted* to look like a corporate gnome.

I held my breath as we navigated another revolving door and only exhaled when I stepped onto plush green carpeting.

Morrison's had the kind of atmosphere that made me feel like a twelve-year-old at a frat party: desperately out of place.

Underdressed didn't encompass the reality of my wrinkled jeans and half-assed ponytail, compared with the starched shirts and smart aprons of the staff.

Why did Neal have to choose a fancy restaurant on Casual Day?

While we waited fifteen minutes to be seated, I counted eleven vacant tables in the front room. The bartender glared past the faux fig trees and brass-trimmed coatracks, snubbing my dampened form at every opportunity.

When I spotted the maître d', the man with the tightest smile and the best-pressed pants, glaring at my oxfords, I had to surreptitiously check my soles to make sure they weren't covered in shit that threatened his freshly cleaned carpets.

When he led us into the dining room without the slightest greeting, I wished they were.

The lord of the lobby seated us in a cavernous booth at the far end of the restaurant, next to the banging and crashing of the kitchen and far from the respectable patrons. Although I had no desire to be seen with Neal, I didn't really want to be alone with him either, and a booth felt much too private for the two of us.

Once we were seated, I looked across the polished marble at my boss, and saw the tabletop was mere inches from his shoulders. I fought the urge to request a booster seat and concentrated on the menu instead.

Neal peered around his menu. "This will be fun." It sounded like a command. "We haven't had the chance to get to know one another."

As if we needed to. "You boss, me employee" was about as much as the king of our corporate jungle had communicated to me in the past.

I nodded halfheartedly and glanced at the booth next to ours, where someone had abandoned a newspaper.

"What looks good?" Neal asked.

The employment section.

"I think I'll just have a side salad." I closed my menu with a sharp snap. It required no preparation time, would take only minutes to eat, and I'd return to freedom with over half an hour to spare for a real lunch at the food fair. A corn dog slathered with mustard. A three-item Chinese combo. Maybe a gyro, dripping tzaziki.

"Come on, Claire. This is a business lunch, no time for skimpy salads. Get an appy and an entrée."

Could he hear the nasal whine when he said *appy?*

"I'm really not that hungry," I lied, cursing my skipped breakfast.

"You women are all the same." He smiled knowingly. "Always watching your figures."

I wished there was a big brass gong I could hit to warn all other patrons of the dick in their midst. Of course, such a gong would probably be sounding constantly at a place like Morrison's, based on the wait staff alone. I faked a smile for a split second before looking away.

"Look, if you're that worried about it, we'll split a starter." He smiled. "How does that sound?"

Like a date. My stomach lurched at the thought.

"Claire?"

I looked into his beady eyes. The faster we ordered, the faster I'd be out of there. "That sounds great, Neal."

"Cheese sticks?"

"Perfect." I was amazed such a pedestrian delight was part of the menu.

Our waitress appeared with ice water and I ordered fettuccine while Neal opted for salmon.

We spent an awkward few minutes admiring the dessert
menu while I waited for him to broach the subject of our meeting and he waited for cheese sticks.

Neal's reward came first.

He bit off a crispy golden end and I watched with grotesque
fascination as strands of melted cheese stretched the full
length of his arm before breaking and dropping against the
front of his golf shirt in a wilted trail.

"Man, I just love these things," he said, while chewing.

I could clearly see the steaming, fried chunks rotating in
his mouth like a pile of laundry in a front loader. Around and
around, growing more mangled by the second.

"Want some?" he asked, taking another bite and repeating
the performance.

"No, thanks."

"Give it a try," he coaxed.

"I don't think so."

"Claire," he said, mock-sternly. "This is your boss talking."

"All right, already," I muttered, reaching for a stick and
taking a bite. I had to admit, it was delicious, despite the sali-
vary sideshow.

"I knew you'd love them." He reached for another and we
chewed in silence.

I watched him double-, then *triple*-dip his cheese sticks in
marinara sauce, growing numb as he licked the grease from
each fingertip.

Had Gord really assigned this man, this double-dipping,
finger-licking *boob*, the task of entertaining our potential
clients?

I glanced at my watch. "It's twelve forty-five," I hinted,

hoping he'd get to the point of the whole damn lunch. "You wanted to talk to me about something?"

"That's what I like about you, Claire." He grinned. "You're a straight shooter."

"Uh, thanks," I said, unsure if it was a compliment.

He offered me the last mozzarella stick and I shook my head.

"You cut to the chase," he continued, taking a bite as our waitress placed our meals before us and whisked the empty dishes away without a word.

I nodded in understanding.

"You make no bones about it." He shoved a forkful of grilled salmon into his mouth.

"Neal?"

"Mmmhmm?" he asked, wiping his lips with a napkin.

"Why did you bring me here?"

"Yes!" He jabbed a finger in my general direction. "That's exactly what I'm talking about. There's no beating around the bush with you, no—"

"Okay, I get it."

"No tiptoeing around the—"

"Neal."

"Right." He filled his mouth with salmon again before continuing, "I've decided to add some new elements to your job."

New elements? "Meaning what, exactly?"

I felt a hollow sensation in the pit of my stomach, and suspected it would take more than a plate of pasta to fill it up.

"I want you to start handling the production sheets. Nothing major, really. Just keeping a record of how many calls people are making and whether they're using time effectively."

I must have winced at the idea of being the company narc,

because he shook his head with reassurance and said, "It's a matter of compiling our existing stats and determining overall efficiency in the office."

"Hmm." I twirled fettuccine on my fork and weighed my options. Maybe it wasn't quite as bad as it sounded.

"I'm asking you after very careful consideration, Claire."

"Really?" I'd assumed the offer was based on seniority.

"You're a good, solid worker."

"Uh, thanks," I said, tasting the rich cream sauce and reluctantly thanking God for Morrison's.

"Not always punctual." He smiled as I blushed in response. "But you're a serious person who gets things done. Just between us, you're a rarity in our office."

I took another bite of pasta, pleased by the compliments.

"I think you have the potential to really go somewhere with this company."

"You do?" The only place I'd thought of going was out the door when I found something better.

"Claire." He took another bite. *"Oh, this is good."* He patted his mouth again and swallowed. "I hope this doesn't sound arrogant, but surely you've noticed that not everyone at Alta Media is cut of the same cloth as you and I."

"Me and you?" I asked, slightly mortified. How on earth were Neal and I alike?

"A lot of people work simply for the sake of a paycheck."

People like me.

"They clock in and out without really giving a damn." He cleared his throat. "Excuse my language."

"And me?" I asked.

"You're smarter than that. You're smarter than ninety percent of the people you work with. Now, normally I wouldn't say that to an employee, but I think you're the kind of person who can keep it confidential." He paused. "Am I right?"

"Yes." I wouldn't dream of telling my peers. They'd be not only jealous, but hurt to know that I was smarter than all of them.

"You're a go-getter, Claire, and I want to give you a chance to move ahead."

Frankly, I was flattered. I'd never expected such praise from Neal. In fact, I didn't think he'd ever noticed me or my work. I had to admit that while I didn't love the job, he was right about me doing it well.

"Hmm." I took another bite and pondered his offer. Maybe I deserved a chance to "move ahead." More important, maybe I owed it to myself to give it a try. "Does added responsibility mean a salary increase?"

"There it is again." He laughed. "Straight to the heart of the matter. You just—"

"Neal."

"Yes." He nodded and licked his lips. "There will be an increase. We'll add fifty-three cents an hour to your base wage. You'll still have to meet department goals, as usual, and exceed those goals for your standard commission, of course."

"Of course." I nodded.

Fifty-three cents wasn't too bad. My last review had only netted me forty-one. I had no problem exceeding production goals, which made me an extra three or four hundred a month, but any added income was nothing to sneeze at.

"I wouldn't ask if I didn't think you could handle it," he assured me through the lump of sockeye in his throat.

He aggressively pumped up my ego for another ten minutes while I weighed the real issues.

A raise. Responsibility.

A raise. Monitoring my coworkers.

A *raise*.

"I'll do it," I said, shoving the pasta into my mouth before I could take back the words.

Neal lifted his ice water in silent salute before unbuckling his belt to make room for dessert.

A real class act.

When we returned to the office after an almost two-hour lunch, Carol handed me another message from Mom.

"Call her," she barked.

"I will."

"*Now*, Claire. I'm sick of talking to her."

I avoided all stares as I returned to my desk, and when Heather lobbed a crumpled note over the cube wall, I knocked it onto the ground and pretended I didn't see it. They'd all know about my job change soon enough. Neal was planning a meeting the following morning to notify everyone.

I called the apartment and Mom picked up on the first ring, as though she'd been hovering over the phone.

"Oh, darling, it's you."

"Yeah, I got *yet another* message from you."

"I'm sorry about that, honey. I was looking for the fabric softener, and couldn't find it anywhere."

"I don't use it." I took a breath. "Didn't we already discuss you *not* calling my office anymore?"

"I just figured if it was one quick question . . ."

"No calls, Mom."

"Carol said you'd gone for lunch with the boss."

"Uh, yes."

"Sounds important," she hinted.

"He's given me some new responsibilities."

"And?"

"And a raise."

"Claire! That's a *promotion!* You've been promoted!"

I hadn't thought about it that way. More money, more responsibility. It *was* a promotion. A smile tickled my lips.

"I never thought I'd hear the words!" Mom continued.

"Thanks." I let sarcasm drip from the word.

"Oh, you know what I mean."

Unfortunately, I did. My own mother was astonished at my pinch of success.

My promotion.

It struck a flat note the second time around. Neal had talked a good game, but did I *want* to be promoted? Did accepting a move up the Alta Media ladder mean telemarketing had become my career? Did it mean that I actually cared about the job?

Impossible. It was all about the money. The whopping fifty-three-cent price of my soul.

"We'll have a celebratory dinner tonight!" Mom said.

"We don't have to do anything special." A party of two would need a dirge for a sound track.

"Of course we do. When is this ever going to happen again?"

"Once again, thank you." I rolled my eyes, but agreed to a celebration, terminating the call before I said something unpleasant.

Knowing I couldn't handle Mom's festivities alone, I called Steph at Cedar Heights, the retirement home where she worked as a nurse. I heard the receptionist page her, and could almost see my sister striding toward the telephone in one of her mandatory pastel pantsuits, white orthopedic shoes squeaking against the shiny linoleum.

After we shared a few minutes of small talk, mostly about the gingersnaps the new cook had made, I got to the point.

"Did you know Mom's in town?"

"Since when?" she asked. The moment she'd stepped out of the closet and fallen from our mother's graces, Steph had adopted a certain paranoia about family matters, as though the heterosexuals were conspiring against her. No matter how many times I told her I was on her side, she couldn't see past our current rankings. I had become the favored daughter, a title that came with no discernible benefits, and, as far as Steph was concerned, my new status meant Mom and I were in cahoots.

"She arrived this morning. I didn't know she was coming."

"Hmm." In that single sound I could hear a battle between relief and disbelief. "What's she doing here?"

"God only knows. Listen, I want you guys to come over for dinner tonight."

"Wait a second. Where's Dad?"

The worst part of our role reversal was that for as long as I could remember, I'd always had the easier relationship with Dad, too. From the moment of her gay awakening, the parental booby prize was all mine.

If I'd won my mother over with some stunning victory, be it career, marriage, children, or whatever, at least I could feel good about it. Instead, I won by default, and it felt like crap to know that all Steph had done to lose her shine was be herself.

"He's at home."

"Have you talked to him?"

"Briefly. Everything seems to be fine there."

"Then what's going on?"

"Other than the fact that Mom's driving me nuts, I don't know. You've got to bail me out, Steph. Please come for dinner."

She crunched her cookie for a moment before asking, "Does she know we're invited?"

"Yup," I quickly lied.

"Don't bullshit me, Claire."

"Okay, so she doesn't know," I admitted. "That shouldn't stop you from coming. She's got to meet Alison sometime, right?"

"Yeah, I'd like them to meet. But not in a lesbian ambush."

"I'll be there to act as a buffer," I assured her.

"You'll be too busy defending your job, your apartment, your single status, and your life to buffer anything."

That wasn't entirely true. I wouldn't have a chance to defend myself. My sister had spent a lifetime protecting me, and showed no signs of slowing down. I just wished I could do the same for her.

"Guess again. We'll be too busy celebrating my . . ." I glanced over my shoulder before whispering, "promotion."

"You got promoted?"

"Yeah."

"At the phone place?"

"Alta Media. For Christ's sake, I've been here two years, Steph."

"I thought you hated it there."

"I do, but—"

"You're always talking about quitting."

Why did she have to remind me of the facts? "I know, but—"

"Is it good money?"

Her salary was probably twice mine, so I wasn't about to mention the fifty-three cents. "There's a little more to it than that." It was vague enough that even *I* didn't know what I was alluding to. "Are you going to come over or not?"

"I don't know. Ali will be all freaked out about meeting Mom."

"Don't tell her. Make it a surprise."

"She'd kill me." Steph laughed.

"Alison will win her over in a matter of seconds. All Mom has to do is see how happy you are together."

"I don't know."

"I'm *begging* you."

"Okay, okay. Sign us up."

I thanked her profusely and hung up the phone, certain it would be a meal to remember.

Due to my extended lunch break, the afternoon passed mercifully quickly, and in the middle of the silent thrill of shutting down my computer for the day, I felt a tentative tap on my shoulder.

"Claire?"

"Yeah?" I stared at my screen, surprised Jason hadn't left already. He was usually out the door and into Pioneer Place, trolling for teenage mall rats, before I'd had a chance to hang up my phone.

"Claire?"

"*What?*" I snapped, hustling my mouse from one icon to the next, glad we were well past the stage of inane pleasantries.

"Sorry to interrupt. I was just—"

"What? For God's sake, spit it out!"

I swiveled my seat, and felt my world blur in slow motion when I saw Adam Carello, the Impossible Dream, instead of Jason, the Impatient Pervert, standing behind my chair. His dark hair was boyishly rumpled, giving him that bed-headed style anemic-looking models had been sporting in all of the fall fashion magazines. On Adam, the chaos of twisted locks and cowlicks was simply charming.

"If this is a bad time . . ." He stuck both hands in his back pockets and started to turn away.

"No!" I yelped, then attempted to control my excitement. *Finally,* he was talking to me. I wasn't going to let him drift away in the middle of our very first conversation, tragically stilted as it already was. "I didn't mean to be so—"

"Rude?" he asked, his smile exposing a chipped front tooth.

If he had been anyone else, I would have slipped in a referral to my dentist, but Adam's imperfection was most alluring.

"Yes, rude." I smiled in return, feeling warmth in my cheeks. "What were you going to say?"

"A few of us are heading down to McMenamins for drinks. I was wondering if you wanted to come."

How many was a few of us? Had *he* decided to invite me, or had he been sent over by some less appetizing coworker? Maybe Daniel, our resident hypochondriac. At that very moment Dr. Death was probably peeking at me over the top of his first aid kit. And *why* was I invited? Was it some ploy to ply me with drinks so I'd spill the beans about my meeting with Neal? Why was Adam the one extending the offer, when we'd never said a word to each other? Why did my mother pick this particular Thursday to darken my doorstep and suffocate my social life before it even had a chance to gasp for air?

"I didn't realize it was such a difficult question."

"Sorry, it's not," I stammered. "My mother's in town and I'm planning to spend the evening with her."

"Oh, that's cool."

Cool? What had Carol told him? Surely she didn't hate me enough to create a Monistat memo. Or did she?

"Thanks anyway, for the invite."

He shrugged and turned toward the door. "Another time, I guess."

When? I wanted to shriek after him. *Name the day and I'll be there!* Instead, I took a calming breath. "Yeah, another time," I repeated numbly.

I sighed as I packed my bag. I'd been daydreaming about Adam Carello ever since Paul Clemens had started to drift away from me more than six months earlier. He had emotionally vacated our relationship, and I'd focused my attention on Adam while I waited for the departure to become physical. It was only a matter of time, after all. If I'd had any guts, I would have left Paul as soon as his eyes wandered to the petite blonde he left me for, but guts were in short supply.

Adam Carello seemed to be just the kind of guy I should have been looking for, if I wasn't so worried about the world's cruelest tag team: rejection and heartache.

I stopped at Safeway on the way home and added four bags of groceries to my load, cursing my luck with every lumbering step. As if dinner weren't going to be awkward enough, I would be missing out on an opportunity that had taken forever to present itself.

A night with Adam Carello, for Christ's sake.

The chance of a lifetime (or at least the past six months), not likely to visit me again in the near future.

Or maybe the ball had moved to *my* court. Maybe the fact that he had invited me out with a group meant I could extend a similar invitation some other night. If I could just assemble a dream team of coworkers nice enough to spend an evening with, but dull enough to pose no threat to a potential pairing of Adam and me, I'd be all set. Heather's "personality" would certainly make mine look spectacular. All I needed were five or six more like her.

I reached my apartment, climbed the stairs, and paused at my door, enjoying a final moment of respite before my descent into hell at the hands of my mother resumed.

FIVE

I opened the door to find shining wood floors and the unmistakable scent of Pledge in the air. My rugs were straightened, pillows plumped, and I could see the creeping brown fern that had been dying by the inch soaking in my kitchen sink.

I lowered my groceries to the floor and gazed around the room in amazement.

A foreign bowl of fruity potpourri had replaced the stack of magazines on my coffee table, a pile of neatly folded laundry piled next to it. The melted wax was scraped clear of the mantel, and a collection of painted picture frames stood in the place of my depleted candles. My brass coatrack was polished, along with the small silver boxes left to me by my maternal grandmother. Framed posters that had spent months leaning against my closet doors were hanging next to my suddenly sparkling windows.

Without the cobwebs, my walls looked even brighter than the area of kitchen linoleum Mom was scouring with the toothbrush I had used that very morning. The toothbrush I'd expected to use that very night.

"Mom?" I wanted to be angry with her for defying my no-cleaning rule, but I was too pleased with the results to bother.

"Oh, I didn't hear you come in," she groaned as she climbed to her feet. "What do you think?"

"It looks terrific." I could hardly believe it was the dump I'd been living in for two years, and I wished I'd taken the initiative to jazz it up myself. "I can't believe the difference."

She nodded. "I was thinking we could stop in at a fabric store on the weekend and find something cheerful for the windows. Get rid of those awful blinds."

"Sounds good." I'd never thought of that.

"And we've got to do something about the rust stains in your bathtub."

"Sure."

"And the way your toilet runs." She wiped the back of her wrist across her brow. "Haven't you mentioned it to your landlord?"

"No, I . . ." My enthusiasm was already waning.

"You know, you've got to clean out the fridge every now and then. The oven may be self-cleaning, but nothing else is." She rolled her eyes.

"Thanks for—"

"I threw out some of your rattier-looking underwear. Honestly, Claire, when the elastic goes, just get rid of it."

I crossed my arms and waited for more.

"I bought some air freshener for your closets. No sense letting your clothes smell musty."

"Anything else?"

"You might consider dusting every now and then."

"Okay, already." It was hard to speak through gritted teeth. "Thank you for your efforts."

"What are mothers for?" she asked, but I didn't dare answer.

I lifted the grocery bags and Mom followed as I carried them into the kitchen and dropped them onto a table surface I hadn't seen for days.

"Why all the supplies?" she asked, pulling a pork roast from one of the bags and setting it on my gleaming countertop.

I figured I might as well bite the bullet.

"I, uh, invited Stephanie and Alison over for dinner."

She swung around to face me. "You *didn't*."

I nodded and avoided eye contact, concentrating on depositing carrots and brussels sprouts in my empty fridge. I was right about the baking soda being the only item left standing.

"You could have warned me." She dumped a bag of russet potatoes on the counter.

"I just did."

"I thought it was going to be just the two of us tonight."

"Sorry, Mom." I put the milk and apple juice on the bottom shelf. "Don't you think it's about time you met Alison?"

"No."

I turned toward her, noting the hands planted firmly on her hips.

"She's very important to Steph, you know."

"*I* used to be important to Stephanie."

"You still are."

"Then why is she doing this to me?"

"Mom, don't be ridiculous. The whole gay thing has nothing to do with you."

She shook her head, obviously irritated. "Do you have to call her *Steph* all the time?"

"I've always called her that. Hell, *you've* always called her that. Why does it suddenly bother you?"

"It sounds so . . . masculine." She frowned as she un-wrapped the roast. "How are we doing this?"

"I'll rub it with herbs and put it in the oven."

"I'll peel the potatoes. You want mashed?"

"Yes, thanks."

We worked in companionable silence, despite the wall of tension that was slowly building around her. As we chopped vegetables and periodically checked the meat, her precise movements were accompanied by the quiet escape of one sigh after another.

Of course, being raised by the woman, I could understand Mom's feelings, unfair as they were. She wanted a picture-perfect family and, in her estimation, a lesbian ruined the shot.

She handed me a bowl and I considered how she must have felt telling her bridge club about Steph. If she had con-fessed the news to anyone, I'd bet on the folding-chair four-some; Muriel, Joan, Joyce, and Nancy. They were closer than the bristles on a hairbrush and shared everything from desserts to desertions with hoarse whispers and delicate peals of laugh-ter. I was almost certain she would have confided in "the girls," but then again, Steph's wedding picture was still on the mantel at Mom's place, a silver-framed beacon of false hope, despite my efforts to get rid of it during my last visit home.

Steph came out to my parents and announced her plans for divorce by telephone a mere week before my arrival and, while I didn't know all of the details, I knew Mom had col-lapsed on the floor in tears and it was up to Dad to finish the conversation. In the following days, Mom mailed Steph pho-tographs of previous boyfriends, then magazine clippings of handsome models, thinking the problem was Marco. Needless to say, Steph didn't respond.

By the time I arrived, I had unwittingly moved up a spot in the McLeod family hierarchy simply by being straight. Mom pampered me by preparing my favorite meals, followed by butterscotch pudding, or lemon meringue or pecan pie. Her hugs were tighter than ever before, and she managed to keep her criticisms down to a handful of jabs per day. Although I hadn't earned the supreme treatment, it was a wonderful change from her usual ways. Of course, I knew the adoration would be short-lived. It was only a matter of time before I tarnished again.

One night, when Mom went to bed early with one of her frequent migraines, Dad and I stayed up to talk.

"Your mom isn't taking this thing with your sister too well," he said, opening a beer and handing it to me before taking one for himself.

"You don't say." I choked back a laugh and Dad smiled.

"Well, you know how she is. Takes everything personally." He lifted the bottle to his lips and swallowed.

"She'll get over it," I told him. "But what about you?" I took a long gulp of beer, shivering as it chilled my throat.

"What about me?"

"What do you think about Steph?"

"I think she's a terrific kid." He closed his eyes as he took another drink.

"Do you wish she wasn't gay?" I knew I did. Not because I had anything against the lifestyle, but because her life would undoubtedly be harder because of it. She was an overnight minority, and I couldn't help worrying about her.

"She's a great person and I'm very proud of her," Dad said.

"But do you wish she wasn't gay?"

"She is."

"But—"

"She is," he said firmly.

The clock struck the hour and the mangled cuckoo popped out of his hole with a couple of monotonous toots.

"That damn thing drives me nuts," Dad muttered, taking a swig.

"Why don't you take it down?"

"Your mother loves it." His shrug seemed to encompass the dried floral wreaths on every door, the potpourri brewing in tiny candle-warmed bowls, piles of knitting patterns on the coffee table, and the prized collection of Hummel figurines scattered throughout the room. The only signs that Dad lived in the house were a set of keys in a pottery bowl at the front door, a Kansas City Royals baseball hat on the counter, and a book of completed crossword puzzles next to the phone. Did he ever question Mom's control over the decor, or did it make any difference to him?

I looked at the man across from me, curious about his inner thoughts. He'd always watched and listened, offering advice only when we asked for it, and I had to wonder how much he knew about all of us from observation alone.

"Did you have any idea she was gay?" It didn't seem likely, no matter how perceptive he was.

"I didn't know for sure, but I wasn't terribly surprised." He straightened the cuff of his flannel shirt.

"You weren't? God, it was the shock of the century to me!" She'd called me too, slightly drunk by the sound of it. I'd asked her when she knew and she confessed to having a crush on Rachel Dugan, her chemistry lab partner, in the tenth grade. My jaw had hung open for three days in response to the news, and I'd be hard-pressed to say whether it was her orientation or her choice of bucktoothed Rachel Dugan that was the bigger shock. And yet, *Dad* had known?

"Well," he said, "Marco talked to me about some things. . . ." His voice tapered off.

"What things? This is no time to start being vague, Dad."

"I don't know." He shrugged as his skin colored. "He just didn't feel like things were quite, uh . . . right. You know what I mean." He took another drink of beer.

"He talked to you about their *sex life?*"

He raised a finger to his lips to quiet me, tilting his head toward the bedroom where Mom slept. "A little bit."

"Jesus," I whispered.

"I didn't want him to, but I couldn't turn my back on him either. I know how much he loved her."

"Are you saying he gave you details?"

"Claire."

"I don't want to know what he said. I'm just trying to picture this conversation."

"Picture it as uncomfortable." He studied the label on his bottle as though it held the secrets of the universe. "There are certain things a father doesn't want to consider when it comes to his daughter. And, uh," he cleared his throat, "intimacy is one of them."

"Does Mom know he talked to you?"

"Well, Marco tried to talk to her first." Dad couldn't suppress a chuckle. "He said they were having some problems, and that Steph wasn't interested in, well . . . sex."

"You're kidding!" I couldn't imagine Marco approaching Mom about something so personal. I wouldn't dare do it myself. "What did she say?"

"She told him to buy Steph some roses and take her out to dinner."

"Great advice," I groaned.

"That's your mother." He smiled. "She's something else."

"Yeah, she's definitely something else." I laughed, and Dad leaned over to clink his bottle against mine.

My mother, a regular Dr. Ruth.

I glanced at her across the kitchen, taking in the frown and furrowed brow, hoping she'd get over her disappointment and move on, eventually.

When six-thirty arrived, Mom pretended to be too engrossed with brussels sprouts to hear the doorbell. Her face was stern, her lips set in a frown.

"I'll get it," I muttered, thrilled to be off to such a fabulous start.

I opened the door to find Steph looking like Casual-Night-Out Barbie, her blonde hair curled against the collar of her fleece jacket, cheeks flushed from the cool evening air, and pale blue eyes—a gift from Dad—searching over my shoulder for a sign of Mom.

I distracted her with a hug. "It's good to see you," I said, releasing her and turning to her girlfriend.

Curious about the introduction to come, I tried to imagine what Alison would look like through Mom's critical gaze. She had *almost* styled her normally limp brown hair by pulling it back from her face, which accentuated what Mom would consider mediocre cheekbones. She wore her usual light makeup, a touch of beige shadow, which, admittedly, did nothing for her gray eyes, and a dusting of unnecessary pink blush. Cosmetology may not have been my strong point, but it was as foreign to Alison as Portuguese.

At first I'd been surprised that Steph hadn't sought out a more glamorous woman, but once I'd had a chance to get to know Alison, her looks were of no consequence. She was unfailingly kind and honest, the sort of person who inspired trust. Unlike me, she would never divulge a secret or act out of spite. She was like the good witch in *The Wizard of Oz*, minus the looks.

I didn't care about the self-conscious way she pulled at her left earlobe when she was nervous, her dedication to Hush Puppies, or the gnawed shreds of her fingernails. None of the superficial business mattered to me.

But it would matter to Mom.

As I reached out to hug her, Alison gave me the most nervous smile I'd ever seen. It struck me that she was about to meet what may as well have been her mother-in-law.

"You look great," I whispered, giving her a squeeze and releasing her. "I love the hair."

"You don't think it's too . . ." She fingered the side of her head carefully.

"No. It's perfect," I assured her, and she let her hands fall awkwardly to her sides.

"I thought I was going to be sick on the way over here," Steph confided, hanging her coat on my rack. "And Alison . . ."

"I threw up in the car." She blushed.

"That bad?" I asked and both women nodded.

"How did she react when you told her we were coming?"

"Pretty well, under the circumstances." I smiled, wishing I were a better liar.

Steph raised her eyebrows. "I seriously doubt that."

"I think the first few seconds will be the worst," I advised. "Like tearing off a Band-Aid. Then it'll be a piece of cake." God, I hoped I was right.

"Well, here goes nothing," Steph whispered before winking at Alison and calling out, "Hey, Mom, we're here!"

Our mother stepped out of the kitchen, wiping her hands

on a dish towel. It was something I'd seen her do a thousand times before, but the simple movement had never looked so sinister. The rolled-up sleeves of her blouse, coupled with a look of fierce determination, made me wonder if I were about to witness a fistfight.

"Darling," Mom said, pulling Steph into her arms and hugging her tightly. "You could do with a haircut."

Steph pulled out of the embrace and offered a tepid smile. She had always been praised for her appearance, her eye for color and the way she managed to pull an outfit together. Mom used to wind Steph's hair into a French braid before school, admiring the sheen and shade of it, matching satin ribbons to her dresses, while my crown of brown was pulled into a practical ponytail, secured by an elastic band.

"I haven't had time for an appointment," Steph mumbled, moving toward Alison in a show of solidarity.

"Make the time." Instead of looking at the couple, Mom picked nonexistent lint from her own blouse.

"So, this is Alison." Steph's tone was one of cautious pride. I felt for her, knowing what it was like to try to please our Queen Bee.

After a moment of deliberation, Mom raised her eyes and gave Alison the kind of once-over she normally reserved for the lower life-forms of waitresses and bank tellers. Her gaze swept from worn suede shoes to black corduroy pants and I regretted Alison's penchant for baggy clothes. She had a nice figure, but did her best to hide it. The only flicker of grudging admiration on Mom's face was in response to the gray mohair sweater visible beneath Alison's coat. Even a homophobe couldn't condemn the craftsmanship. She paused, inevitably, at Alison's hairstyling attempt and I watched Mom's growing frown of disappointment. If I were a mind reader, I'd have bet she was wishing her daughter's girlfriend looked a little more like Heather Locklear.

"It's nice to meet you, Alison." Mom smiled tightly. "You and Stephanie have been friends for some time, I take it." She extended a hand, and the two women shook a slow greeting.

"We're *partners*, Mom," Steph answered before Alison had a chance to speak.

"Partners." Mom offered a short bark of false laughter, dropping her hand. "It sounds like a business." She tucked a loose strand of hair behind her ear.

"Well, we *are* in what you have referred to as 'that homo-sexual business' together."

I could see the strain in Steph's face. She grabbed Alison's abandoned hand, a gesture that prompted Mom to examine her shoes.

"Drinks, anyone?" I asked. "A rum and Coke, maybe?"

"Sounds great." Alison pulled free and followed me into the kitchen.

I found four tumblers in the cupboard and poured a gener-ous splash of rum into each. Alison topped them off with Coke.

"That wasn't so bad, was it?" I asked hopefully.

"Compared to what?" She laughed. "A Pap smear?"

"Come on." I couldn't help smiling. "It could have been worse."

"You're right," she said, lifting two glasses and heading toward the living room. "I bet she's got a mean left hook."

I followed her, clutching the remaining glasses in shaking hands.

"Thank you, dear," Mom said, lifting a drink and swallow-ing it in one long gulp. "I think I could do with another."

I handed her my glass and headed to the kitchen to pour a fresh one, hoping she wasn't planning to get loaded and uncertain of how to stop her if she was.

"Well, congratulations on your promotion, Claire." Mom lifted her glass when I returned to the living room.

Steph and Alison followed suit, offering overbright smiles before settling on the couch. Mom sat in my rocking chair and I took the recliner while we all drank in silence.

"Why don't you guys tell Mom about your new place?" I asked, relieved when some of the life drifted back into my sister as she spoke about their home in Tigard. I gradually relaxed enough to breathe regularly once Steph and Mom had been talking for a while and Alison added details about the renovations they'd been working on.

"It sounds lovely," Mom said, lifting her glass to capture the last drop of rum.

"You should come and see it." Steph sounded hopeful.

"We'd love to show you what we've done," Alison added with heartbreaking enthusiasm. "Why don't you spend a couple of nights with us while you're here?"

"I think the meat is probably ready," Mom said, rising from her seat and walking toward the kitchen without another word. Her braid thumped against her back with each step and I had to fight the urge to strangle her with it.

I jumped from my seat with an apologetic smile for my guests and followed her, noting that Steph looked ready to explode.

Mom took the roast out of the oven and transferred it to a serving platter.

"Listen," I hissed. "I know how you feel about this whole situation, but, for Stephanie's sake, could you just *try* to give Alison a chance?"

"I haven't done anything wrong." She poured brussels sprouts into a ceramic bowl, then did the same with the carrots.

"Can you make an attempt at conversation, at least?"

"Do you have any idea how difficult this is for me?" She mashed the potatoes with unnecessary force.

"Just give her a chance."

"I don't know what you expect me to do."

"I'd like to hear you say one nice thing to her this evening. Give her one measly compliment and you'll be off the hook for now."

She considered the challenge for almost a full minute.

"I'll see what I can do."

When we were all seated at the table, conversation dried up.

"This looks great, Claire," Steph finally offered. "Mom, can you please pass the potatoes?"

The bowl was passed and Mom's gaze lingered on Alison's plate. "Would you like some brussels sprouts?"

"No, thank you." Alison added applesauce to the plate.

"Hmph." Mom adjusted the napkin on her lap with a frown. "Marco loved my brussels sprouts."

My knife blade shrieked against my plate and I looked up to see Alison blushing.

"I always made them," Mom continued, "because I knew how much he loved my secret recipe."

"Marco *ate* your sprouts, Mom." There was steel in Steph's voice.

"That's what I said." Mom liberally salted her meat.

"No, you said he *loved* them. I'm telling you that he simply *ate* them."

"What on earth are you getting at?"

"I don't think we need to get into all of this right now," I said. "Gravy, anyone?"

"Yes, please." Alison reached for the ladle.

"He didn't like them, Mom."

"Are you trying to hurt my feelings?"

"He ate them to please you." Steph turned to Alison and explained, "He didn't want to rock the boat."

"Well," Mom sniffed with distaste at Steph's remarks, "that was a nice gesture. Very thoughtful."

"I'll capsize the fucking boat if I have to," Steph muttered.

"What was that?" Mom asked.

"Nothing."

During the silent meal, Steph repeatedly attempted to touch Alison's hand or pat her wrist, but Alison always pulled away, obviously aware that the affection was only meant to shove the relationship down a certain houseguest's throat.

"This pork is delicious," Alison said.

"We're just a couple of meat-loving *vagitarians,*" Steph muttered.

"What was that?" Mom asked.

"Nothing," I assured her, hoping Steph wasn't planning to run through all of her precious puns.

When Mom finally initiated conversation, it was an invitation to Steph and me alone. She talked about our childhood, and when Alison jumped in to ask about Steph's first dance recital or drama productions, Mom abruptly changed the subject.

Alison made several attempts to talk about current events, entertainment, and even the weather, but sparking a conversation with Mom was like trying to light a wet newspaper.

I waited through the entire main course and it wasn't until dessert that Mom kept her promise of a compliment.

"That is a gorgeous sweater," she finally said, touching Alison's sleeve between bites of apple crumble.

"Thanks. My granny knit it."

"That's wonderful," Mom murmured. "Tell me, does your granny know you're—"

"Size?" Steph asked.

"That wasn't what I was asking." Mom glared at her.

"Yes," Alison intervened, "she knows."

"Alison's family is involved in this crazy thing called unconditional love, Mom. Have you ever heard of it?"

"I don't appreciate your smart remarks," Mom snapped.

"And I don't appreciate your . . ." Steph paused and I held my breath while she contained her anger, "remarks, either."

"More crumble, anyone?" I lifted the bowl, but there were no takers.

I poured coffee and hoped it would thaw everyone out a little.

"I really like your hair like that," Steph murmured to Alison.

"Thank you."

"Hmph," Mom snorted.

"Do you have something to say?" Steph asked.

"No."

"I think you do."

"I was just going to comment that it's very difficult to style thin hair."

"*Fine* hair," Steph corrected.

"Yes, well, it tends to look lank and desperate when it isn't handled properly." She gazed pointedly at the hair. "Quite desperate."

Alison blushed.

"I beg your pardon?" Steph asked.

"Cream? Sugar?" I interjected.

"Just cream for me, thank you," Alison murmured, taking my lead.

"So, uh, what are you guys up to tonight?" I asked, in a desperate bid to redirect the conversation.

"I don't know." Steph shrugged, apparently willing to let Mom off the hook for the time being. "Ali, are you still in the mood for a chick flick?"

The clatter of Mom's spoon against her saucer was enough to turn all of our heads.

"I think that's quite enough." The blood rushed to her cheeks and her dark eyes glittered with anger.

"What's wrong?" I asked.

"What's *wrong*?" she snapped. "Obviously, I don't want to hear all of the gory details."

"What are you talking about?" Steph was clearly as bewildered as I was.

I glanced at Alison, her fork frozen halfway to her mouth.

Mom pushed her chair back from the table and lifted her empty dessert bowl. "I am making an honest effort to deal with this *relationship*." She tilted her head in Alison's direction, but refused to look at her. "And you have to brandish it in my face, doing your damndest to make me as uncomfortable as possible."

"What in the hell are you talking about?" I asked.

"Language," Mom pointed a stiff finger at me while continuing to glare at my sister.

"I have no idea why you're so upset." Steph raised her hands in mock surrender.

Mom stared at the dish in her hand and said, "I don't want to be in your bedroom."

"Well, I don't want you there either," Steph said, shooting me a questioning look I didn't have an answer for.

"For the record, I also don't want you in our bedroom," Alison added, finally depositing the food into her mouth and chewing slowly.

"Then don't talk about . . ." Mom paused and took a deep breath, "*chick flicks* at the dinner table." Her face was almost purple with embarrassment.

"What?" I choked, before the others could speak.

"You heard me. It's hard enough knowing these two live together, and when you talk about . . ." Her voice tapered off.

"Chick flicks," I prompted, finally seeing the light and trying to contain my laughter.

"Yes," Mom hissed, shooting me a dirty look.

"What do you think a chick flick is?" A smile tugged at Steph's lips as she spoke.

"Can we stop using that term?" Mom sighed.

"Can you answer the question?" I asked, feigning innocence.

"I'd rather not. Let me just say that the details of what you girls do in private is of no interest to me whatsoever."

I coughed to cover my laughter.

"And," she continued, "I may not spend a lot of time in the city, but don't think I can't understand your jargon."

"Do you mean Lesbianese?" Stephanie asked, eyes sparkling.

"Or Dyke-lish?" I added.

"*Enough!*" Mom snapped, and I saw the glistening of unformed tears in her eyes.

We had gone too far, and I felt a sliver of guilt. Granted, the results were disastrous, but maybe in her own backward and tactless way, Mom was trying to deal with Steph's new life.

"Mom, it's a movie," I offered.

She looked at me blankly.

"Like a sci-fi flick or a horror flick," I explained. "It's a movie that appeals to women. A chick flick."

"A movie," Mom repeated slowly, and our lesbian guests nodded.

She returned to her seat and scooped another serving of crumble onto her plate. The silence lasted for several minutes as the tension seeped out of the room.

"What did you think it was?" Steph finally asked.

"Never mind." Mom's mouth tightened and I knew she'd never tell us. "I'd just like to know," she said, when she'd regained her composure, "is it so wrong for me to want a normal family?"

"What do you consider normal?" Steph asked.

"Husbands, wives, grandchildren. Where does a gay couple fit in?" She glanced at Alison. "Please, don't take offense, dear. This has nothing to do with you as a person."

I bit my lower lip and waited for Steph's composure to crack.

Instead, Alison's cheeks flushed and her jaw muscles strained against her skin. "I've tried to be as pleasant and polite as possible this evening, Mrs. McLeod." Her hands were shaking. "You're the mother of the woman I love, and I'd hoped we would be able to see eye to eye. I'd *hoped* we could get past at least some of the problems I know you have with this relationship." She took an unsteady breath. "Unfortunately, this has everything to do with me as a person. It's who I am. It's who Stephanie is." She stood and offered me a weak smile. "It was lovely to be here, Claire, but I think I've had enough visiting for one evening."

"You don't have to leave," I said, rising from my seat as Steph followed Alison's lead toward the door.

"Yes, we do," Steph said, giving me a quick hug.

"I'm sorry," I whispered.

"So am I."

I closed the door after them and turned to face my mother, anger welling up inside me.

"I hope you're happy," I snapped.

"Surely you aren't going to blame me for the way this evening turned out." She started clearing the dishes from the table. "That Alison character had some nerve, talking to me that way."

SIX

Mom's behavior had me livid, and while I half expected a knock-down-drag-out over the topic of Steph and Alison, the apartment was curiously calm in their wake. Despite my anger, I was too tired to wrangle with her firmly closed mind and she appeared to have run out of righteous steam.

She washed and I dried the dishes in surprisingly companionable silence, punctuated only by the slosh of a sponge and the gentle chime of clean plates being returned to their stacks.

As we worked, my mind wandered to Tigard, where my sister was undoubtedly apologizing to Alison while cursing Mom's very existence. I couldn't blame her. Mom had treated the apartment like *The Gong Show* set, bashing Alison at every opportunity, and I was amazed the lesbians stayed as long as they had, under the circumstances. Mom had a long history of being demanding, unrelenting, pushy, and manipulative in turn, but I'd never seen her nasty.

When Steph and I were kids, Mom insisted we invite every girl in our classes to birthday parties, and ensured that everyone took home a prize. She deposited loaves of zucchini bread on the doormats of new neighbors and was the first person to approach the freshly divorced or widowed with offers of bridge games then blind dates.

Her treatment of Alison went against everything she'd taught us about kindness.

I understood that she wanted her daughter to be straight and couldn't fathom an attraction between women. Obviously, she wished reality was vastly different for her oldest child, but did she have to be so blatantly intolerant?

She passed me the steak knives, handles first, murmuring, "Careful, they're sharp."

It was as instinctive to her as thrusting her arm across my chest when she stopped the car suddenly, a habit she was still unable to break.

I supposed that need to protect was the core of her discomfort with Steph's lifestyle. Even though my sister and I were adults, roaming free and making our way in the world, Mom still wanted to shelter us, and I honestly loved her for that, but cursed her efforts at the same time. She had ruined everything.

"See how little time it takes to keep things tidy around here?" she asked, rinsing the soapy water from her sponge and squeezing it dry.

I nodded without a word.

"If you did this every night, you'd never have a stack in the sink," she added.

"Ingenious," I muttered. "Now, why didn't I think of that?"

"I'd rather you didn't take that tone with me." She tucked a loose strand of hair behind her ear with practiced precision.

"Then stop criticizing me."

"It wasn't a . . ." She sighed. "Claire, I was just making a suggestion."

"Well, to be honest with you, I'm a little tired of *suggestions* right now." I turned toward the living room.

"Fine," she sniffed, following me.

I glanced at my watch, hoping I could claim exhaustion and sneak off to bed.

It was only eight o'clock.

"What do you feel like doing?" I asked.

"I don't know." She sat on my couch and flipped through the newspaper until she found the entertainment section. After scanning the TV listings for a couple of minutes, while I stared at the floor and wished I were anywhere else in the world, she announced that *Annie* was showing, for what must have been the sixteen millionth time. Despite the odds, neither of us had ever seen it, so, against my better judgment, we spent the remainder of the evening anesthetized by good cheer and positive thinking in the form of a plucky redhead.

Was there any other kind?

When the movie ended in a saccharine-coated finale, I stretched my arms and exaggerated a yawn so there would be no confusion about whether we should stay up and talk.

"I'm beat." I stood and stretched some more, groaning for emphasis. "Do you need to call Dad?"

"No," Mom said, removing the elastic from her hair and loosening the braid with deft fingers. The lamp picked up her red highlights and I admired the rippling length of her hair.

"Oh, you already talked to him?" I hoped she'd called collect. My fifty-three-cent raise wasn't enough to support her gift of the gab.

"No."

"Why not?" I would have expected a courtesy call, at least.

She pushed the hair back over her shoulders. "I'm sure he

knows I got here all right. We don't live in each other's back pockets, Claire."

"No one's saying you do."

"I saw him this morning."

"Sorry." I shrugged. "I just assumed you'd want to talk to him." I checked my watch. "I guess it's pretty late there anyway, isn't it?"

"Yes. Too late."

There was something strange in her tone, an almost melancholy quality I'd never heard from her, but before I could question it, she brought up the issue of sleeping arrangements.

"You take my room. I'm fine out here," I told her.

"I don't want to put you out of your own bed, honey."

"It doesn't matter." An absolute lie.

"No, you go ahead."

"Take the room, Mom."

"You have to go to work in the morning."

"What difference does that make?"

The verbal arm-wrestling continued for several minutes and I began to wonder if insincerity was a genetic trait when we both insisted we preferred the uneven springs of my second-rate couch to the comfort of a queen-sized bed.

Apparently Mom expected the battle to go on a bit longer than it did, offering me a weak smile when I conceded defeat, handed her a couple of blankets, and left her to the living room.

"I'll be just fine," she called after me as I closed my bedroom door. "Don't worry about me."

"I won't," I muttered, before undressing and crawling under the quilted cloud of my duvet. I passed out the moment I hit the pillow.

✑

After a dreamless sleep, my alarm clock announced a new day with its usual obnoxious buzz. I could have set it to play music instead, but the aural assault was all the incentive I needed to leap out of bed and cross the chilly hardwood to turn the bloody thing off. I'd had trouble in the past with snooze bars, relaxing music, and gentle beeps, and I'd learned the hard way that I needed an alarm that was truly alarming, or I'd never leave the sleep-warmed comfort of bed.

I rubbed my eyes and attempted to pat my chronic bed-head into something less frightening, then slipped into a robe and started for the shower.

"Good morning," Mom called from the kitchen, as I caught the scent of eggs cooking.

"Morning." I cleared the sleep from the corners of my eyes.

"Breakfast is almost ready. Do you want me to iron your clothes while you shower?"

"No thanks."

"Are you sure, Claire? I thought you'd want to look sharp for your first day on the new job."

"Right," I mumbled, "the promotion." Neal hadn't mentioned dressing up, but maybe Mom was right. He was giving me more responsibility, the least I could do was look less wrinkled than usual.

"Maybe a blazer?" Mom asked, leaning in the doorway, spatula in hand.

"Yeah, I guess that would be good."

"And a skirt?"

"Well, that might be taking things a little too far . . ."

"Whatever you think, dear." She smiled.

"Maybe I'll—"

"But I would wear the skirt."

"Okay, already." I closed the bathroom door and left the wardrobe details to her.

I ended up cutting my usual shower time in half when, accidentally or otherwise, Mom ran the kitchen tap three separate times while I dodged scorching, then freezing water, banging my head on the mounted metal soap dish when I tried to turn the water off. Statistics on bathtub deaths suddenly made sense.

The scrambled eggs were delicious, a fact I reluctantly confessed to Mom, who embarked on a speech about the importance of breakfast while I ate as quickly as possible. She'd hung my pressed outfit on the back of my bedroom door: a navy blazer, a white silk blouse that must have been crushed to tennis ball size in the bottom of my closet, and a navy skirt with white pinstripes I'd forgotten I owned. I slipped the clothing on, pleasantly surprised at how professional I appeared. Some silver hoop earrings completed the new look, and I stepped into the kitchen for Mom's approval.

"Very nice," she said. "Do you think you should add a scarf?"

"No."

"A little splash of red would top it all off."

"What makes you think I have a red scarf?"

"I gave you one for your birthday last year."

"Oh, yeah." I'd recycled the gift for Heather's birthday and had never seen her wear it, either. "I think I'm okay without it."

"You look terrific," Mom said, with a wide smile. "Good luck wielding your new power."

"Thanks, Mom." I'd expected things to be a little more

strained after last night's main event, especially since we hadn't addressed any of the obvious issues meeting Alison had raised, but I wasn't about to get her started.

I still felt slightly ashamed that I hadn't pushed for an all-night debate on Steph's behalf, but it was too easy to go with Mom's flow.

"Remember the little people," she said, with a wink.

"I'll be tripping over them all day." I laughed, relieved that we were both inclined to act "normal." "See you tonight."

The moment I stepped out the front door, everything went my way. My bus approached just as I reached the stop and, for the first time in months, I got a seat. My stomach was full and my hair was twisted into a rather sophisticated knot, thanks to Mom's expertise. I was pressed, polished, and found myself humming all the way to work. I caught the security guy downstairs admiring me while I waited for the elevator and somehow it didn't matter that he was not only ancient, but myopic.

I ignored Carol's snort as I marched past reception and into an office buzzing with activity.

"Meeting in five minutes," Jason warned from behind the cube wall as I struggled with my bottom drawer.

"We had one yesterday," I groaned, parking my satchel in the drawer, then remembered the meeting was about *me*.

I could hardly wait.

"I know, but . . ." His face loomed over the wall and I noticed his anemic goatee was approaching completion. "Hey, what are you all dressed up for?"

I felt the color rise in my cheeks. "Dressed up?" I scoffed. "I'm hardly . . . I mean . . . I'm not dressed up."

"Could have fooled me," he sang, disappearing into his own work space.

"Hey, Claire," Heather said from behind me. "What are you all dolled up for?"

"I'm not." The last thing I needed was to draw attention to myself before Neal had the chance to tell everyone about my promotion.

"I've never seen you in a skirt before. Oh my God," she gasped, "nobody died, did they?"

"No, I—"

"Because I'm really sorry if I brought it up and you don't want to talk about it." Even her frizzy hair seemed to flinch.

"Well . . ."

"So, are you going to a funeral?"

"Heather, slow down for a second. No one died."

"Whew." She wiped the back of her turtleneck sleeve across her forehead. "By the way, we've got a meeting in a couple of minutes."

"So I hear." I smiled tightly and turned toward my desk to grab a pen and notepad.

"You should have come to the pub last night, Claire," she said as we walked toward the conference room. "It was awesome."

"Awesome, eh?" The last time I'd heard the word used with sincerity was in eighth grade.

"Yeah. Jason, Adam, and I split a couple of pitchers. God, he is so funny!"

"Who?" I asked, kicking myself for missing out. "Adam?"

"No, Jason. He's hilarious. Adam's a little quiet for my taste."

I was glad to hear it. Not that I couldn't give Heather and her rash a run for the money, but I wanted the playing field to be clear of any competition.

We reached the doorway and Heather raced to grab a chair while the rest of us filed into the room.

I wanted to stand, as I always did, at the back, arms crossed in a practiced pose of subtle defiance. But I couldn't. My promotion meant I belonged in a gray area I couldn't yet define, but I instinctively knew crossed arms and an insolent lean were out of the question.

Instead, I stood near the overhead projector, aiming for the look of a casual observer and hoping my coworkers wouldn't be too upset that I was corporate material and they were doomed to remain peons.

"Okay, everybody, pipe down." I couldn't see Neal right away, but eventually spotted his stubby fingers reaching above the crowd to get our attention. Eventually, amid a lot of unnecessary chatter, everyone was either seated or standing at the back of the room, and Neal got down to business.

"I know you're all anxious to get back to the phones," he began, only to be interrupted by barely stifled laughter from around the room. "So I'll make this quick. There are going to be some changes around here—"

"Fresh candy in the vending machine?" a voice called out.

"Something a little more substantial," Neal assured us, rubbing his hands together.

"Flavored coffee?" the same voice asked.

"No. I'm talking about a *staffing* change. I've selected an employee from within your ranks to assist with our production statistics."

"Big Brother strikes again," Jason muttered, making me wince.

"This person will compile stats on each employee, establish a ranking system, and produce weekly reports which I'll review and post next to my office door."

"How many fucking numbers do they need?" Jason whispered in my ear, "and who gives a rat's ass about the results, anyway?"

I held my tongue and waited for Neal to complete his announcement, pitying Jason's bitterness. Obviously, *he* wanted the job. I felt a bit guilty, since he'd been with Alta Media almost a year longer than I had, but what could I do? Turn down the position so a less qualified candidate could have a shot at it? Was Jason even a candidate to begin with? I seriously doubted it.

"Your new department auditor, as of today, is Claire McLeod."

"Jesus," Jason whispered.

I blushed when everyone turned to look at me. I waited for some congratulatory smiles, or thumbs-up, but before my coworkers had a chance to react to the news, Neal barked, "Now back to work, folks."

I started toward the door and the rest of the room stood still, apparently waiting for me to exit first. I took another step.

Of course, I wasn't naive enough to expect a round of applause and a gushing receiving line as I left the meeting, but the eerie silence, coupled with what seemed like an enormous number of fierce glares, took me entirely by surprise. What was wrong with everybody?

On closer inspection, did Heather actually look *disgusted*? Was what I assumed would be jealousy actually, I gulped, *pity*? It was a promotion, for crying out loud! Why did they all look disappointed in me?

As I made my way toward the door with slow steps, I was acutely aware of a roomful of eyes upon me. I felt the kind of embarrassment I associated with the birthday spanking machine I'd had to crawl through as a kid. My promotion should have been something to celebrate, but instead I felt the sickening dread of squeezing between countless knobby knees, while gleeful snickering accompanied a slap on the ass.

How had something so right suddenly become so wrong?

I crept back to my desk, pretending not to notice that no one said a word to me. Before Jason and Heather returned to our workstation, I signed on to my computer and maneuvered my headphones around my cumbersome hair knot. Dammit! I'd dressed up for *this?*

I tried to lose myself in the work and, when the time came, skipped my morning break. I suspected the watercooler was no longer the place for me, but I didn't know where else to go.

I ran through nineteen surveys, mainly because I didn't exchange anecdotes with my work team between calls. I concentrated on the task at hand, certain that once people had the opportunity to accept my upward mobility, things would return to normal.

By lunchtime, my stomach had settled and I'd convinced myself that I was manufacturing feelings of isolation and imagining that the staff reaction was far worse than it really was. There was no hostility, was there?

It was the perfect day for lunch with someone who would assure me that everything was okay in my world. Someone who was even more pitiful than I could imagine being. It was the perfect day to spend time with Heather.

Just before noon I gathered my satchel and coat, walking around the cube wall to wait for her to finish a call. She shrugged apologetically when she saw me, then pointed at her headset, mouthing, "I'm on the phone," as though I couldn't guess.

No matter what happened, I'd never be as desperate to be liked as Heather was—a reassuring thought. When she finally hung up, I made my move.

"Busy day, huh, Heather?"

"Yeah," she agreed halfheartedly.

"I'm starving. What about you?" She was always after me to go to some takeout place or another.

"I guess I could eat." She shrugged, refusing to meet my eyes.

"What do you think about hitting the food court at the mall for lunch?"

"Uh," she scratched the back of her hand absently, "I don't think so."

"There's always bento," I said.

"Not so tempting today," she mumbled as the rough patch of skin reddened.

"Other plans?" I asked, amazed she'd declined.

"Plans? No, I . . . well . . ."

"What's wrong?"

"Sorry, Claire. It's just that . . ."

"What?"

"You're . . ."

"What?" I gasped with exasperation.

"You're one of them now."

What in the hell was she talking about?

"One of who?"

"You know . . ."

"No, I don't."

"Management." She blanched.

"More like middle management," Jason said, peering around the wall and smiling wickedly. "And that's even worse."

"Very funny." I tried to laugh, despite the tightening in my stomach.

"So, Claire," Jason said, "just out of curiosity, what did they give you to narc on us?"

"Narc?"

"How much are you going to make for turning on the rest of us, reporting our every move?"

"Ha." I choked on my own fake laugh. "It's not like that. . . ."

"Is it worth an extra buck an hour, or whatever they're giving you?"

"Don't be ridiculous." My voice shook. "Listen, I'm starving, so I'll see you guys after lunch."

I scurried out of the office, making eye contact with no one, ashamed of the fifty-three-cent truth of the matter and mortified that I'd already accepted the job.

SEVEN

My status around the office didn't improve after lunch and, thanks to a three-item combination plate at Peking Palace, neither did my stomach.

In the space of a few hours, my identity had changed from what had been a frustratingly bland "Claire" to a mocking "she," as in "Who does she think she is, anyway?" or, "Have you seen what she's wearing today?" and, "I saw her stats on the Travel Montana campaign. She sucks."

I wanted to knock the watercooler over and demand some respect, or, more likely, beg for a little slack, but didn't have the nerve. They acted like taking a promotion was the moral equivalent of a double homicide. As if they would have turned down the position if it were offered to them. Of course, Heather wouldn't have been a contender, but Pauline, next to the window? She would have grabbed that fifty-three cents, taking it as incentive to extend her bootleg Eminem collection. Dan Carter, self-proclaimed expert on ink-and-toner cartridges, would have greedily added auditor to his growing empire of job titles, which included break room supply monitor and fire marshall. Even my very own cubemate, Jason, who couldn't see the irony in being president of an anarchist club, would have sported a clip-on tie if he'd thought there was a raise in it. Hypocrites. My coworkers were a bunch of latte-loving hypocrites in twill pants.

I just wished they'd talk to me.

I dove into my work, harassing formerly happy homemakers and retirees with my dental inquisition. I asked about flavors, colors, gels, pastes, packaging, and advertising, filling the blank spaces on my screen as they answered. I completed fifteen questionnaires in two hours, despite four hang-ups and six refusals. I was told to fuck off twice and didn't take it personally.

Steph called around three o'clock and I whispered the lowdown on my miserable peers.

"Give them a couple of weeks," she suggested. "Lackeys don't adapt well to change. Kind of like mothers."

"I'm sorry about last night."

"You've got nothing to be sorry for. Just a sec." I heard a muffled, "Mr. Jarvelle, that's the ladies' room. Go to your left. Left!" before she returned. "Sorry, they switched his medication and he's all messed up. God, I hate swing shift. What were you saying?"

"Last night. I just feel like I should have done . . . something."

"You tried to facilitate an awkward evening, and that's enough. Hold on . . . your *other* left, Mr. Jarvelle!"

"I think she might loosen up, in time," I said hopefully when I had regained Steph's attention.

"I'm not planning to wait for her approval. It's not my problem."

Unfortunately, it was *my* problem, and I had no desire to spend the next decade as a go-between.

"Listen, Mom and I are supposed to go for dinner Sunday night," I lied. "Why don't you come?"

"I think Alison's had enough for now."

"Then come on your own. It'll be fun." Who was I kidding?

"I don't really—"

"I know *she's* upset. I'm living with her, for Christ's sake. And I know *you're* pissed off, not because I'm a supersleuth, but because you make no attempt to hide the fact. You've got to talk to her sometime."

"No, I don't."

"Steph," I whined.

"What time?" She sighed.

"Seven."

"Where?"

"Napoli."

"You're buying," she barked before hanging up.

"I guess she's allowed to make personal calls now," Heather stage-whispered to Jason.

Thankfully, I didn't hear his response.

I finished almost twenty surveys in the last two hours of my shift, counting the minutes until a weekend of freedom. I couldn't believe that one day of being shunned at the office made the prospect of two days with my mother seem tempting.

When five o'clock finally arrived, I feigned interest in the contents of my drawers while everyone around me gathered their coats and bags. If I'd left with the gang, I imagined having half an elevator to myself while they squeezed together in the other half, cringing at the possibility of traitor cooties.

"Are you into Thai tonight?" Jason asked Heather. "A bunch of us are going to try that new place on Twenty-third."

"Sounds great!" she gushed, although I knew she hated Thai. Her screwy stomach couldn't handle anything.

"See you there," he said, then glanced at me. "You're welcome to come too, Claire."

Too.

A mere eight hours earlier, Heather would have been the add-on.

"Thanks, but I've got plans."

"Suit yourself." He shrugged.

"I will!" I almost called after him, but bit my bottom lip instead, drawing blood.

"Have a nice weekend," Heather murmured as she passed my desk.

"You too," I called after her cheerfully, hoping she scratched her rash down to the bone in her sleep.

Mom was sitting on the couch when I got home, apparently anxious for my arrival. Suddenly, I missed my lonely evenings, those bygone days of miserable solitude.

"What do you think?" She raised her knitting needles and waved a delicate rectangle of pale yellow wool.

"What is it?" I asked, fearing the answer.

"A sleeve. I finished the back this morning. Cute, isn't it?"

"Who's it for?"

"No one in particular." She winked. "I'm stocking up."

Ah, the knitting. I could only imagine the state of the spare room at home, teeny lavender and white cardigans piled on my old student desk, the chest of drawers stuffed with impossibly small hats and booties, popcorn-stitched receiving blankets, and Aran sweaters for three- and four-year-olds.

When I was in high school, she'd invited me to sit with her at the kitchen table one evening, armed with a stack of knitting magazines and a black Jiffy marker.

"Tell me which ones you'd like," she said, felt tip poised over open pages.

"I don't think they'll fit, Mom."

"They're *baby* clothes, Claire." She sighed with exasperation. "For your baby."

"I don't have a baby," I reminded her. "I'm in ninth grade."

"Just choose some patterns."

"Why do we have to do this now?" I groaned, knowing Steph was watching *Cheers* in the next room.

"It's fun, Claire," Mom assured me, as though having to tell me didn't belie the words.

"Fine." I stood and pointed randomly at the pictures. "This one, that one, and the cable-knit sweater."

Mom marked each with a black asterisk. "Steph liked that cable-knit too."

"Fantastic," I grunted.

"There's nothing wrong with being prepared, you know. I could get arthritis in a few years and never knit again. Then where would you be?"

"Buying baby clothes at the mall." I shrugged, heading for the family room.

Obviously, nine years later, she showed no sign of slowing down on Operation Impregnation.

"After I finish this one I've got wool for a baby shawl. Pale pink. You'll love it."

"My baby thanks you, well in advance."

"I'd knit you a sweater if you wanted me to." She lowered the needles to her lap in what I could only hope was a gesture of surrender.

Before I could tell her that I'd love one, she added, "But I know you're not interested."

"What?"

"Well, you never wear the ones I made for you." She sighed and resumed knitting.

I'd wanted simple wool pullovers in past years, but she'd insisted on elaborate patterns and fuzzy wool. Garish colors and puffy sleeves. Six sweaters were crammed into my bottom drawer at that very moment, the power of their collective static cling growing by the day.

"They were itchy."

"Mohair's very expensive, you know."

"So I've heard." Fourteen thousand times.

"Anyway, these baby things don't take any time at all. I like making them."

"Great."

"Jen Alder is having a girl in March, you know."

"Is that right?" I mumbled, worrying that the act of unbuttoning my coat would be considered encouragement.

"And Dave Morrison is having a baby in January."

"Well, isn't that a miracle of modern science."

"You know what I mean." She rolled her eyes. "You missed out with that one. His mother told me he had a crush on you."

"I know, Mom. That was in kindergarten. He proposed. I declined."

His fingers always smelled like pee.

"Bet you would have thought twice if you'd known you'd be single this long."

I dug my fingernails into the flesh of my palms.

Remain calm.

"What do you want for dinner tonight?" I asked. "I was thinking it might be nice to hang out here. Get some takeout and a video." I couldn't help but think of Heather and the rest of them ordering spicy dishes and foreign beer while I spent

Friday night with my mother and the ever-growing wardrobe of an imaginary baby.

"That sounds fine, dear."

"I'll pick it up. Pizza okay?" I asked.

"Perfect." Mom smiled.

"What do you want on it?"

"Anything but anchovies."

Ahh. Pet peeve number seven hundred and twenty-nine. When was the last time anyone had been threatened with an anchovy pizza?

"I'll be back in a bit," I muttered.

There was a huge line at Slice of Life, so I decided to hit the video store first. Half of the shelves were empty, which was to be expected on a Friday night, but even a full selection wouldn't have made it easier to find a movie to suit Mom's taste. It took me half an hour to select something that promised no violence or coarse language, no explicit sex scenes (or inferred, for that matter), no Meryl Streep or Sally Field (she had some unspoken issue with both of them), and no subtitles. Then, there was my own opinion to consider. No babies or wedding scenes.

I finally settled on a romantic comedy that, by law, had to star Meg Ryan, and headed for the counter, where an argument between the acne-coated clerk and an overbearing male customer was taking place.

"All I want is my money back." The man's voice was loud enough for the entire store to hear, but only a couple of people turned to look.

"I can't do that, sir."

"Why not?"

"Because the video isn't defective."

"It *is* defective. It was a piece of shit."

That got the attention of the kids in the game section, who giggled as they zapped aliens.

"That isn't grounds for a refund." The clerk's face flushed a deep red.

"Where's your manager?"

"I *am* the manager."

"You've got to be kidding." He snorted. "Listen, I paid good money for this movie and I was ripped off. I want my three-fifty back."

"Sir," I saw the clerk's spine stiffen. "You chose this movie. Nobody forced you to rent it."

I peered over the man's shoulder and saw that the video in question was *Police Academy V.* Dear God. At least he got his money's worth on that lobotomy.

"Can you believe people?" I asked, when it was my turn at the counter. "I mean, pay the fine and move on."

"Tell me about it," he said, with a shy smile.

"And is it that hard to return it on time?"

"We even have a drop box for after hours." He shook his head with disgust.

He scanned my membership card and the computer bleated in response. It might as well have been an air raid siren as it commanded the attention of everyone in the store.

"What's wrong?" I asked.

"You have a late charge." His eyebrows shot up toward his bleached-blond hairline. "A *substantial* late charge."

"How much?" I felt my jaw tighten. I hadn't been in this store since Paul and I were together, and that was ages ago.

"Eighty-two dollars and nine cents."

"*No way!*" I screeched. "For what?"

"*Pee-wee's Big Adventure.* You had it for, let's see, almost three and a half weeks."

"I could have bought it for less than that."

"Maybe you should have." He paused. "Oh, there's an additional fine for not rewinding it."

"What?"

"We put a 'Be kind, rewind' sticker on each cassette." He was almost apologetic. *Almost.*

"Listen. My boyfriend was supposed to return it," I said, barely controlling the rage bubbling inside me. "He told me he'd taken care of it." Just like he was taking care of paying me back the two hundred dollars he'd borrowed during the post-Christmas sales. The worst of it was, I'd wanted him back for months after he dumped me for that stupid, nameless blonde.

"Do you want to call him? Maybe he'll pay the fee."

"No, I don't want to call him. He's not, oh, for Christ's sake . . ."

"We have a payment plan, if you're interested."

"I'll write you a check."

"Sorry, ma'am, we don't take checks."

I yanked my wallet out of my jacket pocket. I needed most of what I had to cover the pizza. "All I've got is twenty bucks to spare."

"Deal." He smiled, and suddenly I knew he was going to pocket the money. "And that'll be three-fifty for the new one."

I dug through the wallet and thrust a crumpled five at him.

"Don't forget, it's due back by midnight tomorrow."

"Thank you," I said, through gritted teeth.

Paul Clemens. That son of a bitch. *Pee-wee's Big Adventure,* no less.

The word *love* had never passed our lips during the six

months we were together, but that didn't mean I hadn't felt it. He was kind, affectionate, fun, and . . . *gone.* An asshole, really. I was probably better off without him. Adam Carello was undoubtedly more my style. Of course, spending Friday night with my mother wouldn't bring me any closer to knowing for sure.

I returned to the apartment, pizza in hand, to find Mom on the couch, bundled in a knitted afghan, watching *Jeopardy.* The sight of her did nothing to improve my attitude.

At least the movie was a distraction, and while we watched it, I tried as hard as I could to pretend I was as impish and lovable as Meg Ryan. It didn't work. Nothing in my life worked.

On Saturday morning, Mom let me sleep in all the way to eight o'clock before banging on my door, opening it before I'd welcomed her in, and parking herself at the foot of my bed.

"Let's have a tourist day!" she said with a wide smile.

I didn't even want to know what that was, and she didn't wait for me to ask.

"We'll spend the day doing all the touristy things you haven't done yet. People travel from all corners of the world to see things locals never make time for. I know from experience."

Was she the traveler, referring to her twentieth-anniversary trip to San Francisco? Or was she the local, honestly believing there were sights to see in Omaha? If so, she was sorely mistaken. The delights of my hometown were exhausted after a field trip to the Kountze Planetarium in third grade, followed by the exact, same field trip in the eighth grade. Did teachers think it was an entirely different experience during puberty?

"Should we go to the zoo?" she asked.

"On a Saturday?" I shook my head. "It'll be packed."

"What about Multnomah Falls? We could hike to the top."

"I don't know if I'm into a big nature trip."

"Let's go to the Saturday market." She was clearly irritated.

"Too many people."

"What about that big-screen theater you told me about?"

"IMAX? I guess we could go there." I sighed, leery of the prospect of a mother-daughter field trip.

We ate a hearty breakfast and when Mom insisted we walk to the show, I humored her for about five exhaust-heavy blocks before flagging down a bus.

The theater was busy, but not the kid-infested mess it could have been, and the feature was an undersea special. We leaned back in our seats and spent a surreal couple of hours with everything from purple and crimson starfish to darting angelfish, mud sharks, and a giant octopus. I could never remember whether sea horses really existed, or if they were among the mystical ranks of the unicorn, until they floated by onscreen. Their rocking bodies and curled tails were cartoon-ish, lacking only enthusiastic undersea cowboys sporting tiny chaps.

The mood of the film had a calming effect on me and I felt suspended in my surroundings, as though nothing from the outside world could interrupt the moment. The stresses of work disappeared as I watched the arms of a pink anemone sway in a mild current.

How many days had I spent moping around the apartment since Paul and I broke up? How much better would I have felt if I'd gone . . . *anywhere?*

"Look at the whales," Mom whispered, quieter and calmer than she'd been since she'd arrived, as the cameras took us to a whole new world.

Suddenly, we were in the company of two swooning, twirling, smiling beluga whales, full of lumbering grace. The male brushed past his partner with a gentle push, and she turned to follow him.

"Reminds me of your father," Mom murmured with a smile.

Her comment would have seemed silly at any other time or place, but seeing her sitting there, the blue water illuminating her face in shimmering reflection, made me look at things differently.

I waited until the movie was over and guided her to a small coffee shop. "How on earth is Dad like a beluga?"

"I don't know." She shrugged, lifting a cappuccino to her lips and blowing to cool it off. "They have a certain gentleness in common, I suppose." She sipped her drink. "We met at a dance, you know." Her tone was dreamy.

"I thought you went to school together."

"We did, but there were a lot of kids. It was impossible to know everyone."

I'd never been interested in their younger lives, assuming they'd been in homeroom together, or saddled with each other for some rotten history assignment. A dance was something altogether different.

"Go on," I said quietly, nodding encouragement when she looked at me uncertainly.

"I wasn't going to go at all, but Rose Carrow convinced me. She promised it would be a night to remember, and it was. I wore a pale green dress with my mother's pearl earrings. You know, the ones Stephanie wore at her wedding." She frowned.

"Let's forget about all that now," I murmured, wanting the soft moment between us to last. "Tell me about the dance."

"Well," she continued, "the decorating committee had filled the gym with streamers and balloons, and Jerry Davis spiked the punch."

Her lips twitched in a smile as she spoke, and I could almost see her as a girl, nervous and excited, standing next to the snack table.

"Someone, I can't remember who, asked Rose to dance, and she left me standing with a wistful group of girls under the basketball net. Every now and then a boy would ask one of us to dance, but return us to our post when the song ended."

"Did you dance?" I asked.

"A few times," she shrugged, "but not with anyone special. Then, when they announced the final dance was going to be slow, I just knew I wouldn't spend the last few moments in anyone's arms."

She reached for the tendril of auburn that was always straying from her braid and absently stroked it, a vague smile on her lips.

"But . . ." I urged her, intrigued by a side of her I'd never seen.

"Robert McLeod, your father, one of the most handsome boys in the school, although he didn't seem to know it, started walking toward the group of us. I think we all froze, hearts racing with anticipation. He passed by the hopeful cheerleaders and a couple of girls I knew from choir who were gathered around the punch bowl, walking slowly but surely toward our cluster under the basketball net. We must have looked like a bunch of near-misses." She laughed. A tinkling laugh I'd never heard before.

"He picked you?" I asked.

"Some of the others had their fingers crossed tightly

behind their backs, smiling the way they'd practiced in their bathroom mirrors."

"Did you practice too?"

"Oh, we all did it. And practiced kissing our pillows." She giggled.

My mother actually giggled.

"So, you were standing there, waiting," I prompted.

"Yes. Frozen in one spot, slack-jawed and stunned."

"Charming image," I offered dryly.

"Anyway, he stopped directly in front of me and said, "Would you mind if I asked you to dance?" and I said, "I'd mind a lot more if you didn't.""

"You brazen hussy!" I teased.

"I still can't believe that's what came out of my mouth, but there it is."

"And you danced."

"Yes." She paused. "We certainly did."

She let her hand drop to the tabletop.

The rest of our day passed in that same quiet mist of camaraderie, and I couldn't remember the last time we'd talked and walked so much, or spent an entire day together. Surprisingly soon, it was six o'clock, so we boarded a bus back to my place, shrouded in a sense of calm.

When we returned to the apartment, Steph was standing at my front door, waiting. I was surprised to see her, and hopeful that she wasn't armed.

"Where have you guys been?"

"All over." Mom grinned. "We saw a film, stopped for coffee, window-shopped, and ate too much."

"Sounds fun." Steph offered a weak smile.

"It was," I assured her, hoping to convey the general feeling of good cheer we were experiencing.

Once we were inside the apartment, Mom decided to have a shower, leaving Steph and me alone.

"So, what's going on?" I asked, once the water was safely running.

"Nothing, really." She sat on the couch and stared at her hands. "I was just feeling weird about last night."

"I think Mom's over it."

"I'm not." Her lower lip trembled. She had always worn confidence like a second skin, and her obvious distress was unnerving.

"Do you want to talk about it?" I asked, feeling like an idiot. Why would she have brought it up if she didn't want to talk?

"Do you know what it's like to feel like your own mother doesn't respect you?"

"Uh, remember who you're talking to here." I sunk into my rocking chair. "I'm the chronic runner-up in this family." Granted, that very day had been a vastly positive and different experience with Mom, but it wasn't quite enough to blot out twenty-three years of nitpicking and criticism.

"You don't get it, Claire," she said, shaking her enviable blonde mane. "This goes way beyond skating competitions and report cards."

"I know."

"You got to hide in the shadows the whole time we were growing up, while I had to carry your weight and mine."

"Excuse me?" I couldn't believe it. "Are you suggesting that my slouching existence and low self-esteem were preferable to being the princess of *everything*?"

"See?" she snapped. "That's the kind of shit I heard every day from kids at school. Princess of everything, my ass."

My sympathy dried up.

"No one *made* you spin that damn baton, Steph. You weren't forced into a life of Brownies, ballet, and Little Miss Beef Jerky pageants. You *begged* Mom to sign you up."

"First of all, there was only one pageant."

"Which you won," I reminded her.

"That's beside the point. There were pressures on me that you can't even imagine."

"Like what? Being prom queen? That must have been so *painful* for you. I should thank my lucky stars I wasn't cursed with your beauty and talent."

"Could you maybe ditch the sarcasm for two seconds?"

"If you visited planet Earth, I might."

She was silent and scowling for a moment, then looked me in the eye and saw that I wasn't backing down. "Okay, we both had problems."

"Thank you."

"But try to put yourself in my shoes."

Did she mean the ruby slippers worn to star in *The Wizard of Oz*, the soccer cleats that scored the tournament-winning goal, or the white satin pumps she walked down the aisle in, for the most beautiful wedding ever recorded?

"I'll do my best," I told her.

"I did *everything* I thought Mom wanted me to do. I didn't care about half of those trophies or ribbons I won. I just tried to make her proud."

"And you did." She made the whole neighborhood proud. No, make that the whole damn *state*.

"That's right. I jumped through hoops for ages. But now? I'm following my own bliss."

Dear God. "Please don't get all New Age-y on me, okay?"

"I'm not getting . . . oh, never mind. Listen to what I'm saying. I finally figured out what I want, and she won't accept it."

"It's a new concept for her."

"It's as old as time, Claire. Look at Sappho."

"For the record, I don't think calling on the powers of ancient lesbians is going to win Mom over."

"It's not like I'm a *serial killer.*" She raised one finger, then began counting on the rest. "I'm not a drug dealer, or a prostitute. I never skipped class, or broke curfew. I followed in Mom's footsteps with nursing, and paid off all my student loans in record time. I got a job and bought a house. I pay taxes and feed parking meters. I eat healthy foods and baby-sit the neighbor's cat, for crying out loud. I'm not a criminal, I'm a *lesbian.* Big fucking deal, right?" She flopped back on the couch.

"It's going to take some time for her to get used to you and Alison. This is just the beginning, Steph. The fat lady isn't singing yet."

Unfortunately, Mom chose that exact moment to break into a rather flat rendition of Neil Diamond's "Shilo," as she splashed in the shower.

While I choked on my laughter, Steph didn't seem to hear her.

"I spent my whole life dancing to her beat, and now that I've found my own rhythm . . ."

"Found your own rhythm?" I rubbed my forehead, hoping she wasn't going to wax poetic all night.

"Now that I've *found my own rhythm,*" she repeated, with a glare, "she doesn't approve." Her hands were clenched in her lap. "What does she expect me to do? Pretend I'm straight?"

"Just give her time."

"That's so typical, Claire."

"What?"

"You," she snapped. "You *would* suggest that I cower in a corner and wait for her to give me the go-ahead."

"I never said—"

"You just fly under the radar, terrified of rocking the boat."

"I think you're mixing your metaphors." I tried to smile.

"I think you're missing my point."

"Which is what?"

"*I'm* the one who was always walking a tightrope and trying to make everybody happy, while you did whatever you damn well pleased."

I tried to remain calm and address only the real issue. "I fully support you, Steph. You know how much I care about Alison and how happy I am that you found her, but let's be realistic here. You're an adult and can do whatever you want. The only problem you've got is that you're so used to being on top of a pedestal, you're terrified of falling off. I'm amazed to see this, because I always thought you were the stronger of us, but you're actually too *scared* of disappointing her to be yourself. You want her to accept your lifestyle, but you pose it to her as a question instead of a statement."

"What the hell are you talking about?"

"Instead of *asking* her if it's okay to be a lesbian, demand that she respect who you are."

"Hmmm." She bit her bottom lip. "The in-your-face approach."

"Exactly." I nodded. "Show her who's boss."

The shower stopped and Steph rose from the couch. "I better get going."

"What? You aren't going to talk to her?"

"I'll see her at dinner tomorrow. Seven, right?"

I confirmed the time and she was out the door, wearing a mysterious smile.

On Sunday night, after Mom and I spent the day organizing closets and clearing out my drawers—a spring cleaning I'd been putting off for six seasons—I realized I hadn't even mentioned our plans for the evening. I announced the dinner reservation on our third return trip from the Dumpster.

"Tonight?" She was touchingly pleased. "Just the three of us?"

"Yeah, we're going to my favorite Italian place. I think you'll like it."

"I'm sure I will." She smiled serenely as I opened the apartment door, and I hoped she didn't think she'd bumped Alison out of the picture.

The light was flashing on my answering machine, and her mood was inexplicably shattered when I played the message back.

"Claire, this is your dad, just calling to say hi. I, uh, hope you girls are having a great time together. I'll be at the Harlowes' for dinner tonight, so I'll try you again tomorrow."

"Why don't you give him a call?" I suggested, as I headed for my bedroom to change.

"I'll leave it for now." Mom's eyebrows furrowed with annoyance.

"Don't worry about the time. Our reservation's for seven."

"He said he won't be home tonight."

"Maybe he hasn't left yet."

"You're forgetting the time difference," she said, yanking a floral scarf from her suitcase with unnecessary force.

"You could at least try," I reasoned. "He sounds pretty lonely. Maybe—"

"Claire, I'm not in the mood. Now, can you drop it?"

She looked upset and I felt a twinge of uncertainty in my chest. Why had she been so sentimental about a pair of onscreen belugas? Where had the sudden warmth toward *me* come from? Why was she upset at the prospect of talking to her own husband?

Something was going on in Omaha, and I was afraid to find out what.

EIGHT

Mom's mood was so dark while we dressed for dinner, I knew nothing good could come from a night out. She insisted on a cab ride to Napoli, claiming public transit was giving her a migraine. If I'd believed a mere bus trip could have ended the evening right there, I would have dragged her onto the first bus I saw.

"I can't imagine living in this city without a car," she commented, once we were comfortably seated in the backseat of a yellow taxi. "Everything is so far away."

"We have exceptionally good public transit." I didn't point out the obvious fact that I couldn't afford a vehicle, let alone insurance.

I was both surprised and disappointed to find that any closeness I'd felt between us over the past two days had shriveled up so quickly. I'd honestly thought we'd had a long-overdue emotional breakthrough, and I was looking forward to forging ahead with a new kind of relationship.

"Another dreary night." She peered through the window at a downpour that had started the second we left the apartment without umbrellas.

"Dreary season," I corrected. "This will go on for months."
Much like her visit, I feared.

"We'll have to get you some bright scarves or something."
She turned and her eyes met mine.

"What for?"

"All that gray you're wearing is too dismal for words, dear."
She squinted at me. "Do you want some of my blusher? You
look a little washed out."

"No, thank you." I sighed.

Screw bonding. We were back to square one.

After several halting attempts to lighten things up and
recapture a brighter mood, I gave up, and by the time we
reached the restaurant I was starving and irritated.

We stepped into the lobby and I watched for Mom's reaction to the decor. I had fallen in love with the rich red uphol-
stery and starched white tablecloths the first time I'd eaten
there. Paul Clemens, Pee-wee Herman connoisseur and all-
around credit risk, had treated me to dinner there for our one-
month anniversary. We'd spent the night leaning toward each
other over flickering candlelight and under a ceiling that
sparkled with hundreds of tiny white lights. We'd whispered
and chuckled about what we would do when we got back to his
apartment, a mere four blocks away, the presence of a roomful
of diners barely registering for either of us.

Paul Clemens.

I suddenly felt like an eighty-year-old spinster, looking
back on my youth, but forced myself to shake it off. I sensed I
had bigger problems to deal with.

Despite the daunting size of the room, the candles and
muted brick walls crawling with ivy gave Napoli the aura of a
cozy bistro. The wait staff were uniformly gorgeous and incredibly efficient, their sleek, aproned bodies coursing between

tables with the sure steps of runway models. Classical music thickened the haze of dinner conversation and tinkling cutlery, while steaming plates of pasta coaxed my senses into acute awareness.

"This place looks awfully expensive," Mom loudly whispered in my ear. The maître d' gave us a withering look, which she missed entirely.

"Don't worry about the price," I murmured. "It's my treat."

"Where's your sister, anyway?"

"She's probably on her way. I'll give her a couple more minutes before calling."

"You told her seven o'clock, didn't you?" She glanced at the face of her watch.

"It's only five past, Mom."

When the wait had lengthened to fifteen minutes and we were about to lose the reservation, Mom was led to our table while I used the pay phone.

Steph herself answered on the second ring, and I had to bite back a scream. *She hadn't even left the house?*

"It's me," I hissed. "Why aren't you here?"

"I'm almost ready."

"Ready for what? A televised pageant? How long does it take?"

"Do you want me to come or not?"

Braving a couple of hours of maternal mood swings was less than appetizing.

"Yes, but can you hurry it up a bit? All I'm getting from Mom tonight is snide remarks."

"And that comes as a surprise?" She laughed.

"Well, no, but everything was going so well earlier and now she's just—"

"Claire, I am so sick of her judging me. I've gone over the

dinner conversation from the other night about a thousand times in my head, wondering why she can't just accept me for what I am. It's driving me crazy."

Didn't we already go over this?

"Me too," I agreed, to speed things along. "That's why I wanted your support here, like twenty minutes ago."

"Listen. I'll make it in time for dessert, okay?"

"Dessert? I don't know if I can last that long."

"*Try*, Claire. It'll be worth the wait. I took your advice and I've got a little surprise for her tonight."

What advice? I had no time to worry about it. "Terrific. Maybe you can cheer her up."

"I doubt it." The laugh that followed was borderline evil.

I found Mom at a corner table, frowning over the gold-tasseled menu. She'd refused the bifocals recommended by her optometrist, due to her own admitted vanity. If she'd only seen herself, head tilted backward and eyelids at half-mast so she could see through the reading glasses propped on the tip of her nose, she'd have begged for a prescription. I told her Stephanie would join us for dessert and Mom shrugged as though it made no difference to her and, before I could say anything more, our waitress appeared with two glasses of ice water. She was a cute little redhead with a bright smile and nickel-sized dimples.

After introducing herself as Brandy and informing us, as if we couldn't guess, that she would be our server for the evening, she rattled off a list of mouthwatering specials. I ordered a bottle of red wine, suspecting we'd need it, and she left us to the agony of making a decision.

"Well, I can see this city still has shock value," Mom said, shaking her head. "I hope you have more taste than that, Claire."

"What are you talking about?" Judging by her sour mood, it

could have been anything from the background music to the table setting.

"That waitress. Didn't you notice?" Her lips pursed with distaste.

"Notice what?"

"Nipples on parade, dear. No brassiere at all, if you can believe it."

Give me strength.

"What are you going to order, Mom?"

"I've no idea." She glanced over the menu, squinting as she scrolled through the italic listings. "What's cannelloni?"

"Ground veal rolled in pasta," I explained, tempted by the thought. Napoli's cheese sauce was out of this world.

"I guess they just slap a fancy name on it and hike up the price." She frowned.

"It's a traditional dish, Mom," I said, wishing she would relax.

"And tiramisu?" she asked.

"A dessert." Didn't she and Dad venture out to eat in Omaha? Weren't there at least half a dozen great Italian restaurants at their disposal? Or were they still stuck in the steak-and-potato rut?

"Good grief. What ever happened to spaghetti and Neopolitan ice cream?"

"Mom," I growled, barely keeping my agitation in check, "in case you haven't noticed, this isn't the Noodle Barn."

"Well, no. Not with these prices." Her forehead creased.

"Can you please ignore the prices and find something you like? I've already said it's my treat. Now, let's try to enjoy our meal."

She sipped her ice water before asking, "Is this one of your usual hangouts?"

"You could say that." Not that I'd been back much since Paul dumped me for that blonde tramp. What was her name? Tina, Cara, or something equally precious.

"If you were a little more careful with your entertainment budget, you could probably afford a nicer apartment."

I gave up and dropped my menu onto the table. "What's wrong with my apartment?"

"Nothing." She gestured vaguely with one hand in my direction but didn't lift her eyes from the menu. "Forget I said anything."

"No, why don't you just tell me?"

"Here's your wine," Brandy announced with an embarrassed smile, clearly aware of the friction between us. "Have you had a chance to look over the menu?"

"I think we need a couple of minutes," I said, with a tight smile of my own.

She disappeared with a quick nod and I turned my attention back to Mom. "Now, what about my apartment?"

"Nothing. It's nothing."

"Fine," I snapped. "I'm sure you'll bring it up again later anyway. So, why don't you just pick something off the damn menu and we can eat."

I poured myself a glass of wine, half of which I downed in one gulp.

When I saw Brandy leave another table a couple of minutes later, I signaled to her and she moved with hesitation toward us. I ordered the cannelloni, which came with salad and a bowl of minestrone, then she turned to take my guest's order.

"Does the minestrone come in a cup?" Mom asked.

"Yes, ma'am. A cup or a bowl."

"I'll have the cup." She closed her menu with a snap and handed it to the waitress, who raised her eyebrows in response.

"That's it?" I asked.

"Soup will be plenty," Mom sniffed, folding her reading glasses and depositing them in her purse.

"It's not a huge cup." Brandy tucked the menus under her arm and tried to illustrate the size with her free hands.

"My daughter is taking me to dinner and I don't want to break the bank."

"Mom!"

Brandy made another quick getaway as my mother inspected a perfectly clean spoon and proceeded to wipe it down with a linen napkin. How could Dad stand her?

I weighed the pros and cons of strained silence while we waited for our meals to arrive, coming to the conclusion that silence was better than criticism. I watched her annoyance increase at the lack of artificial sweeteners in our sugar bowl, then she began fiddling with her wedding band.

"Is something bothering you?" I finally blurted.

"Why do you ask?" Her gaze was steady.

"Because your mood has changed so much since this afternoon."

"I'm fine," she said, firmly.

After a few minutes, our soup arrived, mine in the form of a silver-trimmed bowl the size of a half watermelon, and Mom's in what might as well have been a Dixie cup.

"Pretty small portions," she murmured, liberally salting her miniscule meal before she'd even tasted it.

It was a habit that drove me up the wall.

"She warned you it was small." I tried rather unsuccessfully to keep the "I told you so" from my tone.

"Hmph," she offered between spoonfuls.

My minestrone was fabulous, and I ate slowly, savoring each spoonful and each blessed moment of silence. If I'd been at home, I would have lifted the bowl and licked it clean. Instead, I stared forlornly at the final few drops, which had eluded my spoon.

"Claire?"

I glanced up at the sound of a male voice and saw a shaggy mop of dark hair over sparkling blue eyes.

No!

Paul Clemens stood at the edge of our table, equipped with a broad smile that I grudgingly acknowledged could still weaken my knees.

Of course, the rules of breakup etiquette dictated that Napoli was his territory, since he'd been dining there long before I had. But why did he have to come in on the same night?

"Paul," I murmured. He looked good, and I cursed him for it. May his late charges and failure to rewind videos damn him to a life of overpriced theaters and Channel Twelve's relentless repeats of *Private Benjamin*.

I drank in the sight of his face, from the smooth skin of the forehead I'd stroked a thousand times, to the plump lower lip he always bit when deep in thought.

He looked fantastic.

While we'd always had a lot to talk about, and had more than our fair share of fun together, what I vividly recalled was that the physical chemistry between us had been extraordinary. He had the sort of body I'd seen in magazine ads, but hadn't truly believed existed without airbrushing. His chest was like . . .

Mom cleared her throat loudly.

"Oh, sorry," I felt my cheeks warm, certain that Paul and Mom both knew exactly what I'd been thinking. "I should introduce you. This is Paul Clemens. We used to . . ." What was I supposed to say, *have sex?* "Go out."

"Not as often as we stayed in," he chuckled, giving me a light punch in the arm and a knowing wink.

Lovely.

"Uh, Paul. I'd like you to meet my mother."

"Oh." At least he had the courtesy to blush. "It's nice to meet you, Mrs. . . ." He paused for an outrageous length of time.

Considering he knew more about my nether regions than me or my gynecologist, I was stunned that he couldn't remember my last name. For Christ's sake, I knew his favorite flavor of ice cream. I knew that he wore his socks twice because he thought turning them inside out was the same as washing them. I knew he hit the snooze bar seven times every morning, instead of setting his alarm for a later hour and enjoying uninterrupted sleep. I knew I'd stopped eating at the best Greek place in town because we used to hand-feed each other *dolma-does,* and the thought of a table for one made me want to cry.

I waited as long as I could bear for his memory to serve him, mortified that I had actually thought the relationship had long-term potential. Of course, with a record like mine, long-term meant anything that outlasted the Sunday-morning breakfast rush at Denny's, but I'd thought Paul was different. I'd really believed we had a chance, until he'd run off with that little Cindy—Katie?

I glanced up at him, urging him to remember just who the hell I was, but his eyes were blank.

"*McLeod,*" I offered, clenching my teeth.

"Of course!" He smacked his forehead, punctuating the moment for posterity. "It's nice to meet you, Mrs. McLeod."

"And you." Mom's smile was genuine, despite the cloud of awkwardness hanging over us like a swarm of flies on a dung heap.

"You know, Paul," I said, mortified by his poor memory and insulted by his very existence, "you racked up a late charge at my video store."

Take that!

"I did what?" His quizzical look made me wonder if I'd been speaking another language.

"Late charge. I owed over *eighty* dollars on my account, thanks to you."

"Late charge? For what movie?"

"*Pee-wee's Big Adventure,*" I snarled.

"Oh, yeah." He laughed, rubbing his index knuckle against the wiry stubble on his chin. The beard was new, and I hated to admit I liked it. "Yeah, I love that movie."

Remorse. Where was the remorse?

"Well, I hope you thoroughly enjoyed it."

"I did, but are you serious? They charged you eighty bucks?" There was definite concern in his eyes. Exactly what I was hoping for.

"Yeah." The movement of knuckle against beard distracted me again. Why couldn't I look at his hands without remembering them on my breasts?

"Jesus. Eighty bucks! I can't believe it!"

"Believe it."

"That's criminal. And you paid it?"

"Yes," I said, then reconsidered the facts. "Well, I, uh, paid twenty," I mumbled, feeling the power of martyrdom slipping away. "They kind of wrote off the rest."

"So," he frowned in apparent confusion, "do you want twenty bucks?"

Was that all I meant to him? Couldn't he see that the money was nothing compared to his leaving me for that Tracy, Ashley, whoever she was?

"No." I sighed. How did he manage to make me feel so petty? I had been wronged, seriously *wronged,* and it had taken me months to get over it.

Thank God I was over it.

"I've got it right here . . ." His hand drifted toward his back pocket.

Unbelievable!

"Never mind, Paul. I don't want the fucking money."

"Claire!" Mom gasped.

"Sorry. Look, just forget I mentioned it, okay?"

"Are you sure?"

I nodded.

"Well," he cleared his throat and glanced to the far side of the dining room, "I've got a table full of people waiting for me." He shoved his hands into the pockets of the same jeans he'd been wearing the day we broke up, not that I really noticed. "I just wanted to say hi."

"Hi," Mom and I responded, in unison.

"So, I'll see you around, Claire."

"Yeah." I offered a weak smile and watched him walk away. Not so long ago I'd sat on the edge of his bed while he showered, practicing writing "Claire Clemens" in my journal, like some kind of crush-centric thirteen-year-old. Damn him and Chrissy, Lisa, Becky—what the hell was her name?

"Nice-looking young man," Mom said.

"Nice enough." I shrugged. Gorgeous, really. Wonderful too, at least for a while.

"What went wrong?"

"I don't know. It just didn't work out." I pushed my soup bowl away.

"There must have been a reason."

I glanced toward her and noted one eyebrow raised in accusation.

"You automatically assume it was *my* fault?"

"Was it his?" Her tone suggested it was impossible.

"As a matter of fact, it was."

"He seemed like a bit of a catch," she said wistfully. "Those blue eyes were something else."

"I'm sure the girl he dumped me for is enjoying them now."

If I'd blinked, I would have missed the flash of pain that covered Mom's face.

"Oh, I didn't realize." She touched a fingertip to her lips. "I'm so sorry, honey."

"So am I."

"Was she prettier? Younger? You know I've told you time and time again that something needs to be done with your hair."

My head pounded.

"That's it." I moved to stand. "I'm going home."

She grabbed my elbow and pulled me back into my seat.

"Claire, what on earth is the matter with you?" She loosened her grip, but rested a tentative hand on my arm.

I pulled away from her.

"Could you just get off my back?" I asked, gripping the table with white-knuckled hands.

"What are you talking about? I'm trying to help you." She slowly drew her hand away, dropping it into her lap.

"You're not helping. Constantly criticizing my appearance doesn't do a thing for me."

"*Criticism?* Is that what you think it is? Honey, I'm just

making suggestions. For your well-being. That's what mothers do."

"You've got to be kidding. Mom, you tear me down every chance you get!"

"That's not true, I—"

"You complain about my job, my apartment, my hair . . ."

"Well, your hair is desperate for attention," she insisted.

"That's *exactly* what I'm talking about. I can't even remember the last time I wasn't cringing in your presence, waiting for the next insult. It's impossible for you to be positive about me."

"Can I, uh, take those bowls for you?" Brandy asked with false cheer, her cheeks pink with discomfort.

We held our silence until she had cleared the table.

"You can't seem to see anything good in me." I gritted my teeth as I spoke.

Mom leaned toward me and her voice was stern. "Listen to what you're saying, Claire. All I've heard since I arrived is you complaining about how rotten your life is."

"I never said my life is rotten."

"You don't have to say those exact words for them to come across. I see the way you mope around, expecting the worst from everyone. You don't take any responsibility for your own poor decisions, and when I try to help you change, you don't want to hear it."

"Of course I don't. You don't know anything about me, Mom."

"Here's your, uh, salad." Brandy placed a bowl of mixed greens in front of me. I stabbed at random leaves of lettuce, unable to secure any on my fork.

"I know a lot more about you than you think."

"Don't be ridiculous." I finally hit my target and shoved a

mouthful past my lips. The bitter vinaigrette suited me perfectly.

"You've got a chip on your shoulder the size of a Mack truck, Claire." She folded her arms across her chest and leaned back in her chair to study me. "I want you to do me a favor and name five positive characteristics about yourself."

"What, you think I can't?" I asked, trying to buy some time. For crying out loud. *Five?* Right off the top of my head? I racked my brain. Aha! "I have a good sense of humor."

She shook her head. "Sarcasm isn't humor."

"Fine. I'm . . . reasonably intelligent." Although I was beginning to doubt that. I took another bite of my salad.

"Reasonably isn't good enough. I only want to hear the claims you can make wholeheartedly." She glanced at her watch, apparently timing me.

"I'm . . . a good friend."

"To who? I haven't heard you mention the name of a single girlfriend since I arrived. Who do you hang around with on the weekends?"

Friends?

I was still stuck on positive characteristics, and she wanted me to come up with a secondary list? I spent my weekends alone. The only people I socialized with were at work, and we were all paid to spend time together. Come to think of it, it was pathetic. "I have friends, Mom."

Even I didn't believe me.

"If you aren't good company for yourself, you can hardly be good for anyone else."

"And what makes you such an expert?" I swallowed my greens. "What qualifications do you have to justify criticizing every aspect of my life? Why are you so determined to change me?"

"Because," she said, lower lip suddenly trembling, tears glistening in her eyes. "I don't want you to end up like me."

I was shocked into silence. End up like her? What was that supposed to mean?

Before I managed to form the question, whatever honest moment Mom and I had been about to share was interrupted. As I glanced toward the front of the room, Steph made an entrance I'd remember forever.

"Holy shit," I whispered.

"What?" Mom turned to look. "Oh, my." Her hand reached for her heart.

As Steph swept through the dining room, heads swiveled with alarm at the sight of her black knee-high Doc Martens and the camouflage pants tucked into them. The studded dog collar around her neck was only slightly less alarming than the sudden absence of her trademark blonde mane. Her hair was shaved close to the head, and her cheekbones seemed to jut out in rebellion over the change. If she weren't so beautiful, she would have looked like a teenage boy. I watched lips move as various patrons read the bold print on her white T-shirt, which proclaimed, "I'm not a lesbian, but my girlfriend is."

I groaned.

She was my sister, and I loved her dearly, but a very large part of me hoped she'd swerve at the last moment and join someone else's party.

Nope.

"So, Mom," she said, when she arrived at the edge of our table, "I thought things would be a little clearer for you if the package matched the contents." She squeezed into the booth next to me and I reluctantly made room for her.

"What have you done to yourself?" Mom gasped, her skin losing color by the second.

I was stunned, and if the slack-jawed faces staring at our table as though it were the stage for a burlesque show were anything to go by, I wasn't the only one.

"I'm trying to make a point with you, Mother."

"Your hair," Mom whispered. "That beautiful hair."

"It's gone," Steph said fiercely. "Just like I hope your illusions are gone."

"Illusions?" Mom's voice was barely audible.

"Illusions?" I echoed. Why were we speaking in B-movie dialogue?

"Marco and I aren't getting back together. I love women, not men." Her volume rose, and the woman at the next table dropped her fork with a clatter that stilled the room.

I stared at the hands folded in my lap and prayed it wouldn't get any worse, but who was I kidding?

"Alison and I have phenomenal sex," she announced loudly, just as Brandy appeared with my cannelloni, flinched, and beat a retreat to the kitchen, plate in hand. I lifted my glass of wine, fearing my dinner was lost forever, and took a gulp.

"And, since I know you're wondering," my sister continued in a booming voice, "it's mainly *oral*."

A sudden coughing fit made me choke on the wine and I was deathly afraid I'd spray it all over the table, adding to the main event. I glanced from one end of the room to the other, searching for any sign of Paul, but couldn't spot him. Hopefully he couldn't see us, either. Somehow, I managed to regain my composure and poured myself another glass, pretending I was anywhere but at that table.

Steph turned to face her audience. "What are all of you staring at, anyway? Never seen a real, live dyke before?"

After a brief pause, the chatter surrounding us continued in earnest, and I was pretty sure I knew what the topic was.

From that moment on, I was deaf to the conversation. I know Mom and Steph argued for at least twenty minutes, but I didn't hear a word of it. I just stared at my hands and wondered what had happened to us. The McLeod family was officially falling apart. Even from the perspective of the shadowed sister, it had been a loving household while I was growing up. We'd shared stories around the dinner table and embarked on summer camping trips. We had a cat and a dog, pot roast on Sundays, and played board games in teams of two. When had everything gone so wrong? What was making us so hard on each other?

And then it hit me.

"You know," I interrupted the heated debate, causing Mom and Steph to turn and stare at me, "none of this would be happening if Dad was here."

"Well, he's not here," Mom said quietly.

"And why is that?" Steph asked, looking from Mom to me. Arguing seemed to have worn her out, and I was thankful for that one small mercy.

"I don't really want to talk about it right now."

"I think we need to," I said, sensing there was something substantial on her mind. To my great surprise, I found myself reaching for her arm and didn't notice my grip tightening until she winced and I let go of her.

"Your dad and I are having some problems, all right?" She rubbed her arm absently. "I didn't want to tell you about it because I knew you'd worry."

"What kind of problems?" I asked. *Problems? My parents had problems?* Certainly, Mom was a pain in the ass at times, but Dad was so easygoing, I couldn't imagine them disagreeing over anything more than pork chops or chicken for dinner.

"It's rather personal."

"We're your daughters, Mom," Steph murmured, obviously as intrigued as I was.

"Is it your health?" I asked, and Mom shook her head.

"Financial trouble?" Steph asked.

"No, nothing like that."

"Then what is it?" Exasperation was taking over.

"It's . . . embarrassing." She shrugged, as if trying to shed her discomfort.

Embarrassing?

I could tell by Steph's look that she was worried about the same thing that I was: that we were heading into the uncharted waters of our parents' sex life. I'd hoped that such a beast didn't even exist, and chose to believe that they had only slept together twice, with Steph and me as the result. I imagined it was in a pitch-dark room, mainly so I wouldn't have to deal with troublesome imagery. Did I want to know if they had sexual problems? Not if I could help it.

"If you're not comfortable . . ." I began, hoping like hell that she wasn't.

"Mom, whatever it is, you can tell us," Steph said, straightening her shoulders while I gave her a dirty look.

A sudden movement caught my eye and I saw Brandy and my cannelloni heading in our direction once again. My mouth watered with her every step. I felt a quick surge of guilt that, despite everything that was going on, I was thinking about food. But dammit, I was starving!

"He's seeing another woman." Mom's voice was flat.

I turned toward her. "I'm sure he's seeing them everywhere—" The pained expression on her face stopped me cold. "Oh, my God. You mean *seeing* someone?"

"Yes." A single tear fell.

"Dad?" Steph shook her head. "That's impossible."

Random memories flashed through my mind. Dad's sun-burned neck on a family vacation, his lips kissing a smudge of chocolate frosting from Mom's cheek. I could almost smell Old Spice and Zest soap, hear him whistling "La Cucaracha," see the view when I perched on his shoulders as a child, pulling his ears to steer him in one direction or another.

"There's no way," I whispered. "No way *my* dad would do that."

"He's done it." Her bottom lip wavered. "Your father has taken a mistress."

Mistress? Against all odds, her choice of words made the concept seem even worse, as though Dad were the villain in a worn-out, broken-spined paperback.

Brandy blanched as she heard Mom's statement. She hovered a few feet from the table, my delicious dinner steaming the air, before turning on her heel and walking away.

Shit.

"How do you know?" Steph asked, handing Mom a napkin to dry her tears.

Instead of taking it, she dug a ratty tissue from her sweater sleeve and dabbed at her eyes. "I know."

"There must be some—" I began, but she cut me off by blowing her nose with a startling honk.

"He's having an affair with Joan Salomar." Mom nearly choked on the words.

"Ms. Salomar?" Steph asked as her eyes widened.

"My eighth-grade biology teacher?" I added, utterly shocked.

Mom nodded and began sobbing. Steph reached over to stroke her hair while I sat, stunned once again.

My dad was having an affair.

While that thought struck me like a ton of bricks, my next felt more like six tons. My father was cheating on my mother with the woman who I vividly recalled standing at the front of my science lab, oblivious to the nervous giggles and incredulous stares of her students as she blithely stretched orange and blue latex condoms over a wide, wide assortment of fresh produce and explained the wonders of sexual intercourse. The woman who was fired forty-eight hours later and doomed to manage a Pizza Hut until the end of time.

In the flood of emotions and feelings that coursed through my body, only one clear thought came to mind, and it was less welcome than any thought that had come before.

At least he'd chosen someone who knew her way around a banana.

NINE

Steph and I were mute as Mom looked anywhere but in our direction. Her hands twisted in her lap, seemingly desperate for a set of knitting needles to keep them busy, while her gaze wandered from one table to the next.

The obvious delight in the faces of our fellow patrons chatting, sipping, and chewing was almost grotesque when compared with the grim expressions on my mother's and sister's faces.

All I wanted was some quiet time, to let the information sink in, but Steph just had to jump in.

"Why didn't you say something earlier?" she asked.

"The time never seemed right." Mom dabbed at her nose with her tissue. Her eyes met mine briefly, in accusation. "And I haven't been too keen to talk about it, anyway."

"Who would?" I asked, and Steph jabbed me in the ribs with her elbow.

"Could you be a little more sensitive?" she hissed.

"Am I being insensitive?"

"Yes."

"For asking a simple question?"

"It was a stupid question."

"Well, excuse me, grand wizard of etiquette." I let my eyes sweep the length of her, from the shorn head to the menacing black boots, then glanced at my watch. "When can we expect the next loud and flamboyant demonstration of your four-letter vocabulary?"

"Fuck off, Claire."

"Oh, right on schedule."

Steph reached over and patted Mom's forearm. "I'm sorry she's making this difficult for you."

"Cut the crap, Stephanie."

"Why are you being such an idiot?"

"I'm confused." I frowned, "Am I insensitive, or am I an idiot?"

"Decisions, decisions." Steph tapped her finger against her temple.

"Very funny. Mom, would you tell her to lay off?"

"Mom has to fight your battles for you?"

"Shut up. Mom, tell your daughter she's—"

"I think I need a moment." Mom rose from her chair and walked toward the washroom. Guilt swept through me. What was I doing? She looked unsteady and I almost followed her, but Brandy suddenly blocked my path. She placed my dinner in front of me, and flashed a tight smile.

"Thanks very much," I said, "and sorry about all of this, uh . . ." I couldn't think of a suitable word.

"Can I get you anything else?" she asked, and I suspected she was crossing her fingers behind her back.

"No, I don't think so."

"Well then, enjoy your meal." Her shoulders visibly relaxed as she walked away.

"Hey," Steph called after her, "could we get three coffees?"

Brandy nodded and returned in a moment with steaming mugs.

The heavenly sight and smell of the cannelloni I'd been salivating over for the past forty minutes couldn't tempt me to take a bite. There was too much on the table already.

I pushed the plate away and took a slow sip of water, trying to think of something to say to Steph. I didn't want to fight with her, but I was too full of emotions to think clearly.

"Sorry I bit your head off," she said, and I was annoyed she'd been big enough to apologize first.

She was *always* first with the hugs or kind words. She always managed to smooth things over before I even knew they needed it, and it had never bothered me before. It shouldn't have bothered me then, either. But it did.

"Me too," I admitted.

"I'm in total shock."

Afraid to discuss Mom's bombshell, I said, "So . . ." I grasped for a topic. "How do you like your new look?"

"It's awful." She touched the exposed skin at the nape of her neck tenderly before lifting her shoulders in a shrug that was sheer bravado. "But what's done is done."

"What did Alison say?"

"Well, naturally, she blames you."

"What?" I gasped.

"It was your idea." She frowned. "You told me to do it."

"No, I didn't."

"You told me to stand up to Mom and demand she respect who I am."

"True." I paused for a moment. "But I don't recall telling you to turn into a hard-core femi-Nazi."

"I'm making a *statement.*"

"No, you're screaming an obscenity."

"It got the point across, didn't it?"

"I guess. So, is Alison mad at me?"

"Not really. She told me I was being childish, and I'd never get through to Mom by shoving my lifestyle down her throat." Steph smiled faintly. "She liked the hair, though. She thinks I look like a little pixie."

"How sweet," I murmured. No one had ever called *me* a little pixie.

"But on to bigger fish," she continued. "What do you think about this crap with Mom and Dad?"

I pointed toward the untouched food in front of me. "I think I've lost my appetite."

"And?" she urged impatiently.

"I don't know. It doesn't seem real to me yet. I can't imagine Dad looking at another woman."

"Let alone having a torrid affair?" She tapped the back of a spoon against the tabletop.

"Torrid may be an overstatement, Steph. He's fifty years old."

"And Ms. Salomar's what, maybe forty, forty-five? I think we're still in the realm of torrid." She tapped the spoon harder and faster. "It's disgusting."

"Ms. Salomar." A brief image of her slipping into a stained lab coat and securing her hair with a purple banana clip before passing out petri dishes flashed through my mind. "Do you think she still has a frizzy perm?"

"Probably. And I bet she still chews that goddamn cinnamon gum." Steph paused and laid the spoon to rest before squinting at the salt and pepper, as though she hoped to find some answer there. "Didn't she wear clogs?"

"No, that was Mrs. Jensen. Salomar was culottes."

"That's right. With knee-highs. *Great*. Stellar taste, Dad."
Steph flinched. "Mom's got to be humiliated by this. Can you
imagine the whispering around town?"

"Maybe no one else knows."

"Grow up, Claire. They live in the suburbs. You know how
these things work." She leaned back in the booth. "She was
probably the last to find out. I'll bet he didn't even tell her
himself." She paused to shake her head, and I missed the slow
bounce of her shimmering hair. "Shit! How could he do this
to her?"

I didn't know what to say. An affair was as far removed
from Dad as anything I could imagine. He used to bring Mom
plants because cut flowers didn't last long enough, and his cal-
loused hand had always reached for hers first. He stocked the
cupboards with sourdough bread, even though he preferred
wheat, and let her annihilate the Sunday paper every week as
he waited patiently for the business section. I'd always felt safe
with him, as though he wouldn't let anyone hurt us. The idea
of him sabotaging not only Mom, but all of us, sent a shooting
pain through my heart.

He was better than that.

He let me go to kindergarten wearing jeans under my skirt
when Mom was working graveyard at the hospital. And when
I was older, he waited for me to come to him with problems,
rather than using Mom's technique of interrogating me about
what was wrong and borrowing hormonally charged books
from the library to leave at the foot of my bed as an explanation of what was "happening" to me. He wasn't afraid to look
foolish if it meant we would laugh, and he always, *always* told
us how much he loved us. Dad looked after the things that

mattered while Mom fretted about everything that didn't. They weren't a very likely couple, and, although I was horrified to admit it, on some level, I couldn't blame him for seeking affection somewhere else. Obviously, Mom could be a very difficult woman.

"Aren't you going to say anything?" Steph asked.

I was afraid to share any of my thoughts. What kind of a daughter was I, to side with an adulterer? *Mom* was the one who needed my support, and there I was, trying to justify Dad's behavior. But I couldn't help it.

"Claire?"

"Remember one Father's Day I bought Dad that two-toned green tie?"

"And Mom told you your taste was all in your mouth?"

"Yeah. She wouldn't let him wear it."

"That's because it was hideous." Her laugh was harsh and bitter.

"I'm serious, Steph. I heard them arguing about it the next morning. He was going to wear it to work and she wouldn't let him." I could still remember the sad smile he'd given me when he knotted a dark paisley tie and kissed me good-bye.

"Are you trying to make a point?"

"No, I was just thinking out loud." I ran my fingertip up the side of my water glass, collecting condensation as I tried to sort things through. "Remember the way she used to show him pictures of fashion models? She'd badger him into saying they were pretty, then hold it against him?" I thought of their house, with no outward sign that Dad lived there. "She made him keep his golf trophies in the garage."

"What are you *doing*, Claire?"

"Nothing. It's just that she's not the easiest person to live with, you know."

"Tell me you aren't taking his side." Her eyes were fierce.

"I'm not taking anyone's side."

"Well, not Mom's, anyway," she snapped.

"Calm down. I haven't even had a chance to think about this."

"You shouldn't have to *think*, Claire. Your own mother has just told you she's been betrayed. Your response should be automatic."

"It is. I want to support her, but—"

"God, you were always his favorite." She rolled her eyes.

"That's not true."

"Daddy's little fishing buddy." The mocking tone didn't suit her.

"For Christ's sake, I was eight years old, Steph. And, for the record, he invited you to come along."

"Why are you defending him?"

"Why aren't you?"

"Because Mom needs us."

"And Dad doesn't?"

"In case you've already forgotten, Dad has Ms. Salomar."

It was too much to think about, but my mind raced to the logistics of their courtship. Did they bump shopping carts at the grocery store and flirt outrageously in aisle four, or were they introduced at a cocktail party celebrating someone's birthday or anniversary? Did she remind him of my botched rat dissection over a cognac in some upscale hotel bar? And where was Mom during all of this? Ironing his shirts? Where did Dad and Ms. Salomar rendezvous? Did they have pet names for each other? Did they write love letters? Did they consummate the relationship in my parents' bedroom while Mom was playing bridge with the girls?

I was going to be sick.

"What's wrong with you?" Steph demanded.

"Nothing. I'm too confused to deal with this right now, okay?"

"No, it's not okay. *She needs us.*"

Before I could respond, Mom rejoined our table, her forehead wrinkled with annoyance. "I hope whoever invented those hot-air hand dryers lost out on the patent. They don't work worth a damn." She wiped her hands on her napkin and turned to face us. "You two look like I feel."

"Run over?" I asked.

"To put it mildly." She tried to smile, but her lips quivered. "I gave my life to that man, you know."

"So, what now?" I asked.

"Meaning?" She absently stirred her coffee.

"What are you going to do?"

"I don't know."

"Well, you can't just stay here forever."

Her spoon banged against the side of her cup with a hollow clink. "I wasn't planning on making your couch my permanent home, Claire."

"Of course you weren't." I spoke quickly, seeing the pain in her eyes. Why was I such an idiot? "But you can stay with me as long as you want, Mom."

"Maybe I can spend a couple of nights with Marjorie Walden."

I stared at her. Who on earth was Marjorie Walden?

"We were in nursing school together."

"I've never even heard of her," Steph said.

"I had a life before your father, dear." She sipped her coffee. "And I'm sure I'll have one after."

Life after Dad?

Was this really the end? Could she survive on her own? For Christ's sake, she couldn't even operate the TV remote.

"You don't have to go anywhere, Mom. I've already told you, you're welcome to stay with me."

"You've made it perfectly clear from the moment I arrived that I'm cramping your style."

"No, you aren't . . ."

"Come home with me, Mom," Steph interjected. "We have a real guest room, and a little more privacy than Claire's tiny apartment can spare."

"Thanks a lot, Steph."

"It's true. Mom would be more comfortable at our place."

Considering the reaction to meeting Alison, I doubted it. She could barely handle sharing a table with the lesbians, let alone a shower.

"I'm not so sure . . ." Mom said, obviously thinking along the same lines I was.

"Come on, Mom. We'll take care of you."

"Listen," I said, "your stuff is at my place already. You're all settled in."

"It's a couch, Claire," Steph reminded me.

"It's perfectly comfortable," I snapped.

"Well, that might be pushing it a bit," Mom said. "Maybe having my own room isn't such a bad idea."

"Fine." I waved Brandy over to get a box for my dinner. All I wanted was some time away from both of them, some time to piece the whole mess together. "You can stop by my place to pick up your things."

We finished our coffees in relative silence and when our bill was presented, I grabbed the little vinyl folder before Mom could reach it, reminding her that dinner was my treat.

And what a treat it was.

After a quick calculation, I gave Brandy a twenty-five percent tip. God knows she deserved it.

I'd been so full of tension and bewilderment since Mom made her announcement, I'd forgotten about Paul Clemens until we stood to leave.

When we rounded the wall and moved toward the lobby, I saw him at a table crowded with smiling faces and empty wine bottles, rowdy conversation and laughter audible even from my vantage point. I watched him whisper into the ear of a freckled brunette I'd never seen before. It was hard to watch, knowing at one time I had been that girl. His arm lay casually across the top of her chair, and although I didn't see him touch her, I couldn't help but visualize him caressing her shoulder. In the soft glow of candlelight, she laughed at whatever he'd said, and I could tell she was smitten. I felt a flicker of pity for Tammy, Kirsty, Jenni, or whoever it was he'd dropped me for, knowing she was probably going through the same depression I had experienced. Who did he think he was, anyway? He moved from one girl to the next like a serial heartbreaker.

Thank God I was over him.

I gritted my teeth and trudged behind Mom and Steph, pausing only to glance back at Paul's table once more. At that moment, he pulled away from the brunette's ear and gave me one of the most spectacular smiles I'd ever received, as he raised his hand in farewell.

I pretended I didn't see him.

As I stepped into the cool air outside the restaurant, my thoughts returned to Dad. It didn't make sense. He had coached my soccer team, even though his sport was racquetball. He gave every girl equal time on the field, despite our losing streak, and when my cleats were clogged with mud and grass, he used his car keys to scrape them clean. When we won the last game of the year because the other team didn't show up, he took us all to McDonald's for hot fudge sundaes and congratulated us on a terrific season. All the girls thought he was the best father around.

So did I.

He was the kind of man who floated through life with a smile on his face and patience in his heart. He didn't go out with "the guys" for beer on Friday nights. He didn't sit on the couch, eyes glazed, during football season, or spend money on mag wheels, big-screen TV's, or fancy tools. He hadn't so much as looked at another woman since his wedding day.

Or had he?

I climbed into the backseat while Mom rode shotgun in Steph's Honda for the brief drive to my apartment. Our conversation was limited to new movie releases and varying recipes for spinach dip. I felt like an actress with no script, doing my best to treat strangers as family.

I watched the lights of the city pass in a blur, wishing I had a car of my own, not to mention a life. Another life, with the perfect family I used to claim as my own.

The traffic was heavy with kids cruising, exchanging glances at traffic lights, and moving slowly from one intersection to the next.

Paul Clemens and I used to walk that very street on Saturday nights, stopping for flavored coffees or a quick beer at any number of places, doing nothing but being together.

I didn't want to think about him. It had taken forever to push him to the back of my mind, behind the possibilities of Adam Carello, or the prospect of the hundreds of other fish supposedly lurking in the sea around me.

Sometimes the sea seemed more like a wading pool.

A wading pool full of kiddie pee.

I glanced at Mom's silhouette in the front seat, wondering if being left for another woman was hereditary. Maybe we were predisposed to play the fool while Paul sized up that teeny blonde and Dad courted Ms. Salomar over Chinese takeout and a reproductive special on the Learning Channel.

After what seemed like a lifetime in limbo, Steph double-parked in front of my building and we climbed the stairs to my apartment.

"Why doesn't this place have an elevator?" she asked as we reached my door.

"Because it's only three stories," I snapped, wishing the whole night was over.

The air in my living room was ripe with cleaning solutions and I forced a window open while Mom folded her peach flannel nightgown and placed it in her suitcase, along with her slippers. She surveyed the room for stray Weekender Wear and, seeing none, fastened the clasps on her bag.

"Is this all you brought?" Steph asked, lifting the Samsonite.

Mom nodded. "Except my toiletries."

"They're right here." I grabbed the zippered cosmetic pouch from the bathroom and handed it to her.

"Oh, my knitting bag. Where did I leave it?"

"Next to the coffee table. Steph, can you carry it?"

"I think I can handle it." She smirked and slipped the handles over her wrist. She tilted her head toward the flashing red light on my machine. "You've got a message."

"It's just Dad. We already heard it."

"What did *he* want?" Steph sighed, as though he were no more than an anonymous pest.

"He wanted to talk to Mom."

"*Great.* You aren't calling him back, are you?" She turned to face our mother.

"No, not tonight."

"Good. Well, I guess we're off." She gave me a brisk nod that conveyed only anger and disappointment. "Night, Claire."

"Good night," I said, stepping toward Mom, who hesitated before lifting her arms to hug me.

I'd never felt like such a traitor.

I closed the door behind them, relieved to be alone, but dreading the thoughts that would prevent me from enjoying the solitude. My stomach growled and I unpacked my cannelloni, dumping it unceremoniously on a chipped plate and setting the microwave timer.

I wandered into my room to slip out of my corduroys and into a pair of worn flannel pajama bottoms. My turtleneck landed in the empty laundry hamper and I pulled on a T-shirt I dug out of my dresser. On the way back to the kitchen, I flipped on the TV and channel-surfed until I found a *Friends* repeat.

At the sound of the beep, my plate was scorching hot and the cannelloni only lukewarm, but I didn't care. I pulled one of Mom's knitted afghans over my knees and parked the plate on an old *People* magazine to avoid burning my thighs.

I ate halfheartedly, more for sustenance than pleasure, wondering why food tasted so much better outside of my living room.

I did my best not to think about my parents, concentrating instead on finding the humor in my sitcom. In my sorry state, I only recognized punch lines when I heard the laugh track, then wondered what was supposed to be so damn funny.

I ate the last, tepid bite of cannelloni and left my plate on the coffee table, but as soon as I slumped against the back of the couch, the phone rang.

I muted the TV and leaned over, resting one hand on the receiver, waiting through three sharp trills. I winced as I listened to my recorded message echoing in the room, and then I heard the voice.

"Hi, honey, it's your dad. I uh, tried to reach you earlier, but I guess you girls are still, uh, out on the town."

It took everything I had to leave the receiver in place as Dad continued with what I recognized from years of watching him open Christmas gifts as false cheer.

"Everything's fine here. A bit lonely, of course, but that's to be expected."

I bit my lip.

"Barbara, please give me a call when you get a chance. I don't care how late it is. I hope you're having a great time together and I hope I, uh, hear from you soon. That is, I'd like to hear from either of you and—"

The machine cut him off with a startling beep.

I waited for a couple of minutes, to see if he would call back to finish the message. When the phone didn't ring, I got up and deposited my plate in the dishwasher before returning to the couch, where I wrapped the afghan tightly around me and stared at the silent screen, letting the tears stream down my cheeks.

TEN

I didn't hear from Steph over the next few days, but I wasn't terribly concerned about it. If history was anything to go by, her annoyance would fade within the week and we'd return to our old habit of calling each other every couple of days.

I felt rotten when Dad didn't try to contact us again, but I didn't have the guts to pick up the phone and call him myself. I wasn't ready to hear his side of the story for fear I'd sympathize with him. I felt a moral obligation to get my head straight and support the parent who needed me, but, judging by Mom's defeated confession and Dad's depressing message, I wasn't sure which one that was.

Mom surprised me by refraining from calling. No Mommy messages at work, and no nagging tones on the machine when I arrived home each evening. I ended up stuck in the no-man's-land between relief and anxiety, wondering when the inevitable call would draw me into the chaos.

Unwilling to become more deeply involved with their problems, I decided it was time to look at my own. I took Mom's words at Napoli to heart, rethinking the conversation we'd had before Steph appeared. Her line of questioning had been rude and unrelenting, but she had raised some valid points. I *was* unhappy with almost every aspect of my life, from the few surface relationships I shared with my coworkers, to my dissatisfaction with a job I felt stuck with.

My romantic relationships were few and far between, and the few were, apart from Paul Clemens, brief and superficial. I claimed I wanted a long-term relationship, but I was scared and unwilling to put forth the effort to make it happen. I *did* expect the worst from people, and feeling bitter and jaded at age twenty-three was a sure sign that it was time to make some changes.

In response to the social freeze I was experiencing at work, I'd been tempted to ask Neal for a demotion early the following week so I could return to the anonymity of my old job. Instead, I opted for a change in attitude and embraced the new responsibilities of stat collection and assessment. He was impressed with the new filing system I implemented to keep track of daily, weekly, and monthly numbers, not to mention the suggestions I made for changes to both the telephone and computer systems. He left "Word of Godd" memos on my desk, instructing me (in clichéd corporate jargon) to keep up the good work and lead the office to a new level of performance. As cheesy as it was, I needed the encouragement, which prompted me to race beyond the limitations of what my new position was meant to be, with the hope that a strong work ethic and good ideas could create some upward mobility for me later on.

Later on. I could spend years at Alta Media.

It was scary to think of a future that could actually be realized, rather than daydreaming about quitting my job after being "discovered" by a talent agent in the canned vegetable aisle, or fantasizing about winning the lottery when I didn't even buy tickets. Did upward mobility exist at Alta Media? I was going to find out.

Neal even listened, if somewhat reluctantly, to my suggestions for an employee incentive program. I made the pitch that rewards were appropriate for high-production employees, and dangling carrots could only increase their efforts. On a purely selfish note, my ideas were fueled by the hope that my peers would cut me some slack if I was responsible for office perks that surpassed flavored coffee.

I compiled a ranking of the most productive employees and presented it to Neal for his consideration on Monday. Seeing how seriously I was taking my job, he set up one-on-one meetings between me and each member of the telemarketing team for Tuesday. During brief interludes in a closet-sized office in the back corner, I was supposed to tell them how they ranked statistically and offer suggestions on how to improve their performances.

I was afraid that my peers wouldn't react well to my constructive criticism, and that most were still harboring feelings of ill-will toward me for accepting the promotion in the first place.

As I should have anticipated, the setup on Tuesday morning didn't do much to ease my state of mind. The dusty windows of the tiny office and the wobbly desk I had to sit behind were downright depressing, and even the folders and carefully prepared notes I'd brought with me couldn't alleviate my nervous tension.

I'd been careful with my wardrobe, and I was sure no one could criticize my casual yet classic choice of black slacks, a white blouse, and a gray cardigan. At least, I hoped they couldn't. My hair was locked in its usual ponytail, but, thanks to my program of change, even that would be altered soon. I'd taken Mom's advice and booked a visit to one of the ritzy-glitzy hair salons on the southwest side for later in the month, a leap of faith that required more dollars than sense. As I tucked unruly tendrils behind my ear, I wished I'd been able to book something sooner.

As luck would have it, my first meeting was with Heather. We hadn't spoken since she ditched me for lunch the previous week, but my new life plan left little room for grudges.

She gave me a wary look when I asked her to close the door for the sake of privacy, and I offered a welcoming smile in return. After we exchanged stiff pleasantries, I got down to business.

"I guess we should start with the positive," I began, pulling out her folder.

"Are there negatives?" She sounded panicked, and I couldn't believe it was that easy to start off on the wrong foot.

"Not *negatives,* but there are some areas which could use some fine-tuning."

"Like what?" She absently scratched her rash.

I desperately wanted to slap her wrist and tell her to leave it alone, for Christ's sake, but I took a calming breath instead. "You don't want to go through the good stuff first?"

"Am I being fired?" Her coral nails dug into her skin.

"Fired? No. This is just a meeting, Heather."

"Because you called me in here like I'd done something wrong." She shifted in her seat, her cloud of hair quivering in fear. "And I haven't."

"I'm just letting you know how you're doing compared to everyone else on staff. Let's see," I continued, ignoring her frown, "you make more than the average number of calls every day, ranking nineteenth overall and—"

"That's not *fair.*"

"What?"

"Some of my calls take a long time," she whined, then bit her puffy bottom lip. "Sometimes I have to repeat the questions."

"Everyone does." I nodded with understanding. "We all know that's part of the job."

"But a lot of people hang up on me."

"Heather, everyone else is going through the same thing."

She sniffled and I wished I'd had the foresight to put a box of tissues on the desk. Maybe their weight would have anchored the damn thing.

"I've had this cold for almost two weeks now, you know. It's probably affecting my performance."

"There's nothing *wrong* with your performance. I'm trying to tell you that you're doing fine. There are just a couple of areas that could use improvement."

"Like what?"

"Well, you seem to spend an inordinate amount of time off the phone between calls." I knew she e-mailed friends from her desk, forwarding lists and jokes whenever she had the chance. It hadn't bothered me before, but those social moments added up and diminished her stats. "You really shouldn't use company equipment for personal communication."

"Have you been reading my e-mail?" Her eyes widened as she let out a small gasp.

"No, I—"

"Because there's probably a rule against that. Or a law, even."

"No one is reading your e-mail." Including the recipients, if the stupid jokes she'd sent me and I'd deleted were anything to go by. "All I'm saying is that the time you're off the phone affects your productivity."

I would have kept talking, but she'd abandoned eye contact in favor of staring at her chafed skin. I leaned back in my chair to wait for her attention, but she just sat there.

"Heather?"

"I don't know why you're picking on me, Claire." She finally met my eyes with a look that was part wounded, part defiant.

"I'm not—"

"I thought we were friends." She plucked at her watchband, snapping the metal against her wrist.

"It sure didn't seem that way on Friday, when you wouldn't go for lunch with me." As soon as the words left my mouth, I knew I'd made a mistake.

"Is that what this is about?" she gasped.

"No, I'm meeting with everyone," I hurriedly explained. "Now, let's get back to—"

"I *knew* you'd change when you got this job. You always thought you were better than me, and now you think your big, fancy title proves it."

She paused to cross her arms and lean back in her chair, while I wondered how on earth "auditor" could be described as a big, fancy title.

"Heather."

Her wounded look transformed into one of grim satisfaction. "I know you're jealous of me."

"Jealous of you?" I almost laughed. She was pathetic.

"Yeah, you can't handle the fact that Adam and I are close."

Adam? Since when were they *close*? I could feel the unwelcome tingle of a budding headache.

"Heather, can we get back on track here?"

"I could tell you liked him and now you're going to punish me every chance you get."

"Heather." I had to admit it bothered me to think of them being "close," whatever that meant. I'd been eyeing him for months, but didn't know I'd been obvious enough for Heather to catch on to my secret crush.

"Can I go back to work now?"

"We aren't finished."

"I don't want to take any more time away from the phone. After all, every minute counts, doesn't it, Claire?"

In a flash of mauve chenille she was gone and I sat staring at the number-two pencil on the table. Were all of my meetings going to involve a battle of wills? And, more important, what kind of relationship had she developed with Adam Carello in a matter of *days?*

Unnerved, I called in my next victim and felt relieved when I managed to get through several more meetings with minimal discomfort. A couple of people congratulated me on the new job, or made suggestions about how they thought the auditing should be handled. I took notes, delighted I wasn't the only one who cared about positive change. Regrettably, most of the people I spoke to just sat and nodded as I rattled through their numbers, apparently happy enough just to have a few minutes away from the phone. I pitied those who sat on the other side of the table, looking as defeated as I'd felt a mere week before. Mom's words had sparked the fire under my backside, and I was determined to do my best.

"You beckoned, El Capitán?" Jason appeared in the open doorway after my coffee break.

I tried to smile, but the glint in his eye made me flinch instead. "Have a seat."

He dropped into the chair across from me and draped one arm over the back of it. "To what do I owe the honor?"

"I'm just going over everyone's stats," I said, avoiding eye contact. We'd been friends since I'd joined Alta Media, but I suspected those days were over.

"Stats. Of course. Where would we be without them?"

I cleared my throat. "Can you give me a bit of a break here, Jason?"

"Sitting in here while we're cranking out calls isn't enough of a break for you?"

"Why are you—"

"Because I hate the fact that you sold out."

I should have expected those exact words from the only white-collar anarchist I knew.

"I took a promotion."

"Call it what you will. Christ, Claire, do you get any satisfaction out of this job?"

"I'm trying to."

"You're wasting your time. It doesn't mean anything." He wiped his nose with the back of his hand. "Who gives a shit about surveys and questionnaires?"

"The companies who hire us."

"Big deal. Telemarketers are nothing but phone maggots. We call people who don't want to talk to us and badger them for opinions we don't care about. Where's the honor in that?"

"No one said anything about honor. It's just a job, Jason."

"Exactly my point. You're taking a regular old *job* way too seriously."

"Do you want to hear your stats or not?"

"Wow me." He shrugged.

I checked my list.

"You've got top billing." I sighed. "You're the most efficient employee we've got."

"I figured as much. Now tell me, am I supposed to care?"

"I think you should feel proud."

"Screw pride. Don't you think it's a little fucked up that the best employee here cares the least about this company?"

"That's not the point of the stats. What we're trying to assess is—"

"Jesus." He slapped his forehead. "This is like trying to reason with a fucking Pomeranian."

I rubbed my eyes and tried to clear my head. I was sure my brain was swelling to twice its usual size. The pressure of the past few days had simply been too much.

"Jason," my voice trembled, "I've had a really shitty week."

He leaned forward in his chair, eyes suddenly soft and questioning. "What's wrong?"

Apparently my tone was enough to end, or at least postpone, his tirade. I wasn't sure whether his interest stemmed from genuine concern or his insatiable appetite for gossip, but I was relieved he'd quieted down, if only for the moment.

"I've got a lot going on right now. My personal life is a mess, and work is . . ." I shook my head. "I don't want to go into it. I'm sorry to be the one to break the news that you're an asset to this company, but I'm just trying to do what I was told, okay?"

I could tell by the slight furrowing of his eyebrows that he was truly concerned. The knowledge was enough to ease my headache a little. "You're not upset because of me, are you?" he asked softly.

"No. I'm having a shit sundae and you're just the sprinkles."

"I'm going to pretend there's a compliment in there somewhere." He grinned. "Do you want to talk about what's going on? Not the boring work stuff, but the other? Is it guy trouble? You know I'm an expert on guy trouble, Claire. I've got a bachelor's in heartbreak."

"Shadowed only by your master's in bullshit."

"Ladies and gentlemen," he said, through cupped hands, "she's coming out fighting!"

"Cut it out." I laughed for the first time in days.

"So, you really don't want to talk about it."

"No." I shook my head.

"Well, in that case, are we done in here?"

"I suppose. I'd give you a printout of your stats, but . . ."

"I don't want it." He stood, scraping the back legs of the chair against the floor. "So, are you doing anything for lunch?"

I felt a weight lift off my shoulders at the question. "No." I'd been brown-bagging it all week, eating in my cubicle to avoid a noontime snubbing.

"A few of us are going to that new Greek place on the corner, if you want to join us."

"Who's going?"

"Me and Adam for sure. And I think maybe Chris and David . . ."

I stopped listening the second I heard the only name that mattered. It was about time I had my chance at Adam Carello. "I'll be there." I smiled. "And thanks, Jason."

"No problem." He headed back to his desk.

During the hour before lunch, I met with a few more employees, but had a hard time concentrating on the task at hand when all I wanted to do was count the minutes until I'd be spending some quality time with Adam.

Motivated by my dismal run-in with Paul, I'd spent all of

my spare moments daydreaming about a future with the enig-
matic guy in the back corner. I'd deliberately scheduled him
near the end of my stat meetings so I'd be more comfortable
in my role when the time came, but after a lunch together, I'd
be in even better shape. Six months of silent admiration
behind me and I was finally going to have the chance to get to
know him.

It was hard to believe that taking Mom's advice to change
my life was paying off in dividends so quickly, but I wasn't
about to question my good fortune.

When noon finally arrived, I grabbed my coat and followed Jason to the elevator, where we met Adam. His dark
hair was rumpled, as usual, and the chipped tooth exposed by
his smile was as charming as the first time I'd seen it. How
could anyone so cute be so single? I felt a slow rush of dread.
Was he gay? No. My luck couldn't be that bad.

"I didn't know you were coming with us," he said, with a
warm smile.

I couldn't think of anything brilliant to say, so I nodded
dumbly, already off to a dimmer start than expected.

"Where's Chris?" Jason asked, looking toward her corner
desk.

"Doctor's appointment. And David's meeting his girlfriend
for lunch."

"So, we're it?" I asked, admiring the soft green of Adam's
eyes.

"Yeah, just as soon as Heather gets off the phone."

Somehow, I refrained from rolling my eyes at the news.

"Hey, Claire," Carol called from the reception desk. "I
hear you're part of the management team now."

I turned to see her delicately opening a new Lifesaver roll

with freshly painted algae-colored nails. Her vinyl pants squeaked against her chair as she altered her position for better glaring access.

"I'm just an auditor," I told her.

"Oooh, auditor?" she mocked, popping a candy into her mouth. "So what are you doing now," she tilted her head, "slumming?"

"Slumming? Don't be so hard on yourself, Carol. I'm sure you'll move beyond the lobby someday."

Adam's expression was completely neutral, as though he hadn't heard me, while Jason snickered. Carol shot him a fierce look, but before she could crucify me, our elevator arrived and we stepped inside.

"Hold the door! I'm coming!" Heather called, stumbling as she wrestled with her coat.

"Oh." Her eyes met mine. "I didn't know *you* were coming." They were the same words Adam had used, but forty degrees cooler.

Once outside, we rushed from one awning to the next in a fruitless effort to defy the rain. By the time we reached the restaurant, I felt like a big wet dog, desperate to shake the water off.

During the meal, I tried to think of good topics to discuss with Adam, but I had no idea where his interests lay. I wanted to learn everything there was to know about him, but even his taste in food remained a mystery when he ordered a combination plate while the rest of us ate spanakopita. For lack of stimulating conversation, we reverted to discussing entertainment.

"What's your favorite movie?" I asked him, once Jason had chosen *Communion* and I picked *The Usual Suspects*. If he followed my lead, and explained why he liked whatever movie it was, I would get some idea of what he was all about.

"Oh, I don't think I could pinpoint a favorite," he said, lifting his water glass to his lips.

God, he had beautiful lips.

"Me neither," Heather chirped, smiling at him.

I glared at her and tried to get a top-three list out of him, with no luck. Soon enough, the movie conversation dried up and we were left with the delightful sounds of cutting, chewing, and swallowing.

"So, what do you listen to?" I asked, growing desperate at the forty-minute mark.

"Anything, really." He shrugged.

"Me too," Heather said, with a catty smile. Apparently she thought no opinion was the same as a common interest.

While Heather and I sneered at each other and Adam dug into his souvlakia, Jason chattered away, waving his arms when he spoke, as if the words themselves weren't quite big enough to hold our attention. Of course, my focus lay elsewhere, and I glanced in Adam's direction whenever I thought no one was looking.

He had a certain innocence about him, not that I was some well-versed woman of the world, but watching his shy responses when Heather and I initiated conversation, I could tell he was no ladies' man. I scanned the wrinkles in his pale blue shirt and finally understood why Mom spent so much time ironing Dad's. If Adam was mine, I'd keep him pressed and polished. It was a thought I never expected to cross my mind. Then again, after the seduce-and-destroy tactics of a certain Paul Clemens, I'd never expected to find another man I wanted to get domestic over.

By the end of the lunch hour, I'd asked every question I could think of, and observed as much as I could about Adam, but I'd only discovered three new pieces of information. He was ambidextrous when it came to handling cutlery, which wasn't much, but I (optimistically) hoped it hinted at a keen intelligence. I knew he had a sister in Seattle, which meant he must know a thing or two about women, and, finally, he liked to crunch ice cubes. Not the most sophisticated habit, but certainly better than some.

As we settled the bill and left the restaurant, I decided that the fact that he didn't make his most personal thoughts and feelings known to the general population was a good thing, assuming still waters ran deep, which I was almost certain they did. *Almost.*

When we returned to the office, I met with two more people before it was time for my grand-finale one-on-one with Adam Carello. I dashed to the rest room and splashed some cool water on my face, my temperature already rising. Tearing out the elastic band and finger-combing didn't do much for my hair, but once I'd secured it in a tortoiseshell clip, it wasn't half bad. I paused for a deep breath, squared my shoulders, and darted back to the wobbly desk. I could have had cosmetic surgery in the time it seemed to take for him to arrive at the door.

"You wanted to see me?"

If you only knew.

I invited him to sit down and, after clearing my throat of a nervous lump, explained the stat evaluations. He was glad to hear that he ranked near the top, and my voice grew steadier with every word. I smiled as often as I could, hoping he'd find me warm, friendly, and approachable.

I soon noticed he was watching my lips, and I shivered in response. The longer I spoke, the more focused he became, seemingly mesmerized by the movement of my mouth. Was he thinking the same thing I was? Had he noticed me across the room at staff meetings? Had he been waiting for an opportunity like our Greek lunch hour to come along so we could get to know each other? What information had he gleaned about me over his lamb kabob?

Did he know what that look was doing to me?

I was in midsentence when he lifted an index finger and thoughtfully stroked his bottom lip, while staring intently at mine. The gesture was more than slightly erotic, and nothing could have stopped me from talking.

Nothing but the sound of his voice.

"Claire." He spoke quietly, and all of the numbers I'd compiled slipped my mind. We were in a private room, the door safely closed, and the way my heart was racing, I just knew he was going to kiss me.

"Yes?" My voice was barely a whisper.

His lips opened, just a fraction, and his finger touched the glorious chip on his front tooth.

I felt light-headed, out of breath. Months of furtive glances and daydreaming had led up to this moment, and I was afraid to move for fear of breaking the spell.

His gaze left my lips and his eyes met mine for a heart-stopping second before returning to my mouth. His fingertip moved from the chip toward the softness of his gums and met the junction of tooth and flesh.

I didn't know what it meant, but the movement was undeniably one of the sexiest things I'd ever seen. The temperature in the room felt close to a hundred degrees, but I could have stayed in there all week wearing a parka.

He tapped the enamel once, then turned his finger toward me, pointing at my mouth. Was I supposed to follow his lead?

My question was conveyed in an uncertain smile, and he responded with a nod. It was like learning a new language, all gestures and emotion, curiosity and lust, with no time for thought, no room for inconsequential words.

That is, until he said, "Spinach."

Oh my God.

I clamped my lips together and let my tongue sweep the confines of my mouth. It only took a moment to find and release the morsel, and a matter of seconds for my face to flush with color.

"Spinach," I repeated, dumbly.

"It'll getcha," he said, with a crooked smile. "Every time."

ELEVEN

My meeting with Adam left a sour taste in my mouth that had nothing and everything to do with spinach. For the remainder of the afternoon, I attempted to engage him in conversation whenever he passed my desk, only to be disappointed by the same limp results I'd seen over lunch.

It wasn't fair.

I didn't have high expectations when it came to men. I didn't pant after Herculean bodybuilders, barely contained by their stretch clothing. I wasn't interested in GQ wardrobes in varying shades of gray, cell phones, PalmPilots, or combination-lock briefcases. I didn't seek the life of the party, because of the inevitable romantic hangover, and I steered equally clear of the chronically serious. I'd been sure Adam fit all acceptable gaps in between, but his apparent lack of substance was something I'd never counted on. I felt like I'd bought advance tickets to a rock concert and ended up with Anne Murray. What if he truly had *no* opinions, *no* discernible taste, and *nothing* to say? While I didn't demand an ocean of general knowledge, I wasn't about to settle for a stagnant puddle.

"Hot damn!" Jason said, returning from a trip to the rest room. "Almost four o'clock. Almost time to blow this shit heap and get on with my real life."

I tuned him out, noting that babbling brooks were no prize either.

"So," he said, leaning against my desk. "What's shakin'?"

"Not a lot." I pressed a label onto yet another color-coded file. I wasn't sure whether Jason was the person to talk to about matters of the heart, but the fact that he was the only person still speaking to me lent the idea a certain charm. After a brief internal debate, I took the plunge and asked, as nonchalantly as I could, "So, what do you think about Adam?"

There had to be more to him than a sweet smile and soft voice. There had to be.

"He's a nice guy." Jason shrugged, shoving a piece of spearmint gum into his mouth.

"And?"

He chewed thoughtfully before asking, "What do you want to know? Are you," he raised his fingers and bent them in air quotes, "interested?"

The last thing I needed was a spin through the rumor mill.

"I'm just curious. He was kind of hard to read in our meeting."

"Let me put it this way. You found him hard to read and he *doesn't* read."

"He's illiterate?" It was worse than I'd thought.

"No, just boring."

"Oh, that's much better." I rolled my eyes and fought off despair.

"Don't get me wrong, he's a nice-enough guy, but don't try to talk to him about anything of interest."

How to process that comment? To Jason, "interesting" went beyond the boundaries of normal social interaction. He quoted (I suspected inaccurately) Noam Chomsky and Monty Python in the same breath. He kept a detailed journal of personal injuries, ranging from paper cuts to broken limbs, in a red spiral notebook, not to mention the blue spiral notebook that contained a list of people he hoped would either contract hepatitis or fall victim to spontaneous combustion. Only a miniscule percentage of the population could join the ranks of Jason's illustrious and misguided "interesting" list, so his snubbing of Adam didn't amount to as much as it could have.

However, I hated to admit, my long-distance crush had also failed to say anything of interest to *me*, which was something else entirely. After all, I was easily impressed.

Had I spent months pining for a sap?

"Come back to earth, Claire," Jason sang in my ear before returning to his seat and leaving me alone with my thoughts.

I groaned softly, but barely had the chance to get truly depressed before Neal interrupted my pity party.

"Can I see you for a moment?" he asked, tilting his head toward the corner office.

I followed him to the inner sanctum and planted myself in a heavily padded swivel chair. While he poked around in his mini-fridge, I admired the tomes of his rosewood bookcase: *1-2-3 Success!*, *Lead On!*, and *In Praise of Power* were exactly what I expected, but a slim volume on the second shelf, entitled *Follicle Funeral: Hair Today, Gone Tomorrow*, and a paperback copy of *Short People Have Every Reason to Live* were a revelation.

"So, how are things going?" he asked, offering me a flavored seltzer, which I accepted with a tight smile.

A free beverage. How long was this going to take?

"Fine, I guess," I muttered, wrenching the metal cap with no result.

"Do you want me to get that for you?" he asked.

"I can do it." I tightened my grip and twisted again.

"Are you sure?" He sat behind his desk and opened a drawer.

"Yes." I grunted and twisted, skin burning against the metal.

"Here." Something shiny slid across the surface of the desk and bumped against his tape dispenser before skidding to a stop. A bottle opener. I felt the color rise in my cheeks.

"Thanks."

"You're not one to accept help easily, are you, Claire?"

"Apparently not." I grimaced, cracking the bottle open and placing the tool on the corner of his desk.

"So when I ask you how things are going, and you say 'fine, I guess,' what does that actually mean?"

"It means they're fine." I shrugged. "I guess."

"Can you be more specific?"

"I like the new job." I took a small sip of bubbling lime. "I know it's only been a few days, but I like it."

"That's a start."

"I enjoy working with the stats." A touch of exaggeration wouldn't hurt my corporate climb.

"Good. I sense a *but*."

"There's no *but*." I started to pick at the corner of my drink label.

"Claire." He shook his head slowly. "Talk to me."

Would it be a mistake to discuss my feelings with Neal? Probably. Could he do anything about the annihilation of my social life, or would he come off like a pushy mother, forcing the neighborhood kids to play with her own? Would he let me out of the office without some kind of confession? I glanced up and saw the determination in his eyes and knew the choice wasn't mine. I took a breath.

"I've felt kind of alienated since I took the job."

"Alienated by who?" He pressed his fingertips together in a pyramid and leaned back in his chair.

"Other people on the floor."

"Go on." He nodded solemnly like a cinematic psychiatrist.

"I feel isolated from everyone else now." It was pointless to mention the feelings to Neal. Surely he felt left out all the time.

"That alienation is just one component of success, Claire. Not everyone can be MVP, and that's never going to change. You can't let it get to you."

He lost me with the sports analogy. Was I the MVP, or doomed not to be? "I know I shouldn't take it personally, but . . ."

"Don't. This is an issue of power, not personality."

"That's great, Neal, but—"

"Listen. All you need to do is jump in there and show them that you're still part of the team. I've got the perfect solution for you. A group of us are going to the pub tonight, and I think you should come."

A group of us? Who the hell invited *Neal* and not me? The situation was worse than I'd thought.

"I don't know . . ."

"Claire, you brought up these feelings of isolation."

"Yeah, but . . ."

"*But* is a three-letter death sentence. Either you want things to improve, or you don't."

"I guess you're right."

"You know I'm right." He leaned forward and rested his elbows on the surface of his desk. "Now, can I count on you to join us tonight?"

"Okay." I nodded and got up to leave. Just as I reached the door and turned the handle, he spoke again.

"There are worse things in the world than being disliked, Claire."

I thought of the way we all used to talk about him when his door was closed and winced. "I'm glad you feel that way, Neal."

I marched back to my desk feeling moderately hopeful. Naturally, I wasn't thrilled that Neal had been the one to invite me, but once I got to the pub, I suspected I could win a few people over between drinks.

When five o'clock finally arrived, I was pretty enthusiastic about an evening out. While Mom's fleeting presence in the apartment hadn't exactly cramped my single lifestyle, it certainly hadn't helped. Granted, the missed opportunity to go out with Adam on Friday night wasn't quite as devastating as I'd first thought, now that I knew what he *wasn't* made of, but watching *Annie* was no social coup, either.

As I signed off the computer and gathered my things, I wondered if Mom was having more fun with Steph and Alison than she'd had with me. Sure, she had traded my couch for a real guest room, and Steph's cooking skills were far superior to my own, but it seemed unlikely that her homophobia could be cured in a matter of days. Or could it? After a twenty-three-year climb to reach top billing of the McLeod sisters, had I been bumped by a queen-sized mattress and a cheese souffle?

Probably.

The longer I went without talking to Mom, the more tempted I was to call my father. My loyalty to Dad had never been called into question before, but the disappointment I felt at his betrayal was like poison in my stomach, eating away at me, and I wanted some kind of relief. I was gradually reaching a point where I wanted to hear his version of events, and I'd almost picked up the phone twice to call him, but I was too afraid that hearing the words of betrayal come from his mouth might turn me against him forever. As long as I was in limbo, I didn't have to make a decision. I didn't have to lose him.

"Cheer up, for pete's sake," Neal said, nudging me with his elbow and propelling me toward the elevator. "It's Friday night! You can have a few brewskis. Heck, you can party all night if you want to and sleep all day tomorrow."

"It's Tuesday, Neal."

He raised his wrist to squint at one of the many dials on his flashy watch. "So it is," he murmured. "Oh, well, a couple of drinks never hurt anybody, right?"

I nodded, but he was too busy stabbing the down button with his index finger to notice.

As we made our descent, I pushed thoughts of my family to the back of my mind. It was time to have some fun for a change. I could return to my world of worry in the morning. There was nothing wrong with letting loose and enjoying myself for one measly night.

"There's next to no parking, so I'll leave my car here, if you don't mind walking," Neal said, and I nodded assent.

The rain was still sprinkling and, judging by the darkened sky and blustery wind, we were in for a downpour. He opened a pocket-sized umbrella, assuring me that it was big enough for both of us. The black nylon offered about as much protection as a paper parasol in a girly drink, although it did manage to keep my right shoulder as dry as the roof of my mouth while we waited at crosswalks and stepped over sloshing gutters.

We arrived at the pub a little breathless and I paused to compose myself as Neal shook the drops from his umbrella. I made a mental note that I had nothing to worry about. I'd gone out for drinks with the gang before, and I was perfectly capable of handling myself. Neal had presented me with an opportunity to turn things around, and I wasn't about to miss my chance.

"I've never been here before," I said, watching him push the damp hair off his forehead and waiting for the stubborn raindrop on the tip of his nose to fall off.

"It's great." He smiled and the movement set the drop free. "I come here a lot."

He held the door for me as I stepped into a dimly lit room and a blast of blaring eighties pop immediately weakened my resolve. It wasn't exactly the kind of bar my coworkers usually hung out in. I glanced from the brass-rimmed booths against the far wall to the bar stools and empty dance floor, searching for familiar faces, but found none. The bartender, posed in front of a wall of booze that seemed to shake with every deafening drumbeat and bass chord, smiled and waved at Neal.

"What time were we supposed to meet here?" I shouted in Neal's ear.

"Mostly burgers," he shouted back.

"What?"

"Pub food. You know, burgers . . ."

"Oh, never mind." I shook my head and brushed past the reaching leaves of plastic ferns on my way to the bar.

"I'll get this round," Neal's stale breath caught up with me. "Do you want a wine cooler or something?"

Yeah, right.

"I'll have a double rum and Coke."

"Oh." He lifted his eyebrows in surprise. "Something a little stronger. I like it."

We were soon seated at a booth facing the front door, sipping our drinks and watching for any sign of our crowd.

"What time are they supposed to be here?" I asked, taking a final swig of my delightfully stiff drink.

"There wasn't a specific time."

"Don't you think they should be here by now?"

"I would have thought so, but I don't mind waiting. Do you want another drink?"

"Sure." I pulled my wallet out and handed him a twenty. "I'll buy the round. I'll have the same thing, and get us some chicken wings or something. I'm starving."

Mercifully, someone turned down the music about twenty minutes later, when we were midway through our third round. The music was still horrid, but tolerable, much like Neal.

I excused myself to use the rest room, where I admired the healthy flush in my cheeks brought on by mild intoxication. The areas where my hair hadn't unraveled felt tight and sore, so I let it all down, wishing I carried a brush to tame it. After shrugging and grinning at my vaguely blurry reflection in the mirror, I bought a couple more drinks on my way back to the table.

"Still no sign of them?" I asked, handing Neal his beer.

"Nope."

"Losers," I scoffed. "We'll just have to have fun without them."

And we did. Neal proved to be quite a storyteller when he loosened up. On our fourth or fifth drink, the animated face across the table seemed to belong to a stranger. A rather cute stanger, as a matter of fact. I'd never noticed what a nice smile he had, or the way his eyes crinkled when he laughed. I felt guilty for the way I'd written him off as a jackass and never given him the chance to prove he was anything else.

"You're not at all who I thought you were," I said, when he had finished his story.

"Meaning?"

"You're more entertaining than I expected."

"Entertaining. I sound like a circus performer."

"I don't mean it like that."

"What did you think I was like?"

"I don't know . . ."

"Yes, you do. Just tell me, Claire."

"I guess I thought you were a little . . ."

"I know I'm little." He looked wounded.

"I said *a little*. I thought you were a little uptight."

"That's exactly what Danielle says."

"Who?"

"My girlfriend. We're having some problems."

"Oh." I'd forgotten about the girlfriend, who I'd always assumed was imaginary.

"I say we have an intimacy issue, she calls it a sex problem." He took a long drink.

Oh, God. "Neal, I really don't think I'm the person to talk to about this."

"She says I don't communicate well." He banged his empty glass against the tabletop. "Can you believe that? I get *paid* to communicate."

Sex problems and communication. I wondered if he left

"Word of Godd" memos on the bedside table. *For better results, lift right leg higher.*

"Maybe you should be talking to her about this."

"I can't. We end up arguing every time it comes up. She's not rational, like you are."

"I am?"

"Yes. Rational. Sensible. Levelheaded. Do you want another drink?"

"Sure."

I watched him weave through the increasingly crowded dance floor and wondered why Danielle had trouble communicating with him. I found him incredibly easy to talk to, not to mention a pleasure to be around. Did she think she was going to stumble on to somebody better? I gulped the last of my drink. I'd been single and hopeless long enough to know that good men were few and far between. Who did she think she was, criticizing a catch like Neal?

She didn't know how good she had it.

Just after midnight, we decided it was time to leave. We both had to be at work in the morning, and a well-rested hangover seemed more promising than the alternative.

"My car's still at the office," Neal groaned when we reached the sidewalk on unsteady legs. He dug his keys out of his jacket pocket and started walking back toward work.

"I don't think you should drive."

"Why not?"

"You've had too much to drink."

"Oh, Claire." He paused for a few seconds, then grinned. "Hey, isn't that in Wisconsin?" His giggle was less than infectious. "Come on. Don't be such a worrier. Drinking heightens my senses."

"What?"

"I'm actually an overcautious driver after a few drinks."

"Let's just split a cab." I had just enough cash to get home, and my apartment was on the way to Neal's place in Beaverton.

"If you insist."

He flagged down a Yellow Cab and, after a fair bit of clumsiness, we were in the backseat and on our way.

"That was a great night, even though nobody else showed up," I murmured, leaning my head against the cool windowpane.

"I'm surprised they didn't make it," Neal said. "I gave really clear directions."

I turned toward him, the movement blurring my vision.

"Do you mean this was *your* idea?"

"Yeah."

"*You* did all of the inviting?"

"Mmmhmm."

No wonder.

Neal dozed as we sped through the slick city streets, and when we arrived at my apartment, I woke him with a tap on the shoulder.

"Thanks for everything, Neal. I had a good time."

"Where are we?" he mumbled.

"My apartment. Just tell the driver where you need to go and I'll see you in the morning." I climbed out and started to close the door.

"Claire, wait!"

"What?" I turned to see a panicked look in his eyes. "What's wrong?"

"I can't go home. She kicked me out."

"Danielle?" What on earth was that woman thinking?

"She told me not to come back."

"Why didn't you mention this earlier?"

"I don't know." He sighed and leaned his head against the door frame.

"Is there someone else you can stay with?"

"You tell me."

"What?" It took a moment for his point to come across, stabbing me between the eyes. "Oh, you want to stay here?"

"Hey, thank you, Claire. I really appreciate it."

"I wasn't—"

"I'll cover the cab." He handed the driver some bills.

"Neal, I don't think this is—"

"I'm really tired of thinking, aren't you?"

"I guess so." Too many drinks, too much to think about.

I led him up the stairs, stumbling at the landing. As I fumbled with my door key, Neal's hands gripped my shoulders.

"Claire?"

"Yeah?"

"You look really pretty with your hair down." His hands slowly moved up and down my arms in a soothing motion.

"Neal . . ."

"Really pretty." His fingertips grazed my cheek with aching softness.

It had been a long time since anyone had touched me like that.

He gently tucked some stray hair behind my ear and I found myself leaning toward him. He wrapped his arms around me and I was amazed at the solid strength of his body. He smelled like new rain, some kind of expensive musk, and sweet, sweet rum. After holding on for a moment, he released me and we faced one another at close range. If I bent my knees a little, we were almost at eye level. *Almost.*

It was almost impossible to believe, but I wanted him to kiss me.

Very slowly, his face lifted toward mine and I lowered my chin toward his. It seemed like minutes passed before his dry lips pressed against mine.

Suddenly, it all felt terribly, terribly wrong.

"Whoa." I pulled away from him.

"What's wrong?" His eyes were still half-closed.

"I don't think we should do this." Even in my inebriated state, I *knew* we shouldn't.

He glanced down the hallway. "Out here?"

"At all." I bit my lower lip.

"Really? I thought we were . . ."

"So did I, but we're not."

"Are you sure, because I know I felt . . ."

"It's a very bad idea."

"I see." His shoulders sagged and a silence fell between us.

"You can still stay here, if you want to."

"Okay." His eyes brightened a bit and I unlocked the door.

"Nice place." He scanned my living room, and somehow his perusal of my home was worse than Mom's. I had the distinct feeling his lair was filled with black leather and chrome.

I hurried to remove the pile of magazines from my couch and placed them on the overloaded coffee table. Much of Mom's cleaning blitz had already worn off.

"I'll just grab a pillow for you." I started toward the linen cupboard.

"I don't get a bed?"

"I don't have a spare room."

"But that couch doesn't have sheets," he whined. "I need Egyptian cotton."

"Ha! I'll get you some sheets, Neal."

"I could probably make do with a three-hundred-count percale."

"You get what you get."

"I'm sorry if you think I'm being difficult, Claire, but up until a couple of minutes ago I thought you and I would be—"

I stopped him right there.

"I don't want any awkwardness between us, Neal. We almost made a mistake. Can we just leave it at that?"

"I guess so." He shrugged off his overcoat while I searched for clean bedding.

"So, there won't be any trouble at work, right? We'll never talk about this again?" I asked, handing him a stack of mismatched linen.

"Contrary to popular belief, I'm not an asshole, Claire." He crammed his pillow into a case and set to work with the sheets. "Excuse my language."

I felt a new surge of guilt. He really was harmless. "Of course you aren't. I'm sorry. I'm being stupid about this."

"Let's just forget it. Do what you suggested and never talk about it again."

"Thanks, Neal." I sighed with relief. "The bathroom is down the hallway and to your left."

"Do you have a spare toothbrush?"

"No."

"You don't keep an extra one around?"

"No, I don't."

"No bed, no toothbrush . . ."

"Good night, Neal," I said, through gritted teeth.

I stripped out of my smoke-scented clothing, crawled into my flannel pajamas, and practically fell into bed. I could feel the probing fingers of nausea in my stomach and did my best to ignore them, slowly falling into a troubled and restless sleep.

✍

I awoke to the normally delightful smell of bacon cooking, and thought I might be sick. Groaning, I wiped the sleep from my eyes and sat up in bed, sheets twisted and tangled around my legs.

The alarm clock I'd failed to set the night before read seven thirty-five.

"Shit!"

I jumped out of bed and raced toward the bathroom, but spotted my mother in the kitchen on the way.

"Mom?"

Wasn't she supposed to be at Steph's?

"Good morning!" she called, incredibly loudly.

"Morning," I mumbled, reaching for the bathroom door knob, just as the shower was turned on. Who in the hell had Mom brought with her?

"I met your boyfriend, Claire. He's short but sweet."

In my morning-after state, her voice seemed suited to a Broadway stage.

"What are you doing here? I thought you were staying at Steph's."

"Things didn't really work out. I let myself in. It's a good thing I had a key made the other day."

Great, she had her own key. I was so distracted by that horrid detail, it took a moment for her earlier words to sink in. "You met my *boyfriend?*"

"Neal," she said, eyes bright with hope.

"God," I mumbled. Was he still here?

"Right. Neal Godd."

"I mean, God. As in *oh God.*"

"Oh."

"Mom, he's not my boyfriend. He's my boss."

"That's a shame." She made a disappointed clucking sound.

"Yes, it is, and not the way you mean it."

"He's having a shower."

"So I gathered."

"Would you like some juice? I'm making bacon and eggs."

My stomach lurched. "No offense, Mom, but what happened? Why are you here so early?"

"Like I said, things didn't work out over there."

"In what sense?"

She flushed a deep, rich red. "Steph's walls aren't as thick as she might think."

It took a moment for her meaning to sink in. "Oh, you mean you heard them, uh . . ."

"Yes." Mom bit her lip. "Loud and clear."

Before she could say much more, the shower stopped running and Neal appeared looking damp, but dressed. I would have offered to iron his suit jacket, which looked like he'd slept in it, but there was no time for niceties.

"How do you like your eggs?" Mom asked.

"To go," I told her, pointing at the clock. "We're going to be late."

I dashed into the shower while Neal ate breakfast and chatted with Mom. After throwing on some relatively clean clothes and wrestling my wet hair into a ponytail, we were out the door and hailing a cab.

On the way to the office I suggested that I get out a block before our building and walk the rest of the way for the sake of a separate entrance.

"Don't be ridiculous," he said, straightening his tie. "No one will even notice us coming in together. I never guessed you were so paranoid, Claire."

"Well, I am."

Neal paid the driver and I checked my watch. Ten minutes late. As we made our ascent, I hoped everyone would be concentrating on calls already, too focused to see us come in.

I tucked in my blouse as the elevator door opened and we stepped directly into Carol's glare. A flicker of knowledge danced in her eyes as they slowly meandered from Neal's wrinkled suit, obviously worn the day before, to his damp and freshly combed hair.

"Sleeping your way to middle management, Claire?" she hissed.

I tried to ignore her and stepped into the office with Neal too close by my side, striving to act natural and holding my breath as almost all of my coworkers turned to stare.

Judging by the nudging, I'd made a very big mistake.

TWELVE

It only took about two seconds for speculation that Neal and I *might* have spent the night together to become certainty that we had sweated and grunted well into the wee hours, a tangle of motivated limbs and breathless abandon. Heather's gaping blowfish mouth and the wrinkled brows of our two newest hires were some of the milder signs of shock, dismay, and, ultimately, disgust I witnessed in those first ugly moments.

"Let's get busy, folks," Neal barked, snapping his stubby little fingers.

"Looks like someone got busy last night," a voice muttered from the vicinity of the recycling bin.

I clenched my fists and started to walk toward my desk. The crowd parted like an old zipper, their stiffness only loosened by a couple of jerks.

"I hope she got a raise out of him," Anthony Carter said, nudging Pete McChord.

"Shit man, I doubt she even got a *rise* out of him," Pete snickered.

Oh, the hilarity of it all.

I pretended not to notice the whispering and giggling that increased in volume as soon as Neal was safely ensconced in his corner office. It was a source of great frustration that while *I* was doomed to spend the day as an open target, *he* could close the door for as long as he damn well pleased.

I tossed my hair in a miscalculated demonstration of nonchalance, only to curse the effort when the damaged, wet ends of my ponytail hit me in the face.

Typical.

I knew that any hope I had of making it through the day depended on my ability to paste on a smile and carry on as if all were well in my world. If people had nothing better to do than sit around gossiping about the office romance that wasn't, I'd just have to talk to Neal about raising the call quotas in our department.

Of course, that would require a private visit to his well-insulated corner fortress, a trip I suspected could only make matters worse.

I sighed and logged on to my computer, adjusting my headphones and preparing for the day.

"So, Claire . . ." Jason whispered, a conspirator's smile on his lips as he peered over the cube wall.

"I don't want to hear it." I dug around in my drawer for a pencil, staples, anything to convey the air of a busy worker with no time for chatter.

"Then you'd better buy some industrial earplugs."

"Jason," I warned, gripping an eraser in my right fist.

"What do you expect after an entrance like that? Half of this office would consider reruns of *Mr. Belvedere* entertaining, and you've given them live drama."

"I really don't want to—"

"Man, this one's going to take months, even years to die down."

"Can you just get to whatever point you're sharpening?"

Jason frowned, obviously disappointed to have his stage time cut short. He ran his nail-bitten fingers through the wiry depths of his hair before looking at me.

"All I want to know," he shook his head, undoing his efforts to smooth his curls, "is what the hell you were thinking. I mean, it was bad enough when you took on the new job, but shit, Claire, you've already *got* it. There was no need to screw that midget bastard."

"I didn't." My knuckles whitened at his choice of words.

"Okay, okay." He rolled his eyes. "We'll get all PC for the sake of your delicate sensibilities. You didn't need to 'make love' to that fuckin' digital wiener."

Digital wiener?

"Will you shut up? I didn't have sex with him, Jason."

"What do I look like, an idiot?"

"Well . . ." I eyed him suggestively.

"Never mind. Don't answer that."

"What's the point of answering anything if no one will believe me? The fact is, he spent the night on my couch, and if you can't handle that . . ."

"Hey," he raised his hands in mock defense, "whatever you say, Claire."

"No, listen to me." My ferocity caught his attention. "He slept on my couch. My mother made him breakfast, for fuck's sake."

"Whoa, Claire. I could use a little less venom."

"I give up." I turned away from him and toward my monitor. "I've worked with you for two years. I thought we were friends."

"We *are* friends. And I'll have you know, I don't say that about many people."

"That's really heartwarming," I snapped, shooting him a fierce glare. "Do you consider your other friends liars?"

"I never said—"

"I don't have time for this. I have work to do."

I had no one on the phone but began my toothpaste survey to dead air.

"Claire?" Heather's breathy whisper smelled like stale coffee.

"Yes?" I asked, pulling my headset away from one ear.

"I was just wondering if you wanted to, uh . . . *talk*."

"About what?" I aimed for an expression as blank as her mind.

"About, well, *you know*." She wiggled her eyebrows.

"About my night of raunchy and sordid sex with Neal?"

"Was it?" Her eyes widened with shock and delight.

"For God's sake, Heather, we didn't have sex."

"But you just said . . ." Her voice trailed away and she bit her lower lip with uncertainty.

"He had too much to drink and I let him sleep on my couch."

She gave me a vague stare for a moment, before nodding slowly and winking at me. "Gotcha," she said, leaning in close to my ear. "So, how was he?"

"I just told you that nothing happened."

She paused, then whispered, "To tell you the truth, I always thought he was kind of cute." She giggled. "I guess you did too."

"Yeah, Heather. He's a fucking Adonis."

"You think so?"

"No, I don't."

"But you just told me you—"

"Sarcasm, Heather. Try to keep up."

"You mean you slept with someone you weren't even attracted to?"

"We didn't sleep together." I wanted to beat my head against my keyboard, or strangle her with my mouse cord. "I swear to you that nothing happened between us."

Nothing beyond an extremely chaste and fleeting kiss, anyway, and that was a secret I would guard with my life.

"Do you really expect me to believe that?"

I looked her straight in the eye. "Yes."

"Hmm." She frowned with consternation and turned away without another word.

Finally, I got down to the task of organized phone harassment, but only managed to complete nine surveys in two hours. Between calls, I prepared myself for the realities of going about my day. As much as I dreaded the prospect, "acting normal" had to take place beyond the carpeted walls of my cubicle.

I made a beeline for the watercooler on my morning break, greeting everyone I passed with a bright smile and a cheery hello, slightly more manic than my usual behavior, but a far cry from cowering at my desk.

I was given a wide berth and a number of baffled looks as I filled a paper cup and leaned against the wall to sip my drink in silence. The threesome huddled next to me briefly showed an interest in my presence, until it became apparent that I wasn't about to spill my lurid beans, and they returned to the hushed tones of their conversation.

I held out at the water cooler for as long as I could, which turned out to be three of the fifteen minutes my break consisted of, before returning to the safety of my desk and the welcome distraction of work.

Shortly after eleven o'clock, Carol sashayed over to my desk with a pink message slip and a smirk.

I finished my call, face reddening in anticipation of the damage about to be done.

"Give it to me," I snapped, reaching for the paper.

"I think Neal already did." Her smile was tight, her cheeks a shade lighter than her pancake makeup could conceal.

"Very funny."

"Very *pathetic*," she scoffed, then glanced at the note. "Mommy called to say that *our boss* left his watch on your breakfast table."

"Thank you, Carol," I said, with all the bravado I could muster, taking the message and placing it on my desk without a glance. I wouldn't give her the satisfaction of seeing me squirm.

I waited for her to return to her foyer of evil, but she stood glaring at me instead.

"Look, you delivered your message and had your fun. Why are you still standing here?"

"He doesn't care about you." Her arms were crossed tightly across her chest, red fingernails digging into her black acrylic sweater sleeves.

"I never said he did."

"He'll never love you."

Certainly the least of my worries.

"Why do you care?" I asked, taken aback by her bitter tone.

Her knuckles whitened as her nails dug deeper.

"You're making a fool of yourself." Her skin was as pale as

the puddle of dried whiteout I'd spilled on my desk, and I suddenly realized something I'd never have believed if I hadn't seen it myself.

She was *jealous*.

I had the upper hand.

Antagonism had been building in my system for a full two years, and suddenly I had an opportunity I couldn't resist. A glorious outlet I could and would put to good use.

I had to think quickly if I was going to win this round, and while my mind raced, I smiled softly, hoping to convey the appearance of postcoital contentedness.

"I never knew he had such strong hands," I murmured, leaning back in my chair. "And such a sensitive touch."

"He . . ."

"Those lips," I closed my eyes briefly in pseudo-remembrance, "they were practically lethal."

"He used you," she snarled, and I knew I had her.

"Well." I sighed. "Just between you and me, Carol. If I'd known being used felt that good, I would have—"

Before I could finish my fabrication, she stormed away from my desk in a blur of black fury.

For the first time that day, my smile was genuine.

I made a valiant effort to stay focused on calls, but the gods were fully committed to working against me. My morning was interrupted once again when Steph phoned me on her morning break, a note of panic in her voice. Apparently, all hostility over our divided loyalties was forgotten and she needed my help. I encouraged her to slow down and, when I was finally able to understand what she was babbling about, I assured her that Mom wasn't missing in action, but camped out at my place.

She breathed a long sigh of relief. "Thank God. I got up this morning and she was gone. I freaked out."

"Not as much as I did, waking up to find her in my kitchen."

"What?"

Coming from Steph's end of the line were the sounds of paper shuffling and some kind of public service announcement blaring from a TV in the background. Most of the residents of Cedar Heights had trouble hearing, and Steph was constantly dealing with the shrill bleating of overextended hearing aids.

"Nothing. I was just surprised to see her this morning."

"What?" Steph asked.

I waited for the background noise to die down before speaking again.

"So, what's going on?" Steph asked. "She left without even saying good-bye."

"She was upset." The last thing I wanted to do was discuss the details of what had prompted Mom's departure.

"She told me she didn't like the potpourri in her room. Now, tell me, Claire, who the hell is offended by lavender?" she scoffed.

I was hard-pressed for an answer.

"Anyway," she continued, "I moved it into our room. What more did she want?"

"It wasn't the smell." I gritted my teeth. "It was the noise."

There was a pregnant pause before she responded, and I could almost hear the gears of her brain creaking. "Uh, could you be a little less cryptic? This is a coffee break, not my lunch hour."

I briefly and awkwardly explained that Mom was uncomfortable because she'd heard Steph and Alison having sex.

"When was that?"

"Last night."

"Yeah, right. We haven't had sex since she moved in."

"Steph, I know you, uh, *do it*, so don't feel like you have to cover it up for me. I'm not, uh, bothered by your sex life." At least I hadn't been until her "mostly oral" proclamation at Napoli. There were certain things I simply didn't need to know, not that I hadn't wondered from time to time what exactly the two of them got up to in the wee hours.

"Well, I am. Alison's all nervous about doing anything with Mom in the next room, so every night we've put on our pajamas, crawled into bed, and slept like a couple of nuns. It's pissing me off."

"Even last night?" I asked, thoroughly confused.

"No, last night we . . . oh my God." She snorted with laughter.

"What?"

"There's no way she could have thought . . . oh, shit. That is classic Mom!"

"What?" I snapped.

"We were moving our furniture around. Alison wanted the wardrobe by the window, so we had to move the bed and chest of drawers. The bed weighs a ton, so we were grunting and swearing as we tried to get it turned around."

"And she thought you were . . ." A smile crept onto my face.

"I remember at one point Alison was gasping and saying something like, 'a little more to the right, just like that, ooh that's perfect.' Then we bumped the frame against the wall a couple of times." She snickered into the phone, "Poor Mom."

"Do you want me to tell her the truth?" I asked.

"No, let it simmer. Maybe she'll get over the shock."

"But in the meantime, she's all mine."

"Sorry, Claire."

"No, it's okay. I've been thinking about her today and I can see that you were right to defend her the other night. I should have been supportive of her right from the start, and now I feel shitty about it." I waited for her to assure me that I wasn't a horrible person, but it didn't happen. "Did you manage to get any more Dad info out of her?"

"She's not talking. I kept telling her I was there for her no matter what, but she wouldn't open up."

"Well, I'm going to make her talk tonight."

"Has Dad called again?" she asked.

"Nope. It's just as well, though. I don't know what I would say to him."

"She's shattered."

"I know."

"I never expected to see her like this."

"Neither did I." I sighed. "And I never thought Dad would . . ." I couldn't find the words. "I feel like he's a stranger." It was like the father I knew had died, and I was in mourning.

When I hung up the phone, I felt a surge of panic at the thought of actually losing my relationship with Dad. I was almost certain he'd betrayed all of us without a second thought, and I suddenly felt the overwhelming need to know if it was true. I also needed to know what had made him do it.

He loved my mother. He chose her as his partner for life, and I needed to know what had driven him away. Of course, I didn't have the luxury of choosing the woman who would give birth to me, so the mother-daughter relationship was bound to be rocky, but my parents were adults when they made the decision to marry. They were fully formed people who assessed each other and made a conscious decision to spend their lives as one. They signed a contract, bought a house, built a family.

After all of these years together, what had changed Dad's mind?

Before I could talk myself out of it, I was dialing Omaha, praying he would answer before I lost my nerve.

When he did, I almost cried at the sound of his mild "Hello?"

I couldn't speak.

"Hello?" he asked again.

"Dad?"

"Claire! Are you all right?"

"I'm fine," I lied, then didn't know where to begin, or where I wanted the conversation to go. "I got your message, but I haven't had a chance to—"

"That's okay. I know you're busy." He cleared his throat. "How's your mom?"

"Mom? She's . . ." What was I supposed to say? I took a breath and tightened my grip on the phone. "She told me." The words came out in a rush.

"Both of you?"

My heart sank when he knew exactly what I was referring to.

"Yes, Steph too. At dinner the other night."

"I'm surprised." His voice was flat.

"She needed to talk to someone."

"Yes." He cleared his throat. "And it should have been me."

"Dad. She's having a really hard time."

"We both are."

"What's going to happen?"

"I don't know, but I think this is a temporary setback. We can get through this."

"A temporary setback?" I gasped.

"These things happen, honey."

"That's all you have to say? Surely you don't expect things to go back to the way they were. You don't expect her to just forget about it, do you?"

"People do, Claire. Affairs happen every day and marriages survive."

"That's a pretty pat answer," I said, suddenly very angry. "*Affairs happen every day?* Not in my family, they don't."

There was a lengthy pause before he spoke again.

"This is exactly why I wanted your mother to stay here." He sighed. "This is between her and I."

I wanted him to beg for forgiveness, or acknowledge that what he'd done was wrong, but there was no emotion in his voice. It was like talking to a goddamn robot.

"I don't know how you expect to stay married."

"You think we should divorce?"

How could he be so calm?

"Right now, I don't know what to think."

"I think you should talk to your mother, Claire. If she could just get over it . . ."

"Get over it? Jesus, Dad. How callous is that?"

"I'm being realistic. We've been together for twenty-odd years, and I have no intention of giving up on this marriage."

"I don't think it's your decision." *Who was this man?*

"You're probably right."

The conversation was not going the way I'd hoped, and all

I wanted was to get off the phone, but I couldn't leave him without addressing one very real, nagging issue.

"Dad, for Christ's sake. Why her?" He couldn't miss my meaning, and didn't.

"Joan Salomar?" he asked, the words rolling across the miles like they were nothing. "I don't know. She's young and pretty." He confirmed my worst fears as I held my breath in disbelief. "What can I tell you, it was crazy."

"I have to go," I said, hanging up before he could say good-bye.

I thought I was going to be sick, and I clutched my stomach with both arms. How could he be so cold and uncaring? Had he actually said that Mom should just "get over it"? No wonder she'd left home in favor of Steph and me.

Shit.

She'd traveled across the country, seeking comfort and understanding from me, and I'd completely failed her. I'd been so caught up in viewing her as a pain-in-the-ass mother, I'd ignored the fact that she was a woman as well. A human being, with the same range of emotions and feelings as me. I let her down when she needed me most.

"Claire, can I see you for a minute?"

I glanced up and saw Neal at the corner of my desk, apparently confused by my crumpled form. I lifted myself into a properly seated position. "Uh, sure."

"In my office," he said, over his shoulder as he turned and retreated.

I felt the eyes of every Alta Media employee upon me as I followed him, but after my conversation with Dad, none of it mattered. They could think I was a corporate-climbing slut for all I cared. The man I respected more than anyone in the world had betrayed my mother, and I, in failing to support her, had done the same.

Neal closed the door behind me and offered a seat.

"Are you okay?"

My mind was still reeling from Dad's admission. Joan Salomar was "young and pretty"? That was all it had taken to lure him away from his marriage? A horrible thought flashed through my mind. Was she the only one, or had he been cheating on Mom for years with any willing and able body in Omaha?

"Claire?"

"I'm fine," I muttered absently.

"That's what you always say, but I'm really asking if you're okay."

"No . . . yes, I mean, it's just some family stuff."

"Your mom?"

"I don't really want to talk about it."

"She seemed nice. Great eggs."

"Legs? What kind of a pervert are you?" First hit on the daughter, then the mother?

"I said *eggs*, Claire."

"Oh." I took a deep breath. "Sorry."

"Apology accepted." He dropped into his swivel chair.

"Is that all you wanted to talk to me about? My mother's cooking?"

"No."

I waited, but he didn't offer any additional information, and I was in no mood for guessing games. "What is it, then?"

"This new position of yours . . ." He frowned. "I'm not sure it's working out."

The words caught me completely off-guard. "What, the auditing?"

"Yes." He nodded solemnly.

"It's only been a few days, Neal. And I thought it was going extremely well."

"It was."

"Was? As in past tense?" My stomach tightened.

"Things aren't going the way I'd planned."

"What are you talking about?" If he thought he could take away the only thing in my life that was *almost* working, he had another think coming.

"Maybe you're not the right one for the job." He folded his stubby hands together and I shivered at the thought of them caressing my body less than twelve hours earlier.

"Wait just a second, here. Maybe I'm not right for it?" I could see where he was going, and I didn't like it. "Is that because I wouldn't sleep with you?"

"No!" His eyes bulged like a startled cartoon character's.

"Are you actually going to *demote* me," I tried to control my increasing volume, with no success, "because I wouldn't *fuck* you?"

"Claire!" His index finger shot to his lips in a shushing motion. "Jesus, do you want everyone to hear you?"

"If I'm right, hell yes!"

"This has nothing to do with what happened last night."

"Nothing happened last night!" I shrieked. He, of all people, should have known that!

"I know! Take a breath, Claire. You're all worked up."

"Of course I'm worked up! The day after we don't sleep together, I'm being demoted?" My head was pounding. "Dammit, if one more thing goes wrong today, I'm going to lose it!" I was close to tears, but didn't want to cry in front of him.

"Why don't you take the rest of the day off," he offered quietly.

"I can't, I need the—"

"With pay. You need to go home, Claire."

"But I—"

"I'll see you tomorrow."

I wanted to fight the suggestion, but I was so tired, so worn out by the events of the past few days, that I simply couldn't do it. By the time I pushed back my chair and stood up, I was so busy trying to leave his office with a teaspoon of dignity, I forgot to demand a reason for the potential demotion.

"Where are you going?" Jason asked, as I gathered my things and logged off the computer.

"Home."

"You're walking out?"

"Neal gave me the rest of the day off."

As I walked away, I heard Heather's hoarsely whispered, "I guess that's just one more perk of sleeping with the boss."

It wasn't until I was halfway down my hallway that I saw a man hunched in front of my apartment, hastily shoving something under my door.

"Hey!" I shouted, before giving a thought to my personal safety. "What are you doing?"

As the man climbed to his feet, my hands scrambled in my bag for my umbrella, a book, or a nail file, anything I could use as a weapon.

Countless times Paul had warned me to carry a whistle or a personal alarm, and I'd always ignored him, sure he was fearing the impossible. Why was I incapable of taking good advice? Why was I having such a bad week? Was my life going to continue spiraling downward indefinitely, or was I doomed to a gruesome death in a third-, no, fourth-rate apartment building?

The man stepped toward me and I wanted to scream, but couldn't make a sound. I was frozen, mute, and scared to death.

He took a couple more steps, and his face was illuminated by the dinky lightbulb over apartment fifty-one.

My prowler was none other than Paul Clemens.

THIRTEEN

If I hadn't been enraged by the scare he'd given me, Paul's tentative smile would have had me swooning. I clung to my anger, knowing I was an emotional wreck, and that any sign of kindness from him would only hurt me in the long run.

"What the hell are you doing, sneaking around like that?" I demanded.

He frowned, and I was such an idiot, I couldn't help admiring those damn lips. I couldn't help remembering the way they brushed against my ear when he whispered during movies, or how soft they felt when he kissed my shoulders, my wrists, my . . . everything.

Shit!

"I'm not sneaking around," he said.

"Oh, that's right. *Now* you don't have to." I sniffed. He certainly didn't have to hide anything from me anymore. No more sneaking around to save my feelings. No more lies. Of course, cute little Tina, Ashley, Susie, whatever her name was had already been replaced by that brunette at Napoli. It served her right.

His shrug implied that he didn't get my meaning, and if he wanted to play dumb, that was fine with me.

"So, what are you doing here?" I asked, pulling the keys from my purse and walking past him to the door. God, he was wearing the aftershave I gave him for Valentine's Day. That woodsy smell made me crazy.

"I was just dropping something off."

I opened the door and stepped inside, noting and appreciating Mom's absence. I stooped to pick up a white legal envelope and he followed me into the room, closing the door behind him.

"What is it?" Before he could answer, I tore open the envelope, hoping, against all reason, that it was a formal apology for the way he had hurt me. Instead, it was a bunch of twenty-dollar bills.

"I borrowed a couple of hundred bucks from you after Christmas. You know, before we . . . broke up." He paused. "I just wanted to pay you back."

"Thanks a lot," I mumbled.

"I hadn't forgotten about it or anything. I just haven't had the money until now."

"Well, thanks." I stood facing him over several planks of polished hardwood and several months of longing, wishing he'd shaved his head so I wouldn't have to look at the dark hair I used to touch when he slept.

"The place looks nice." He smiled, and it felt like my heart was being wrung by strong and determined hands. "You finally hung that Klimt print."

Those eyes. They were the feature I'd been most attracted to in those early days, when watching him tell a story had been the highlight of my day.

Against my better judgment, I offered him a drink.

"Have you got any chocolate milk?"

I was thinking more along the lines of a shot of just about anything, but I nodded. Of course I did. When we first started seeing each other, I'd gone years without chocolate milk, but he'd transformed me into an addict in a matter of weeks.

He sat on the couch while I prepared drinks in the kitchen, my hands shaking more than I cared to admit. It had been difficult enough seeing him in a public place, but alone in my apartment?

Pathetic.

My saving grace was that Mom could walk in at any moment, and that possibility was enough to keep me clothed.

At least I hoped it was.

After a quivering breath, I returned to the living room, unnerved by how right he looked propped against the embroidered pillows on my couch. How many nights had we spent snuggled under a blanket watching court dramas and sitcoms? More important, how many nights had we skipped the TV in favor of rambunctious physical activity on that very same blanket?

I handed him a glass, and our fingertips brushed. I almost jumped out of my shoes (which, under the circumstances, would have been a lot better than, say, my pants), embarrassed as hell that something so minor and unintentional could have such a startling effect.

Paul had always been affectionate, more of a "toucher" than I was. He liked to hold hands, rub shoulders, nuzzle necks.

Necks. The plural factor was what I needed to concentrate on.

"So, how have you been?" he asked.

"Better."

"Oh." He looked oddly disappointed.

"No, not better than when we . . . I mean, I've been better in the past than I am now."

"Oh." His smile returned for a split second before a look of concern appeared.

"I'm sure everything will be fine," I said, mustering what little optimism I had left. "It's just a rough patch."

"If you ever want to talk . . ."

"Thanks. Thanks a lot, but I think I can handle it."

"I mean it, Claire. I'm here for you."

His eyes were so sincere, and his voice so soft, that it was all I could do not to slump against his chest and hope that he'd hold me.

How could such a good guy turn out to be such a bastard?

I realized, with a shiver, that Mom was probably asking herself the very same thing.

"I went back to school over the summer."

"You did?" He'd always talked about wanting to be an electrician, but I'd never taken him seriously.

"Yeah. It's going really well."

"That's good."

"Mmmhmm." He nodded. "How's your work going?"

"I got promoted."

"That's great!"

"But I think I'm being demoted now."

"Oh." The apartment was so quiet, I could hear my Timex ticking on my nightstand.

It was hard to believe that after hours of talking until we were hoarse, and evenings of filling each other in on the day's events, we hadn't seen each other for months and somehow had absolutely nothing to say.

"I've been meaning to come by and see you," he said, then sipped his drink. He was left with a chocolate mustache I would have kissed clean in another life.

But everything was different. He had a beard.

He had a girlfriend.

Or girlfriends.

"You don't have to say that." But I was glad he did. At least he was thinking of me. I hoped he'd regretted leaving me and that his thoughts were, like mine, fond and filled with what could have been. The fact that he'd been meaning to come by was something, anyway. Had he considered trying to get back together? Was he making an attempt at that very moment? Was that the reason for stopping by?

"I left my brother's Discman here, and he's been asking me about it for months."

"Oh." My response was stifled by the lump in my throat. "It's in my room. I'll grab it."

In an attempt to compose myself, I took longer than necessary locating the device on top of my dresser.

"Excellent," he said, when I returned. "This'll get him off my back."

I had loved this man, and somehow, that hadn't been enough.

Why wasn't *I* enough?

We talked about a big bunch of nothing for the next few minutes, slurping chocolate milk during the inevitable awkward pauses in conversation. Despite the disjointed words and mixture of emotions swirling around in my mind, I began to loosen up a bit and I was almost feeling normal. That is, until

Paul asked if I still had his favorite suede jacket. I didn't know how to answer the question without revealing too much.

"It might have been burned." I stared at the neat double knots of his Vans, too ashamed to meet his eyes.

"It *might* have been *burned?*" He leaned toward me, and that damn evergreen scent surrounded me.

"I, uh, *might* have doused it with lighter fluid and burned it in my sink after you left." I could still remember the frustration of trying to pry open those goddamn childproof lighters I'd dug out from under the couch cushions and pulled from the pockets of discarded jackets and tote bags. The smoke set off my fire alarm, which I dismantled with a well-aimed broom handle as my kitchen filled with the stench of burning hide.

"I can't believe this." He rubbed his forehead. "You *burned* it? Are you some kind of nut?"

"I was upset." I shrugged halfheartedly. It had seemed like a good idea at the time.

"So you destroyed something you knew I loved?"

I didn't answer him right away.

"Claire?"

"Well, yeah." I'd destroyed a jacket, while he'd destroyed *me*. "I thought you deserved it."

"What?"

Again, I didn't answer, so he continued, "I never would have expected that from you. I thought I knew you, Claire."

I almost choked on my own disbelief.

"You're coming off a little holier-than-thou, considering you had trouble remembering my name at Napoli the other night." My cheeks flamed at the memory. Did he honestly think he could play victim after everything he'd put me through? Son of a bitch!

I'd cried for weeks when he walked out the door. I'd questioned every bit of the relationship, playing it over, moment by moment, in my mind like a video that never had the right ending.

I'd questioned, then hated, myself in those first weeks, devastated that he'd looked for someone else because he didn't care about me. I'd loved him, and mourned the sorry sack of shit when he left me. There was only one victim in our equation, and that was me.

"Of course I knew your name at Napoli," he barked.

"Sure, somewhere in the dark recesses of your mind. In case you've forgotten, I had to prompt you when I introduced my mother."

"I knew your name." He paused. "Better than you knew mine."

What was that supposed to mean?

"And that girl you were with?" I asked. "The fawning brunette?"

"The brunette?" He paused, apparently requiring some time to figure out which brunette from his cast of thousands I was referring to. "She's a friend."

"Bullshit."

"For crying out loud, Claire, I thought you were the one."

"The one?" I asked, voice trembling with rage. "The one what? The one you left in the dust? The one you pretended you cared about? The one you couldn't get away from fast enough?"

"The one I thought I'd marry." He glared at me, a look that tore through me faster than his words.

Did he say *marry*?

I dropped my glass and it shattered on the hardwood, a brown puddle racing toward my knock-off Persian rug.

"What are you talking about?" Blood rushed my ears with a steady rhythm.

"I think that was a pretty clear statement, Claire."

"Marriage?"

"Yeah, well." The muscles in his jaw were working overtime. "Things change, I guess."

"Hold on." I grasped for understanding. "You thought you might marry me until you met that Cindy, Janie, Judy . . ."

"Who?" He sounded genuinely baffled.

"That perky blonde. The one you left me for."

He raised his hands in confusion. "I don't know who or what you're talking about."

"That girl, that *woman* you left me for."

"Are you talking about Christina?" he finally asked.

"How the hell should I know what her name is? I'm talking about the woman I saw you with at the Golden Dragon, then at McCormick and Schmick's." I'd been totally shaken by the sight of them laughing and whispering mere days after we'd broken up.

"I didn't see you." His eyebrows furrowed.

"Obviously."

"That was Christina. Chrissy."

"Just the proper name is fine, thanks." My voice sounded dead. Now I knew what that bitch's name was.

"My sister-in-law."

"You had an affair with your sister-in-law?"

"No, Claire." His lips thinned in annoyance. "I planned a surprise birthday party for my brother with her."

"Oh." All of the rage drained out of me and I couldn't think of anything to say. It didn't make sense.

We sat in silence until I finally got up the nerve to ask a question I'd been sure I knew the answer to. I cleared my throat.

"So . . . so then . . . what went wrong between us?" The question sounded stupid as soon as the words left my mouth.

He turned to stare at me in disbelief. "You don't *know?*"

"Uh, no." Up until three minutes earlier, I'd thought he ran off with someone else. I'd spent six months believing I'd been thoroughly wronged and run over. There had been no need for a secondary theory.

"You don't know." He shook his head slowly from one side to the other before rubbing his forehead with his hands.

Such beautiful hands.

"Paul." I almost reached for his arm. "Can you just tell me? Was it something I did?"

He left the couch and walked toward the window, leaving me to wallow in uncertainty. I didn't know what to say or do because I couldn't imagine what I could possibly have done to sabotage the relationship. *I* was the insecure half of our partnership, never sure of how I'd managed to snag him. *I* was the one hoping with all my heart that he hadn't met someone else when he started to pull away from me. How could the breakup be my fault? It couldn't be.

It wasn't my fault.

"You called me Adam," he said, softly enough that I barely heard the words.

"Adam?" I swallowed hard. Impossible!

"Yes, Claire. Adam." His lips twisted as he said the name.

"When did I . . ."

"When I was under the impression we were making love and your mind was obviously somewhere else." He turned toward me, cheeks flushed with anger, embarrassment, or both.

I felt like I'd been turned upside down and shaken by my ankles.

"You must have misheard me, Paul." Had I really said it? Yes, I'd been considering Adam an option for the inevitable moment Paul would leave me for the mystery girl I was sure he was seeing, but I didn't have any feelings for my coworker at that time.

I called him *Adam*?

It was *my* fault?

It wasn't fair.

I was trying to save myself from the looming heartache I knew Paul was going to cause me, and Adam was just a distraction. I had to think there was some hope for life after Paul, so I'd pinned that hope on Adam Carello. The one I wanted didn't want me, so I had to want someone else.

It wasn't fair.

Had I *really* said it?

"So, if I did call you by another name, which I doubt very seriously," I tripped over my own tongue in an effort to justify my stupidity, "that's hardly a reason to end the relationship."

"Are you joking?"

"No, I mean, if it happened, it was . . ." How to make it sound as harmless as possible? ". . . one measly slipup."

"The third time was the charm." He turned toward me and grimaced before looking away again.

"What?"

"You heard me."

Shit.

"Paul, I . . ."

"Do you have any idea what it feels like to love someone and find out that they want someone else?"

I sure as hell had thought I did.

"Uh . . ."

Life with Paul was over because of stupid, boring, blank-

slate Adam Carello? My big mouth had blown the best relationship I'd ever had? It was ridiculous! It was impossible!

It was so fucking typical of my week, it had to be true.

"But Adam is just—"

"I don't want to know." His sagging shoulders were too
much for me.

"But he's—"

"Don't."

"Paul, can't we talk about this?"

He finally turned to face me. "I think we just did."

"Paul, just give me a chance to explain." The desperation
in my voice was pitiful, but I didn't care.

"No," he said, moving toward the door.

"Couldn't we just . . . don't you think we could give it
another try?"

"I've spent the last six months moving on with my life."
He reached for the doorknob.

"So have I, but now that I know there was a misunderstanding, two of them, actually, when we count the sister-in-law . . ."

"It's too hard." He opened the door.

"But Paul, I—."

"It's too late." And he was gone.

I stood for a few dumbfounded moments at the front door
before moving on unsteady legs to the safety of the couch. I
leaned against the pillows that still smelled like him and struggled to remember every word of our conversation. The fact
that there had been no other woman was bad enough, but coupled with the knowledge that I was the one who had inflicted
the wound, the situation was mortifying.

He'd never given any indication that I'd called him by another name, but had given me a second chance, followed by a third, and I'd blown them all.

I couldn't imagine what I would have done if he'd used someone else's name when we were in bed.

He'd called it "making love."

He'd wanted to marry me.

Of course, marriage wasn't my ultimate goal, and I had some serious doubts about women who made a proposal their top priority, but the thought of spending the rest of my days with Paul Clemens had crossed my mind more than once. I had several journal pages of "Mrs. Paul Clemens" and "Claire A. Clemens" autographs to prove it. My daydreams about a life with Paul had left no room for hyphenated, just-in-case surnames or doubts about other fish in the sea. I'd wanted us to belong to each other. It was that simple and, thanks to my unbelievable stupidity, it had become that impossible.

As I willed away the threat of tears, I heard a key in the lock and the rustling of plastic bags before Mom stepped into the living room, grocery-laden and obviously surprised to see me.

"What are you doing here?" she asked, carrying her load into the kitchen.

Apparently she'd forgotten it was my home.

"Nothing."

"Well, I can see that," she said, poking her head around the corner.

"Neal sent me home."

"Why?"

"Because I'm a wreck."

"You're not a wreck."

"Mom," I said, as the tears started.

She left the groceries and came to sit next to me on the

couch. I fell against her and she wrapped her arms around me, smelling of reassuring rose water. She cradled me as though I was fragile, or very young, and I felt an almost overwhelming sense of security. The experience was familiar, but almost forgotten, until I realized it was the way she'd held me when I fell off my bike, right before she spread iodine on my wound and blew gently to ease the sting. It was the way she held me when I cried over a *D* in math, and when I awoke from terrifying dreams and crept to her bedroom for solace.

How had I forgotten her long history of comforting me?

"You can't hold it all in," she murmured against my ear, and I wished like mad that I was a little kid again with problems that only lasted as long as commercial breaks.

"I'm sorry," I whimpered, overwhelmed by guilt over Paul and the fact that I'd let her down.

"You have nothing to be sorry for."

"You needed me for the first time, and I wasn't there for you." My fingers brushed the tip of her braid.

"I can take care of myself, honey."

"But I want to help. I'm so sorry that Dad did this to you." A fresh batch of tears blurred my vision.

"Let's not talk about that right now." She cleared her throat. "Tell me about what happened at work."

That glimmer of encouragement was all the incentive I needed to pour out my heart and soul. Mom listened to me prattle on about my new sex scandal, possible demotion, and peer alienation, offering only supportive murmurs and sympathetic clucks. I must have talked for two hours, outlining my worries and fears, and hopes.

It wasn't until I told her about my visit with Paul that she jumped in.

"It sounds like he really cares."

"*Cared.* And I ruined everything."

"From what you've told me, I think he still cares."

"Even if he does, he made it very clear he doesn't want anything to do with me."

"Maybe he just needs some time."

"Is that what you need? I mean, with Dad?" I didn't want to talk about Paul. It hurt too much.

"No." She sighed and sunk back into the pillows. "You and Paul had a misunderstanding. In our case there was, well . . . intercourse." She blushed.

I tried, unsuccessfully, to hide my discomfort.

"I spoke to Dad today," I said, hoping she'd be willing to talk about it.

"He called again?"

"I called him." I tried to gauge her response, but her face was expressionless. "It was a very weird conversation. He was distant, like a complete stranger. I was so angry, I didn't—"

"Don't be angry with him, Claire." She rested a hand on my forearm and gave me a pleading look.

"How can you expect me to be anything else?" I blew my nose with the crumpled tissue she pulled from her coat pocket.

"This entire mess is between the two of us. I wasn't going to tell you girls anything about it, but at dinner the other night it all just spilled out."

"You need to talk about it, Mom."

"I don't want you to turn against him, honey. He's your father."

"And he's totally betrayed you." What was she talking about? Forgiveness? *Hell, no.*

But wasn't forgiveness exactly what I wanted from Paul?

"Claire, you love him. So do I."

"Still?"

"Of course. I've always loved him." She smiled sadly. "To much, really."

"But the affair . . ."

"I'm not saying we'll stay together, dear, just that I love him."

"You're going to file for divorce?"

"I don't see how we could possibly get past this. I love him so much it almost kills me, but the trust is gone."

"Will you stay in Omaha?"

"I don't know. This is so fresh I haven't given much thought to the details of what comes next."

"But what about—"

"I don't really want to talk about this right now, dear."

"Sorry."

"Stop apologizing." She reached over and gave me another hug. "You haven't done anything wrong."

If only it were true.

I thanked her for listening to my weep session and let go of her to stand and stretch my aching body. Spilling my guts had left me feeling both cleansed and hungry. "Do you want something to eat?"

"I'll make us some sandwiches," she said, heading for the kitchen before I could stop her. "You know, I might be able to help you with a new job. While I was at Stephanie's, I called Marjorie, the one from nursing school, and her daughter works here in Portland. I understand her company might be looking for someone."

"It's okay, Mom." The last thing my career needed was middle-aged meddling.

"I'm just trying to help."

"Thanks, Mom. But I really think this is something I should handle on my own."

While she spread mustard and mayonnaise on the eight-grain bread I suspected would taste like kibble, she told me what a good cook my sister was.

"So, up until today, did you have a nice visit with them?" I asked.

She hesitated before answering. "I suppose so, yes."

"How did you like Alison?"

"She's . . . *different*." Mom smiled tightly.

"Different meaning a lesbian, or—"

"Just different. She was polite and made me feel at home." It was more than I'd expected her to admit.

"And?" I couldn't help pushing.

"She makes wonderful cheesecake," she confessed, and I knew what that compliment must have cost her.

After all she'd done to help me that afternoon, I decided to cut her some slack.

"You know, Steph called me at work today, worried about where you'd gone."

"I left a note on my pillow." She waved her hand dismissively.

A note. Passive-aggressive, but effective. "I guess she hadn't found that yet. Anyway, I wanted to tell you that the noises you heard weren't of a, uh, *sexual* nature. Steph and Alison were just moving the furniture around."

"I see." Her lips tightened into a straight line.

"I was hoping that would make you feel better about everything."

"Well, the fact that they weren't doing . . . *that* last night doesn't mean that they don't do it at all."

"Yeah, I guess that's true."

"And the fact that I like Alison's cheesecake doesn't mean

that I like *her.*" She slapped the top piece of bread onto the meat and sawed with surprising vigor.

"I never said it did." I tried not to smile.

"And don't get any funny ideas just because I'm knitting her an afghan."

I bit back a laugh. "I won't."

"I think this whole gay thing between the two of them is just plain wrong."

"Okay, Mom."

"I'm only knitting the blanket because Stephanie keeps the heat turned down so low."

"I know she does."

"It's ridiculous."

"I know."

"Alison gets cold when they're watching TV."

"I see."

"I'll have to get that cheesecake recipe."

Maybe there was hope, after all.

FOURTEEN

After a pleasant lunch, sprinkled with light conversation that couldn't quite mask the deeper issues we didn't want to discuss, our stark realities caught up with us. Despite the comfort of knowing we had, in my case, family, and in Mom's, both relatives and friends, at our disposal, I think we both felt quite alone in the world. I knew nothing we said to each other could change our situations, and talking about it seemed pointless.

We spent the late afternoon in matching states of melancholy, which couldn't be lifted by TV, books, or any of the usual distractions. While she distractedly worked on Alison's afghan, I sat in the kitchen, staring at my tablecloth fringe and trying to conjure up the words that would give me another chance with Paul. It was like trying to channel-surf with no remote, and all my efforts managed to produce was a gnawing hunger that finally prompted me into action.

I was sure that making dinner would occupy my mind, so I dragged myself off my chair to chop vegetables and season the chicken breasts Mom had bought. I tried to find glee in rosemary, or even a subdued happiness in thyme, but my numbness conquered not only the wonders of the spice rack and my lazy Susan, but my ability to find a bright side as well.

Soon, the apartment was filled with the smell of roasting chicken and the windows were steamed by my boiling saucepans. Unfortunately, the feelings of contentment I'd hoped the imminence of a hot meal would provide eluded me.

When we finally sat down to eat, the only sounds between us, aside from the occasional blare of traffic from the street below, and the *Entertainment Tonight* theme song bleeding through the wall from next door, were the off-tune clink and clank of silverware and our respective gulping noises, the result of squeezing poultry past the lumps in our throats.

Watching Mom across the table, heavily salting her chicken, I acknowledged that my assumption that Paul had cheated was just as damaging as Dad actually doing it. We lifted our forks at an equal pace, eyes downcast, as we focused on honeyed carrots and quartered red potatoes instead of the men not quite in our lives.

Although we had both been defeated by the pitfalls of love, I had to believe that we still had a chance to make things work. After all, the game wasn't over yet, and the fact that my punctured and deflated ball lay in Paul's court didn't mean that Mom couldn't lob hers over the net.

As the thoughts trickled through my mind, I cursed Neal's penchant for sports analogies.

"Do you think you could ever forgive him?" I finally asked, resting my fork on my empty plate. As concerned as I was about what would happen between her and Dad, I was also asking whether Paul would forgive me.

"I don't want to talk about this right now," she said, resting her knife and fork across the center of her plate.

"I think you should."

"Claire." Her voice was firm, and mildly threatening.

"You're going to have to talk about it sometime."

"Not now." She rose from the table and carried her plate to the sink.

Apparently, the conversation was over.

I cleared the rest of the dishes and Mom filled the sink with hot water. I watched her hands, so like my own, pour dish soap, and wondered how someone so strong could end up a victim.

She washed while I dried and several minutes passed before she spoke again.

"I never thought he was mine to keep," she said quietly, rinsing our glasses.

"What do you mean?"

"It was only a matter of time before he left me."

She handed me a plate and I gingerly took it from her. "How can you say that?"

"It's something I always knew in my heart. I knew he was too good to be true the moment he asked me to dance."

"Mom, he *married* you."

Her smile was slight. "You know, I didn't think he would show up at the church. I was actually surprised when I saw him standing next to the minister." She paused. "Surprised, and happy." She handed me another plate.

"I'm sure he was happy too. I've seen your wedding pictures, Mom."

There was one photo in particular that stuck in my mind. It was taken in the churchyard, right after the ceremony: a snapshot that caught the moment before the formal picture. Aunt Paula, who hated her bridesmaid dress, was rolling her eyes, my grandfather was trying to corral a screeching flower girl and the already grass-stained ring bearer into the frame, and the rest of the wedding party were growing impatient for the open bar at the reception. There was a sense of either frustration or exhaustion in every face but the bride's and groom's. In the midst of chaos, Mom was gazing dreamily into Dad's eyes and he wore a smile of wonder, as though he couldn't believe she was really his.

"You both looked love-struck," I assured her.

She pulled the plug from the drain and spoke over the sucking sound of escaping water. "Always remember, Claire, that love has to be felt equally on both sides or it can never work."

"That's ridiculous." I shook my head and put the last plate away. "You can't measure love."

"Sure you can." She shrugged and wrung out the dish cloth. "I loved him more."

"For God's sake, Mom. He loved you. Loves you still, I'm sure of it."

"But he chose someone else." She choked on the words and I froze in front of the open cupboard. Her face crumpled and, for the first time in my life, I reached over to hold and comfort her.

The embrace lasted several minutes, and I felt her body shake, felt her warm tears against my neck, amazed that in a few short days we had reached a point in our relationship where the moment was possible.

I waited for the gentle heaving that signaled she was finished crying and I continued to hold her, considering her uncertain future and trying to imagine what the next step should be.

Although he'd nearly destroyed her, Robert McLeod was my father. That enchanted groom in the dark suit had loved her so dearly he'd committed himself to a lifetime of Old Spice and just last year traded his Ford pickup for a Toyota Corolla because Mom preferred a trunk to a truck bed. He'd knelt to bandage her feet when her high heels raised blisters, and he'd combed her hair when she sprained her wrist. He called her "my girl" and waited to eat dinner with her when she returned from a graveyard shift. He made her countless pots of Earl Gray, touched her, listened to her, laughed with her.

Loved her.

"Don't you think," I eventually murmured into the thickness of her hair, "you should hear his side?"

She pulled away from me, her face a mask of dejection, and said, "What makes you think I haven't?"

Before I could respond, she retreated to the washroom and started filling the tub.

I waited for her to come out and tell me more, fill me in on all of the details and finally get everything off her chest, but she never opened the door. I sat on the edge of the couch for ages, but her bath lasted so long I went to bed without brushing my teeth.

FIFTEEN

Overnight, thanks to utter exhaustion and a fitful sleep, my mood changed drastically. My aching sadness over the events of the past week transformed into a sudden and remarkable wave of anger.

I awoke incensed at the relentless bleating of my alarm clock, the irregular water pressure in my shower, and the expiration date on my milk carton, which indicated I only had three days left to finish it off.

I declined Mom's offer to make breakfast, advising her to rest instead, and left home without eating a thing. My stomach soon joined the ranks of the enraged with a growl that could have been heard for miles.

During my commute, I knew that instead of sitting back and watching my life fall apart, it was time for me to hold on to everything I had left and fight for whatever else I wanted.

The first thing I wanted was Paul Clemens.

I arrived at Alta Media with no patience for an elevator wait that would only delay the phone call I hoped would change everything, and opted to take the stairs instead. It was a plan I regretted by the fourth floor and abandoned on the fifth in favor of the elevator.

When I finally reached the reception area, I was rewarded with the sight of a glowering Carol.

"Claire" she began, but I cut her off.

"No time. Sorry." I breezed into the main office, crossing the room in several long and hurried strides. I didn't care about the trail of snickers I left behind, or the curious looks from all corners. I was on a mission.

I nodded in response to Jason's greeting, dropped into my chair, and put on my headset before dialing Paul's number. My fingers shook as I pressed the keys and I willed myself to breathe steadily, think clearly, and say all the right things.

The phone rang and I bit the inside of my cheek, drawing blood.

It rang again and my right knee started to bounce up and down at a tremendous rate.

The phone picked up after the fourth ring. My throat constricted at the sound of his voice, until I realized it was an answering machine message. I listened to the message and briefly considered leaving one of my own before deciding that spilling my guts to a machine would not be a stroke of genius.

"Dammit," I snarled, disconnecting the line.

"What's wrong?" Jason appeared next to my cube with a bottle of water and a cinnamon bun.

"Nothing. I'm just going to get some coffee."

"Good reason to be pissed off." He smiled, and I wanted to knock his teeth out.

"That's not why I'm upset."

"See? I was right." His smile widened to a grin. "Something *is* wrong."

"I know." I glared at him.

"Want to talk about it?"

"No."

"I'll be relentless in my pursuit of the facts."

From past experience, I knew it was true.

"It's Paul." I sighed, my newfound anger draining at the sound of his name.

"Ex-Paul?"

I nodded. "I saw him."

"And?" He waited, but I didn't say anything. "Well, did you bite his head off and tell him what a shit he was?"

"No."

"Why not?"

"Because it turns out that the shit was me."

His eyes lit up at the prospect of hot gossip. "What's that supposed to mean?"

"I made a mistake. A *big* one."

"Do I get to hear the details?"

"No."

"Not even a little?"

"No."

"Hmm." He frowned with disappointment. "It's going to be hard to give you advice without the whole story."

"Then it's a good thing I'm not looking for your advice."

"So, did you apologize for this mysterious shitty behavior?"

I had to think about that one. I had denied, distracted, and distanced myself from the fateful Adam utterance, but had I apologized? "I'm not sure."

"So, it's your fault you broke up, you didn't apologize, and now you're going to let him get away?"

"I hope not, but whether we're together or not is up to

him." And it was. Despite my brief flurry of determined energy, the truth was that I could do my best to come up with the magic words, but the decision was Paul's to make.

"That's a real top-notch plan, Claire."

"Like I said, *I* was the shit. It's up to him to take me back. I can't *make* him do it." As much as I would have liked to tie him to a chair, using some elaborate and impossible knot, and force-feed him a steady diet of reasons we should be together, I could barely manage to double-knot my own shoelaces, and hadn't yet composed the speech necessary to win him over.

"So, if he doesn't take you back, where are you going to find another Paul?"

"Thanks, Jason. That really helps."

"Don't blame me. You're the one who didn't even try to keep the thing going."

"I *begged* him to come back."

"No, you didn't."

"How do you know?"

"I know how you women operate." He shook his head. "You think you did everything you could, but I bet you're wrong."

"You want me to beg some more?" Not that I wouldn't consider it.

"Do what you have to do. But take some advice from a master of testosterone: there aren't many guys like Paul around. You'd better scoop him up before someone else does."

"I know." My voice was almost as forlorn as I felt. "I just need a chance to talk to him."

I threw myself into my work, caught between the possibility that I could win Paul back with a few choice words and the likelihood that he wouldn't give me a chance to say them.

As I ran through surveys, I noted that it was the last day of the toothpaste campaign, and as of Monday I would leave the dental dialogue behind. According to the "Word of Godd" memo topping off my In box, our next contract was about television programming, which would be a nice change of pace.

As my call numbers grew, I noticed that Heather was spending a ludicrous amount of time standing and stretching at her desk. While it was quite necessary to limber up on the job every now and then, Alta Media frowned on excessive stretching, and Heather's efforts were certainly over the top. Every few minutes she'd pop up, roll her shoulders, bend at the waist from side to side, flex her arms, and punctuate the routine with a toss of her fuzzy mass of hair.

After the eighth or ninth stretching session, I told her she was too distracting.

"Then don't look," she snapped, disappearing behind the wall, only to make another appearance ten minutes later.

I focused on the task at hand, the hours passing with moderate speed, and before I knew it, noon had arrived.

I desperately needed the break, but just as I was grabbing my bag for yet another solo lunch, Adam Carello appeared at my desk. For the first time I'd ever witnessed, he looked like he actually had something to say.

Painfully aware of the fact that I was entirely to blame for the breakup with Paul, and despite all reason that would make me feel otherwise, I suddenly loathed Adam Carello and the wrinkled clothes he wandered around in.

Whether it was intentional or not, my misery was *his* fault.

He offered a fleeting smile and I couldn't help but compare his stupid chipped tooth to Paul's pristine wall of enamel. Adam's charming cowlicks were suddenly juvenile and sloppy as I wondered, for the umpteenth time, just what in the hell I'd been thinking.

I said his name?

"So," he said, shoving his hands into his back pockets and rocking back on his heels.

I forced an expectant smile and waited for more, but it was slow coming.

"So," he repeated.

"Knit," I answered. "Macramé."

"Huh?"

"Needlepoint."

"Oh." He nodded. "You mean like, *sew*. Good one."

"Is there something I can do for you?"

"Actually, I just have a quick question."

I begged to differ, but waited as patiently as I could for him to get to the point.

Was he finally going to ask me out, now that it wouldn't mean anything? Was his striped tie a special effort for my benefit? Was he going to suggest a movie, a concert, or another awkward Greek lunch?

"What is it?" I finally snapped, eager to break his wretched heart.

"Is Heather . . ."

Annoying? Irritating? Contagious?

"Yes?" I asked.

"Is Heather, uh, single?"

"What?" Where on earth had that come from?

"Heather." He bobbed his head toward the cube wall that separated our desks. "Is she seeing anyone?"

Who cared? "Not that I know of."

"Excellent." He grinned. "Thanks, Lara."

I'd thought they only existed in movies, but I actually did a double-take.

"Claire," I corrected.

"Huh?" His jaw slackened.

"My name is *Claire*."

"It is?" He frowned.

I nodded, watching his brow furrow before he turned and walked away without another word.

Could it get any worse? He didn't even know my fucking *name*?

I wanted to scream until my tonsils were bloody and raw, but went for Thai at the mall instead. It wasn't quite as satisfying as an emotional catharsis, but it came with a free Coke.

I sat at a table full of abandoned trays and balled-up food wrappers, watching the people around me talk, walk, and shop as if they hadn't a care in the world. I took the opportunity to make an important mental list.

I began with the "pros."

I still had a job, and would hold on to my promotion with a steel-fingered grip. I still had one friend in the office, and I could overlook the disappointing fact that it was only Jason. I was building a new relationship with my mother that exceeded any expectations I'd ever had for us. Steph and I were back on speaking terms, and Mom was on the verge of accepting, or at least tolerating, Alison. I had a hair appointment in a couple of weeks, and Paul hadn't cheated on me.

The "con" list came to me quickly.

Fighting for my job didn't mean I would keep it. Most of my coworkers either disliked or hated me, and I was the star of a most horrifying office rumor. My parents' marriage was falling apart. My mother had nowhere to go but my couch. My father, my hero, had betrayed us, and I doubted my ability to forgive him. My Pad Thai was too spicy and the man I loved thought I was a dirtbag.

The sense of calm I'd hoped the list would provide was not forthcoming, and heartburn was setting in.

By the time I returned to my desk, I felt horribly depressed, but the aura of tragedy I sported didn't stop Neal.

"Have you got a minute, Claire?" he asked.

I nodded, acknowledging that I had a lifetime of minutes to look forward to, basking in loneliness and wishing I were dead. The worst of it was, other than my mother, there was no one around to sympathize with my plight or console me with kind words and support.

As I followed Neal across a room filled with people who didn't care how rotten I felt, I noted that the worst thing about a pity party was the poor attendance. Most of the guests never showed up.

Neal left his office door open, to curb speculation—a preventative measure that came way too late.

I slumped in his guest chair and waited for him to speak, certain that my demotion was the order of the day.

"Watch," Neal said, and I swiveled in my chair to obey the order, resenting his monosyllabic approach.

All I saw through the open doorway were the same old people in the same old cubes.

"What am I looking at?"

"Do you have my *watch*?" Neal whispered, lifting his wrist as a visual aid.

"No."

It was hard to miss the exasperation in his sigh. "I left it at your place."

"Sorry." I made a point of staring at the digital clock next to his wilted fern. He knew what time it was. "I forgot to bring it in."

"It's a very expensive watch."

"Geez, I'm not pawning it, Neal."

"I would really like it back."

"I would *really like* to return it," I snapped. "And I will do so. Tomorrow." My "con" tally flashed in my mind and I knew it was time to take the bull by the horns and fight for what was mine. "In the meantime, I'd like to know what's happening with my job."

The pause was long, and his chin-rubbing methodical as he worked out a response. "I think it's too much for you."

"Actually, it's all I have."

He raised an eyebrow and I took it as encouragement to continue. "I'm having some personal problems right now, and—"

"If this is about the other night . . ."

"It isn't," I assured him.

"I need you to know that Danielle and I are working things out."

"That's great, Neal," I managed, through gritted teeth.

"That kiss was a mistake."

Nothing like stating the obvious.

"I know." I nodded.

"I hope I didn't lead you on."

"Uh, in case you've forgotten, *I'm* the one who slammed on the brakes."

"I guess you might see things that way."

"That's exactly what happened, Neal."

"Hey, I'm not here to argue with you."

"Then stop re-creating the facts."

"Fine." He shrugged. "Have it your way."

I waited for him to continue, but he stared at the stationery on his desk instead.

"Why don't you think I can handle the job?"

His gaze settled on me. "You've been overwhelmed and agitated since you took it on."

"I can handle it."

"Look, I know people are giving you a rough time, and if you're uncomfortable . . ."

"What happened to the big pep rally you staged at Morrison's to talk me into the job?"

He smiled sheepishly. "I blow a lot of smoke."

"No shit." I let out a sharp laugh, surprised to be speaking to my boss that way, then leaned toward his desk. "Now, why don't you tell me what's really going on?"

He pondered the question for a full minute, weighing the sides of some internal debate I had no time to deal with.

"Can't you be straight with me?"

It sounded like something Mom would ask of Steph.

He sighed, shook his head slowly, then looked into my face. Whatever he saw there dragged the words out of him. "The CEO is moving back to town."

"Gord?" I never thought the mention of the old windbag would feel like a breath of fresh air, but suddenly spring was upon us. "I thought he put you in charge so he could stay in Sacramento."

"So did I." Neal grimaced.

"But why does Gord have anything to do with my promotion?" It didn't make any sense.

"I just think that it might be better if the leadership is clear when he comes back."

"Meaning?"

"This is a one-horse town."

"With enough manure for a whole damn state," I countered. "What are you trying to say?"

"If it looks like I need help to run the office, Gordon will question my abilities."

"You *do* need help."

"That's beside the point."

It finally dawned on me. "Wait a second. You're actually willing to demote me just to save face?"

"Well . . ."

"Forget it, Neal. I earned that promotion, and if you try to take it away from me, I swear I'll take legal action." With Court TV as my guide, I didn't stand a chance.

"Don't be ridiculous. This is a matter of fifty-five cents."

"Fifty-three, actually. And I'll fight for every penny."

"Claire, be reasonable."

"Neal, be a man."

I returned to my desk with a straighter spine than I'd had in days and gave myself a pat on the back for a job well done.

The pink slip on my desk indicated Mom had called, yet again, so I phoned her right away, hoping for some new and fabulous development.

Unfortunately, there was no news on her marriage front, and no message from Paul, but she did suggest we invite the lesbians for dinner, mentioning something about wanting Alison to try her French onion soup.

Ah, progress.

SIXTEEN

Between phone surveys, I tried to reach Paul all afternoon, with no luck, but when I left work I found myself climbing on a bus that would take me to his place. If I wanted him back, I couldn't just sit around and do nothing. Mom had dinner under control, and our guests weren't due until seven-thirty. I had ample time to grovel.

As the brakes groaned at one stop then the next, doors opening with a loud swoosh, I daydreamed about how our conversation would play out. Paul would let me explain my asinine blunder. We'd laugh about what fools we'd been. We'd go to the coast for the weekend. We'd spend the rest of our lives together. It was as simple as that.

It was almost six o'clock when I rode the elevator to the fourth floor of his building, nervousness spreading in my stomach like a virus. I strolled down the carpeted hallway to number 428 and rapped my knuckles against the wood.

"Coming!" he called from inside.

He was home! Despite my determination, I hadn't really expected the chance to use my carefully scripted dialogue so soon.

I pasted what I hoped was a confident smile on my face, and by the time he opened the door, my eyes were watering from the effort.

His hair was slightly rumpled, as though he'd been running his fingers through it. His new beard was gone and, as much as I'd liked it, the sight of his smooth, shaved skin was a pleasant surprise. He was dressed in baggy brown corduroys, with thick grooves, and the dark green wool sweater I'd given him for Christmas. The sweater had to be a good sign. Hell, the fact that he was home at all was a good sign.

"What are you doing here?" he asked, his tone about as welcoming as the tattered newspaper he used as a doormat.

"I stopped by to talk," I said hopefully.

"I'm about to eat."

It didn't sound like an invitation, so I fished for one by sniffing the air appreciatively. "Smells good. What are you having?"

"A TV dinner and a Bud."

He wasn't giving me much to work with.

"I hope you didn't get one of those chicken ones. I can never tell what those pieces are supposed to be." I forced a laugh.

"Claire." He sighed, folding his arms across his chest and leaning against the door frame, barring my entry.

"I mean," I babbled, "I've never seen a chicken with square limbs." My God, I was desperate.

"I don't really have time for this." He stepped back into the room and started to close the door.

"Paul," I pleaded. "I only need a minute."

I hoped he wouldn't dig an egg timer out of his utensil drawer and hold me to that claim.

"We have nothing to talk about. I already told you that."

"You didn't give me a chance to explain about Adam."

I didn't want to have the conversation in the hallway, but the choice didn't appear to be mine. He was back to blocking the doorway like a bouncer.

"Did it cross your mind that I don't want to know about him?" He tried to close the door again, but I stopped the motion with my foot.

"If I could just—"

"I don't want to know." He sounded firm, bordering on angry.

"Listen!" I scrambled to cut through my uncontrolled chattering. "Adam Carello is a moron I work with, who couldn't form an opinion if he had a mold."

He shook his head in apparent disbelief. "And yet, you fantasized about him while *we* were having sex?"

"Yes. I mean, no, I . . ."

"Tell me, Claire," his smile was as cold as his eyes, "is flattery as foreign to you as monotony?"

I started to answer, but didn't understand the question. What did my tone have to do with anything?

"Monotony?" I asked, genuinely baffled.

"Monogamy," he barked.

"But you said *monotony*."

"You know what I meant." He rubbed his forehead.

"Monogamy happens to be my strong point." I lifted my chin in proud defiance.

"Well, I hate to think what your weak points are."

I'd had it. All I wanted to do was give him a simple explanation.

"Listen, you can give me all the crap you want, but it's not going to get us anywhere. God, I came here for a dialogue and all I'm getting is criticism."

"Now you're mad at me?"

"Of course I am." The temptation to stamp my foot was overwhelming, but I doubted it would aid my case.

"Hold the phone, here, McLeod. I'm the one who has the right to be pissed off."

"No, you don't. Well, you do, but not as much as you think. It was a *misunderstanding*. A stupid, goddamn blunder. I was thinking about Adam because I knew you were planning to leave me."

"I wasn't planning anything."

"I know. Geez, I know that *now*, but at the time I thought you were, so to comfort myself, I started—"

"Seeing someone else?" he sneered.

"No! Nothing happened between us. I just used him, well, the *idea* of him, really, to distract me from thoughts about you. He was kind of a backup."

"Is this supposed to make sense?"

"I started thinking about him because I didn't think I could have you."

"You had me." He glared at me and I felt it to my core. It was too much.

"You aren't listening to me!"

The past few days had been riddled with so many idiotic conversations, I didn't think I could survive another one.

At this point, I did stamp my foot, an effort that came off as even more juvenile than I'd anticipated, and caused me to lose my balance.

He stifled a laugh, but caught my arm before I could fall. Hope did a little jig in my chest, but he set me free as soon as I was steady again.

"What are you doing?" he asked.

"I'm trying to talk to you! Why won't anyone listen to me when I'm trying to explain the simplest bloody things? All I need is a couple of minutes and you're too goddamn stubborn to give me the time!"

"Are you quite finished?"

"No, I'm not *quite finished*." I took a ragged breath in preparation for a verbal flood. It was my big chance and I had to make it count. "Paul Michael Clemens," I savored each name as it rolled off my tongue, "I want you to know that my mistake was big, but innocent. I want you to know that I was so afraid of losing you, I couldn't see straight. I want you to know that I *never* meant to hurt you, and I've done more damage to myself over this than you can even imagine."

At that point he raised one eyebrow in mockery, but I kept going.

"I want you to know that I love you and I'm not going to give up until you give me a chance to prove it to you. I'm not about to let you slip away."

Take that!

His face was suddenly void of emotion. "Claire Alyse McLeod," he said, softly, causing me another outbreak of hope. "I want *you* to know that I've got a TV dinner in the oven, and I'm going to eat it."

With a soft thud and a click of the dead bolt, he closed the door in my face.

I walked to the elevator and quietly exited the building without looking back. The conversation had been humiliating, but worthwhile. At least I'd expressed, albeit spastically, most of what I needed to get off my chest.

The bus that would take me home was approaching, but I didn't bother trying to flag it down. I had no desire for either fluorescent lighting or a crowd of commuters.

I walked slowly but deliberately in the direction of the apartment, trying to look forward to a pleasant night with Mom and the lesbians.

It was no easy task.

When I was halfway there, the rain started, first as an occasional drop but quickly accelerating into a veritable downpour. My fellow pedestrians whipped out umbrellas or darted to the safety of brightly colored awnings, but I kept a slow and steady pace. The way my life was going, the last thing I had to worry about was getting wet.

After about twenty minutes, "soaked" turned out to be a little closer to the mark, but I didn't mind. I walked the slick city streets, watching lights reflect in the wet pavement. While car tires splashed through puddles, I felt cleansed by the steady drum of raindrops rolling down my skin.

I took a long and circuitous route home, passing steamed restaurant windows and cafes filled with boisterous crowds, content to wait out the rain. I thought about Paul's rejection and chalked it up to hurt feelings. If he needed time, I could give it to him. It wasn't like I was short on personal issues to resolve. I had more than enough to keep me busy, and in the meantime, I could be patient. Maybe, when the time was right, we could work things out.

Once I'd accepted that there was no need to rush him, I felt a quiet peace come over me, and I was relaxed for the first time that week. He still cared, and that was all that mattered.

I climbed to the second floor of my building, wishing my personal space was empty so I could explore this new sense of calm. *Maybe I should start taking yoga. Or tai chi.*

"What happened to you?" Steph asked, when I opened my door and stepped into the apartment.

"It's raining." Stupid questions deserved stupid answers. I

shrugged out of my coat and carried it into the washroom, hanging it on the showerhead to drip dry.

"We're having lasagna," she said, when I returned.

"What happened to Mom's French onion soup?" I whispered.

"Ali's allergic to onions."

Terrific. World War Three would erupt over a bulb.

"How did that go over?" I was almost afraid to ask.

"Surprisingly well." She raised her eyebrows. "I think Mom likes her more than she likes me."

"They're really getting along?" It was too good to be true.

"Hard to believe, huh?" Steph smiled.

"So, you must be quite the happy camper."

"Well, my sex life's been restored, if that's what you're asking."

"It isn't," I mumbled, feeling thoroughly creeped out. I cleared my throat. "I see the hair's growing in nicely." I reached over and rubbed the fuzz of her scalp.

"You're full of shit."

"I know." I laughed and made my way to the kitchen, where the rich smell of Mom's tomato sauce filled the air.

Alison offered to pour me some wine, and I sat at the kitchen table to watch her work with my mother.

"More oregano?" Mom asked, lifting a spoon to Alison's mouth.

A pink tongue darted out for a taste. "Just a smidge."

"I always add sweetener to my sauce," Mom confided, reaching into her purse for a pink packet. "It takes the edge off."

"I'd never thought of that," Alison said. "Good idea." She stirred the sauce and opened a box of noodles. "Do you cook yours first?"

"The pasta? Of course, don't you?"

"I find the noodles get a bit soggy, so I don't."

"Do they soften in the oven?"

"Yeah. There's enough juice in there to take care of it, and I think it's easier to cut and serve when it's done."

"Uncooked noodles." Mom shook her head in amazement. "That's ingenious."

I left them to their culinary exchange and joined Steph in the living room.

"They're trading cooking tips," I said. "Mom told her about the sweetener." That was a secret she'd refused to tell her own sister.

"It's unbelievable." Steph leaned toward me and whispered, "Any breakthroughs while she's been here?"

"A couple. I'll fill you in later."

"Dad left a message at my place this morning." She frowned. "Bastard."

"Steph." I didn't want to hear it, no matter what he'd done.

"What? He is, Claire. After what he did to Mom, I can say whatever I want about him."

"But he's your father."

"Genetically speaking, yes. Emotionally, no."

"What, you're going to write him off?"

"It's already done." She rose from her chair. "I need another drink."

On some level I wished I could see things the way she did, in strict terms of black and white. Then again, gray areas never hurt anybody. Sure, I was angry at Dad, but disowning him hadn't crossed my mind, and probably never would.

Instead of Steph returning to the living room, Alison joined me.

"The lasagna's in the oven," she announced, drink in hand as she sat on the chair opposite me.

"And Mom's in your back pocket." I smiled.

"No. Well, maybe." She laughed. "Despite our rocky start, she's really not bad at all."

"Hey, I agree, and no one's more surprised than I am. Our rocky start lasted twenty-three years."

"Do you think your parents will work things out?"

"I don't know." I shrugged.

"Steph's furious about it."

"But she hides it well, doesn't she?" I rolled my eyes.

As Alison raised her glass in agreement, there was a knock at the door.

"If this is number forty-nine wanting to borrow another roll of toilet paper, he can forget it," I said, rising from my chair and crossing to the door. "He can steal it from Denny's, just like everyone else."

I undid the bolt and swung open the door to find, not number forty-nine, but a familiar Carhartt jacket and a nose that matched my own.

"Dad!"

I stepped out of the way so he could enter the room.

"Claire." He nodded, expression somber, then glanced at the figure in the recliner.

"Alison," I said, by way of explanation.

"Mr. McLeod." She smiled tentatively.

"Robert?" Mom gasped as she walked into the room, dish towel in hand and my sister at her side.

"Barbara," he said softly.

"What is this, the fucking Name Game?"

"Steph!" I snapped.

"Yeah, I think that's everyone," she said, seating herself on the couch with a scowl. "We can probably move on now."

"Your hair . . ." Dad murmured, studying her shaved head.

"That's the least of your worries." She folded her arms, effectively shutting him out.

"What are you doing here?" Mom asked, lifting her hand to the security of her braid. Her skin had paled by several shades and she appeared to be shaking.

"I came to see you." His hands hung at his sides and his shoulders were sloped in a manner of defeat. He looked more tired than I'd ever seen him, but it was a kind of weariness I couldn't attribute to the rigors of air travel.

I wanted to hate him, but his sorry state made me worry instead. This was a man filled with pain and regret. This was a man who wanted his wife back.

"She doesn't want to be seen," Steph said, refusing to make eye contact with him.

"This is between your mother and myself," Dad told her, slowly unwrapping his plaid scarf and leaving it to dangle limply against his chest.

"We're all in it now," Steph argued.

"Honey?" he asked, looking to Mom, and I flinched at the endearment. He'd have to earn the right to call her that again.

"Robert." She looked shell-shocked and unsteady. "I can't."

I moved to her side, effectively stating my support, and put my arm around her waist. "Dad, this might not be a good time."

"There isn't going to be a good time," he sighed. "Believe me, I know."

Alison attempted to leave her chair, obviously uncomfortable in the midst of our stilted family scene.

"Stay," Steph urged her, and she settled back onto the cushions.

"Girls, I see that you want to support your mother, but she and I really need to talk alone."

"We already know what happened," Steph growled, practically baring her teeth.

"Does anyone want a drink?" I asked, desperate to leave the room so I could breathe. No one granted my wishes with a cocktail order.

"We know you had an affair," Steph continued, never one to mince words.

She was slumped in the chair, her body language expressing nothing but cool indifference, but I knew her too well to believe she was unaffected by his arrival.

"I didn't have an affair." Dad spoke slowly, weighing each word.

Who did he think he was kidding?

"Dad, we know all about you and Ms. Salomar," I reminded him.

"Joan Salomar." Dad took off his glasses and rubbed his eyes.

I held my breath as her name echoed in the room.

"Mom told us *everything*." Steph hurled the words at him, her facade already crumbling.

"Barbara."

"I had to." Mom's lower lip quivered.

"Why did you drag them into this?" he asked.

"She needed to talk about it." I was amazed by his lack of understanding. "We're her *family*. We're *your* family, Dad."

"Yeah, right." Steph sneered. "A regular Brady Bunch."

"Robert . . ." Mom's voice was shaky and I tightened my hold on her.

"Why did you have to go screwing around with Ms. Salomar?" Steph asked, barely containing the rage that was just below the surface.

"I didn't," he said, forcing her to look at him.

I was confused. He and I had already discussed Joan Salomar.

"Dad, it's too late," I said. "We all know about your affair."

"Barbara," he said, "can we please speak in private?"

"She's been devastated by this," I told him. "If she wants us here, I think we should be here." It was my chance to stand up for her, and I wasn't about to let her down.

"Maybe I should just . . ." Alison began.

"Stay here," Steph ordered.

"But the lasagna . . ."

"Please stay."

"The affair . . ." Mom began, but couldn't finish the thought.

"Go on, Barbara."

"Don't push her, Dad." Steph's voice was fierce.

"I thought . . ." Mom's eyes were welling up with tears.

"I know," he said.

"Can somebody please tell me what the hell is going on here?" I asked the room.

Dad's voice was soft as he began to speak, staring straight into Mom's eyes. "You thought I had an affair with Joan Salomar."

"Dad!" He was denying it?

"What is this, some kind of brainwashing technique?" Steph added.

"Please, just let me finish." He took a breath before continuing, his gaze still fixed on Mom. "Just like you thought I'd done with Patti Morrison, Fran Helms, and Donna Peterson." He took off his hat and held it with both hands. "Not to mention two of the cashiers at Food-4-Less, a waitress at the Jade Palace, and the senior loan officer at the bank."

"What?" I almost laughed, but the sound caught in my throat.

"Ask her," he said, eyes never leaving my mother's.

He was serious?

"Mom?" I waited for her to explain, and my arm dropped away from her body as she remained silent.

What in the hell was going on?

"Does anybody here speak in complete sentences?" Steph snapped, clearly shaken by the new, yet terribly vague, developments.

"I didn't have an affair," Dad repeated.

"You didn't?" Steph asked, apparently as confused as I was. "He didn't?" She turned to Mom, who closed her eyes briefly before looking at Dad and shaking her head.

What?

"Mom, how could you . . . why would you *tell* us that?" I couldn't believe what I was hearing. If Dad didn't have an affair, why had she left him?

"I . . . I . . ." Mom stammered.

"Did you lie about it?" Steph rose from her chair and took a step toward her.

I'd never seen Mom look so uncertain. "It wasn't a lie, so much as a . . ."

"*You lied about it.*" Steph stopped midway across the room. "You told us this whole horror story, got us all upset and worried, and it wasn't even true?"

"He didn't have an affair," I said, my mind numbing at the news.

Mom turned to face me, a look of panic flashing in her

eyes. "But I *thought* he had. It's the same thing!" She gripped the dish towel so tightly her knuckles whitened.

"No, it isn't," Dad said quietly.

"I told you how much I love your father," Mom said, tears welling in her eyes as she glanced from Steph to me, searching for support.

"And you told us he'd cheated on you," I reminded her.

"I love him to a point that probably isn't healthy." The tears streamed down her cheeks. "I thought he betrayed me and I didn't know what to do."

"Barbara," Dad said, taking a step toward her. "The girls don't need to hear any more of this."

"Yes, they do."

"There's more?" I asked, dreading the prospect.

"I was upset and confused . . ." Mom began.

"And *hurt*." Steph's tone was sarcastic. "Don't forget hurt."

I was amazed by how quickly she could transfer her allegiance.

"Don't speak that way to your mother," Dad told her.

"Who's side are you on, anyway?" she asked.

"There aren't any sides."

"Mom, what's going on?" I rested my hand on her wrist.

"I didn't know what to do, or how to react." Mom wrung the dish towel with both hands. "My whole life was falling apart. I felt like the joke of the neighborhood, the last one to know." Her breathing grew ragged. "I thought people were looking at me strangely, everywhere I went. Even the bridge girls seemed to be pitying me." She frowned at the memory. "I'd given him everything I had, and he'd turned to someone else."

"Don't do this, Barbara," Dad pleaded.

"Do what? Where is this going?" Steph's arms crossed her chest, her hands gripping her elbows.

"I was embarrassed," Mom continued in a shaking voice. "So angry I didn't know what to do."

"Barbara, please." Dad reached for her, but she pulled away.

"So," her voice was shrill, "I slept with Don Estes." She choked on the name. "There!" she shrieked in awkward triumph. "I've said it."

I almost fell over.

"You *what?*" Steph screeched.

"All I could think about was revenge." One fat tear fell from Mom's chin.

"You had sex with Steph's father-in-law?" I gasped, barely able to breathe.

"You're still married?" Alison asked.

"*Ex*-father-in-law," Steph corrected, eyes wide with shock.

"Whew," Alison breathed.

"It was a mistake," Mom sniffled.

"No shit," Steph snapped. "Does Marco know?"

"Polo," I mumbled, unable to contain it.

"I don't think so." Mom's eyes were cast downward.

I glanced at Dad, whose grim expression told me Marco knew, and so did the rest of the neighborhood.

"Don Estes," I repeated. The jovial man who'd toasted his son's marriage so many times he had to be carried out of the Masonic Hall at the end of the night. He had a big, round belly, like a hard-boiled egg, and I couldn't quite fathom the gymnastics required to pair his nether regions with my mother's.

I shivered at the image. *Dear God, why was I trying?*

"Barbara, we need to talk alone." Dad stepped toward her and she pulled away from him again.

"There's nothing to talk about. It's over. The trust is gone."

"I'll be the judge of that." Dad sighed. "Honey, we're talking about twenty-six years."

"I've ruined everything." Mom bit her bottom lip. "It's over."

"We can get past this."

"Don't you see?" Mom wailed. "I never thought I deserved you, and now I've *proven* it. I can't look you in the eye without being torn apart by guilt."

"I forgive you, Barbara."

"You can't forgive me. Dammit, I'll never forgive myself."

A loud knock interrupted them, so I rushed to shoo whoever it was away as quickly as possible.

I opened the door and found Neal standing in the hallway.

"Oh, God," I muttered.

"That's right. May I come in?" he asked.

"Actually, this is an extremely bad—"

"Something smells *fabulous*." He brushed past me and stepped into the living room.

"Neal, I don't think—"

"Mrs. McLeod, nice to see you." He offered Mom a wide smile, oblivious to the stifling tension that filled the room. He didn't notice Mom's tears, or Dad's annoyance, but it took no time at all for him to spot Steph. Even bald and stressed out, she was radiant. "Claire, aren't you going to introduce me?"

"Uh, sure. This is my Dad, Robert." Dad accepted Neal's offer of a handshake and shot me a bewildered look. "My sister, Stephanie." I pointed, but Neal was already devouring her with his gaze. "And this is Alison." Neal couldn't tear his attention away from Steph long enough to acknowledge her girlfriend.

"Neal is my boss," I explained.

"Neal." Dad cleared his throat. "It's nice to meet you, but we're in the middle of—"

"Would you like to join us for dinner?" Mom asked brightly, wiping her eyes. "There's enough lasagna for everyone."

"Ohh." Neal clutched his chest. "I *love* lasagna."

"Mom. I think we need to—"

"Set the table? You're right, dear. Maybe Neal can help you."

Her smile was one of genuine relief. Neal's presence would put an end to the family meeting, at least temporarily.

I led the little twerp into the kitchen, where I whirled around to attack him. "What are you doing here?"

"I came to get my watch, but dinner sounds great."

"There's a lot going on right now. You've walked into an emotional tornado here, and I think it would be best if you—"

"Garlic bread!" He peeled the foil away from the loaf and inhaled deeply. "Heavenly."

I wanted to scream, cry, or both, but Neal started rifling through my cupboards for tableware.

"You didn't tell me you had a sister."

"Then I probably didn't mention she's a lesbian."

"Ouch." He winced, then looked pensive. "Any signs that she might reconsider?"

"Uh, no."

"Hey, it can't hurt to ask, right? Maybe she hasn't met the right guy."

I sighed and handed him the cutlery.

I couldn't physically shove Neal out the door, and Mom probably wouldn't let me try anyway, so I figured I might as well get something out of his visit.

"Since you're here, I want to confirm that I'm keeping the auditing position."

"Geez, Claire, I'm not sure if—"

"Look, you can stay for dinner and ogle my sister if I get to keep my promotion."

He peered into the living room to give Steph another once-over. "Deal."

"But don't hang around afterward, okay?"

"What kind of hostess are you?"

"I'm serious, Neal." I ushered him out to the table before he could argue.

While setting the table, I glanced at Dad and winced at the pained look on his face. I'd have to make sure dinner was quick and get everyone out of the apartment so he and Mom could talk. Surely Steph would let me spend the night at her place.

Don Estes. I couldn't believe it.

Mom found some forgotten candles in a kitchen drawer and ordered everyone to the table while she served the meal.

Just as I passed the salad down to Dad, there was yet another knock on the front door.

SEVENTEEN

I pushed back my chair, afraid to imagine who was on the other side of the door. All I needed was for Jason to show up for a political debate or, God forbid, Heather to make an appearance.

I opened the door and my breath caught in my throat at the sight of Paul.

"What are you doing here?" I asked. It had certainly become the question of the night.

"Hi to you, too."

"Oh, sorry." Why was I such an *idiot?* "Hi."

He shoved his hands into the pockets of his cords and cleared his throat. "I've been thinking about what you said to me earlier."

"You mean tonight?"

"Yes, Claire. Tonight." He rolled his eyes.

"Of course." I blushed.

"Anyway, it took me a while to put all of the pieces together, and—"

"I was rambling." I winced at the memory.

"I know."

"Sorry about that."

"Would it be okay if *I* talked for a minute?" he asked.

"Go right ahead."

"Anyway, when I had a chance to think about all of the things you said, the most important being that you, uh, *love* me . . ."

"Claire?" Mom called from the table. "Who's there?"

"It's Paul." *It's Paul!* "I'll just be a minute."

"Invite him in, darling. We're all waiting to eat."

"Are you in the middle of dinner?" he whispered. "I can come back later if this is a bad time."

"No!" If he walked away he'd have time to rethink what-ever he was going to say, and I had a feeling it was something good. Surely having a chance to think about what I'd said meant he'd reconsidered. Didn't it?

"There's plenty of food," Mom called, obviously eager to fill the table with extra bodies.

"Just a minute," I managed, through clenched teeth.

"It's getting cold, honey."

"Oh, for crying out loud," I groaned. "Come in for dinner, Paul."

He already knew Steph, Alison, and Mom, so I introduced my father and Neal before shuffling my seat over to make room for the man I couldn't believe had made an appearance.

I sat within inches of him, our sleeves brushing against one another as we settled into our chairs, and I couldn't wait for the meal to be over.

I cut a piece of lasagna for him and placed it on his plate. "Better than a TV dinner?"

"I threw most of it away." He smiled and helped himself to some garlic bread.

Paul Clemens was eating dinner with my family! I was

giddy, until it struck me: *Shit!* Paul Clemens was eating dinner with *my family.*

I had no control over any of them. I was completely at their mercy, and knowing that Steph had an ax to grind was enough to make me nauseated. What horrifying scene would she create, and *when?*

"This smells delicious," Paul said, then whispered to me, "and so do you."

I laughed nervously.

It was too good to be true. There had to be TV cameras hidden somewhere, so I could make an ass of myself in front of the whole damn country and spend the next decade trying to live it down. Paul Clemens couldn't possibly want me back, not after the week I'd had.

Despite the fabulous sight and smells of the meal spread out before us, none of the McLeods was eating.

But that didn't stop Neal.

"This is terrific," he said between mouthfuls.

"Thank you." Mom smiled tightly and took a sip of wine, careful not to look at the rest of us.

"There's something about it that's kind of different." He thought for a moment. "Maybe the sauce?"

"I add sweetener to it," Mom said, obviously pleased he'd noticed.

"Sweetener?" He chewed slowly. "Is that what it is? I would have thought that would ruin it."

"Why ruin the lasagna when you can ruin everything else?" Steph muttered.

Here we go.

Mom's face flushed with color and Dad shot Steph a warning look. "I think that's enough."

"Oh, so you're drawing the line now?"

"Stephanie." Alison covered my sister's hand with her own.

"What? I'm just amazed that Dad is taking a stand over something as trivial as meat sauce."

"Am I missing something?" Paul whispered in my ear.

I nodded. "I'll fill you in later."

"I don't think we need to discuss this right now," Mom said, hands clasped in her lap.

"Of course you don't." Steph glared at her.

"I'm going to have to try out that sweetener trick," Neal said, apparently unaware of the tension.

"Just a smidge," Mom advised him, breaking eye contact with Steph. "You don't want to overdo it."

"That's right. Mom never overdoes it." Steph's sarcasm kicked in with a vengeance.

"So, Stephanie, are you as good a cook as your mother?" Neal asked. "Maybe you can give me some lessons sometime."

How could he possibly think the time was right to hit on her?

"I don't really cook," she told him, clearly annoyed by the interruption.

"Actually, I do most of the—" Alison began, but Neal cut her off.

"Maybe we could take a class together, then."

"Maybe you and *Danielle* should take a class," I suggested, thoroughly pissed off. "Whatever happened to her?"

He glared at me. "Things are kind of touch-and-go at the moment."

"Is that right?"

"Actually, they're more *touchy*-and-go." He paused for dramatic effect. "She was upset about the other night, you know, with us, and we had a big fight." He gave Steph a doleful yet lusty look. "She left me."

"I'm sorry to hear that," Mom murmured.

"Yeah, that's a shame," I said, rolling my eyes. "That relationship really seemed like it was built to last."

I felt Paul's body tense. "What happened the other night?"

"Nothing," I assured him. That goddamned kiss was the biggest mistake of my life! That, and calling Paul by the wrong name. Oh, and letting Neal Godd sleep over. Not to mention taking the fucking job at Alta Media in the first place. And waking up every morning, of course. Yes, waking up was the biggest mistake of my life and I just kept on doing it.

"Claire?" Paul nudged me.

"We had a few too many drinks, and—" Neal began.

"That's pretty much it," I blurted. "We went out after work and drank too much."

"Was it a staff party?" Paul asked.

"Kind of," I told him. "Can you pass the salad, Dad?"

Dad lifted the bowl and handed it to Alison, who passed it to me.

"Kind of?" Paul pushed.

"It was *really* nothing." I dug into the food, despite my lack of appetite.

Conversation pretty well dried up, and other than the screech of cutlery against plates and the occasional compliment to the chef, the table was quiet.

I slowly worked my way through my dinner, hoping that everything was going to be okay between Paul and me. Hope was all I had.

Mom struck up a conversation with Neal, who seemed to be the most receptive to chatter, and I watched her eyes dart to Dad and away again every few seconds.

I was surprised to realize that I didn't hate her for what she'd put us through. Steph was a seething ball of rage, but I could actually sympathize, seeing the price Mom was paying in guilt for her infidelity.

Don Estes!

I still couldn't come to grips with her choice of partner, but I had some understanding of her motivation. Thinking Dad was cheating on her had made her crazy with jealousy, and the only counterattack she could think of was to cheat on him.

With Don Estes.

I couldn't escape the connection of father and son sleeping with mother and daughter, and hoped Marco (Polo) and Don hadn't compared notes on bedding the McLeod women.

As I tried to swallow one mouthful after another of lasagna, I envisioned Mom tarting herself up for a secret liaison. Did she make a special effort with her makeup? Buy sexy lingerie? Did they meet at her place, or have sex in his RV, famous for a well-stocked bar and plush furnishings? Did she return home afterward and climb into bed with Dad, or did she drive around for hours, hating herself for what she'd done?

I wondered how Dad had reacted to the news, and how he'd found out that she had strayed. Was there a blowout fight? Probably not. Would he have stepped outside for a cigarette and a chance to cool down, or was he immediately forgiving? Had he confided in any of his friends? Had he thought about leaving her? I couldn't fathom the two of them living separate lives. Steph and I would have to spend Christmas with one parent and New Year's with the other. We'd have to be careful never to mention Mom around Dad, and vice versa. No more family pictures. No more matching knitted sweaters. *No more McLeods.*

I was eternally grateful that Dad was capable of forgiving

her, but at the same time, I worried that even if they did stay together, Mom's affair would undermine the marriage. Things would never be the same, would they?

It was too much to think about, so I switched gears and considered what possibilities existed with Paul.

If only I'd heard the rest of what he wanted to say at the door. I suspected that we were on the brink of getting back together, but I wanted the suspicion confirmed. *Immediately.*

The meal seemed to stretch on for hours, and the only guest who opted for a second serving of lasagna was Neal. I wanted to stretch my legs under the table and kick his shins. Hard. When the time finally came to clear the plates and serve dessert, I almost cheered. Instead, I stood to help, but Paul grabbed my elbow.

"Can we talk privately for a second?" he whispered.

I excused us both and led him to my room.

My nerves were jangling, my mind racing, and I closed the door behind me, praying for privacy.

"I didn't think we'd ever be alone," he said, reaching for my hands.

Holding hands was definitely a good sign.

We stood still for a moment, and I absorbed the warmth of his skin.

"I've missed you," I whispered.

"So have I. I was thinking we should—"

"Claire, where's your ice cream scoop?" Mom called from the kitchen.

"In the utensil drawer," I shouted, biting back a curse.

"I don't see it." I could hear her rattling around.

"Top drawer," I shouted, then smiled tenderly at Paul. "Sorry about this."

"I can't imagine why you don't use that spoon holder I sent you for Christmas," Mom continued.

"She passed it on to me," Steph told her, and I knew I'd never hear the end of it. Mom loathed gift recycling.

"I love that thing," Alison said, in an effort to smooth things over. "It's even got a spot for measuring spoons."

"That's what I liked about it, too," Mom agreed.

Paul drew me close and I inhaled the woodsy scent of him.

"I think the scoop has a red handle," Alison said.

"No, it's black. I saw it just the other day. I can never find anything in these drawers," Mom groaned. "So much clutter."

"You should see her desk," Neal piped in. "She's a piler, not a filer."

I closed my eyes, murmuring, "That is a total lie."

"Just use a regular spoon, Barbara," Dad suggested. "Run it under hot water."

"It's not strong enough. This ice cream is rock hard."

"So am I." Paul's breath tickled my ear.

"Pervert." I lightly slapped his shoulder and laughed. "Are you sure you want to get involved with me, knowing these lunatics are part of the deal?"

"Pretty sure." He nodded. "Although I might need some convincing."

He started to lean toward me just as the door creaked open.

"Sorry to interrupt," Neal said, without a trace of remorse, his unrepentant gaze observing the intimate scene. "Your mom says my watch is in here."

What compelled her to move it from the breakfast table to the bedroom?

He surveyed the pile of freshly folded clothes at the end of my bed, the stack of books I'd probably never read on my bedside table, and the lacy underwire bra hanging on my doorknob.

"It's on the dresser," I growled, pointing the way with my suddenly free hand.

I glanced at Paul, and saw his expression darken, his hands back in his pockets. What had I done now?

"If you don't mind my asking, I know you work together, but who exactly are you, Neal?" Paul's voice had an edge to it.

"My boss," I answered for him.

"Why is your *boss* picking up his personal effects at your apartment?"

"It's just a watch," I shrugged, then saw Neal bristle at my description of his beloved timepiece. "He left it here the other night."

"The other *morning*, actually," Neal corrected, apparently offended enough to sabotage my rekindled romance.

Son of a bitch.

"I see." Paul's gorgeous lips formed a tight line.

"Believe me, you don't." I attempted a laugh, but failed to produce the sound.

"Claire and I—" Neal began.

"Don't say another word," I threatened. Nothing he could say would help, I was sure of it.

Thankfully, he respected my wishes and made a beeline from the bedroom.

"I think I'd better go." Paul's voice was tight.

"Paul, please don't get the wrong idea."

"It's pretty hard not to."

"He stayed on my couch the other night, too drunk to drive home."

"And his watch *somehow* ended up in here," he scoffed.

"My mom's a neat freak. She probably put it there for safekeeping."

"Speaking of your mother, I thought *she* was sleeping on your couch."

"She was at Steph's." I sighed. Did we even stand a chance of making it? "Are you going to be this suspicious about everything?"

"If it's this suspicious, yes."

Couldn't life just go back to the way it used to be?

"Aha!" Mom called. "I found it! Don't worry, Claire."

It was easier said than done.

"I've got to get out of here." Paul turned toward the door.

"Paul, please."

"No, I'm done." He rubbed his forehead and gave me a long, hard look. "I don't know what I was thinking, coming over here."

"Just give me a chance to explain."

"Why is it that every time I see you, you've done something that requires an explanation?"

"I don't think—"

"No, you don't."

And he was gone.

I stood in my bedroom for a miserable five minutes, trying to compose myself so I could get through the rest of the hellacious evening.

"Claire? Are you coming?" Mom called. "Your ice cream is melting."

Tears welled up but didn't fall, and I knew I'd have a weepy and sleepless night when I was finally allowed to go to bed.

I returned to the table and glared at Neal.

"Paul left in a hurry," Mom said.

"Yes, he did."

"Is everything okay?"

I stared at her in disbelief.

"How can you ask that?" Steph seemed as shocked as I was. "*Nothing* is okay. This whole situation is such a fucking mess, I can't believe I'm still sitting here."

"Steph," Alison said, reaching for her hand.

"I mean, Mom drops a bombshell, and we're all supposed to sit here eating ice cream?"

"Everything's going to be just fine," Dad told her.

"Are you kidding?" she scoffed. "Forget it, Dad. We're leaving." She rose and crossed her arms, waiting for Alison to do the same.

"I'm sorry about this," Alison said, as the two left the table.

"It's not your fault," Mom said apologetically.

"No, it's *yours*," Steph snapped, pulling Alison toward the door.

Dad stood to follow them. "You won't talk to your mother that way!"

"I won't talk to her at all." Steph slammed the door.

And then there were four.

"More ice cream for the rest of us, I guess," Neal said, digging in with his spoon.

I glanced at my parents. There was nothing I could do to help them sort things out. What they needed was time alone.

And what did *I* need? The man who'd just walked out of my life. Again.

All I wanted to do was run outside and catch up with Paul, but I knew it wouldn't do any good. I'd ruined everything. Instead, I covered my ice cream with chocolate syrup and tried not to think about him.

As we ate, Mom fingered the end of her braid and said nothing. Dad watched her from across the table, and the determination I saw in his face assured me that he would do everything in his power to save the marriage. His expression, and his acceptance of what she'd done, proved to me, for what must have been the thousandth time in my life, what a good man he was.

It was hard to look at him without being crushed by my own guilt for believing he was capable of cheating on her. Granted, I found some solace in the fact that it had taken a while for Mom to convince me of his betrayal, but I hated the fact that I'd lost faith in him.

I wasn't sure I could forgive myself, either.

Paul was as good a man as my father, and I couldn't believe I'd destroyed my chance at happiness with him. I probably deserved to be miserable and alone.

"Can you pass the chocolate syrup?" Neal asked, and I almost punched him.

I was finally able to usher my illustrious boss out the door, just after eleven o'clock.

"Thank you so much for the dinner," he said, over his shoulder. "I had a wonderful time."

"Yeah, whatever."

"I'll see you tomorrow morning, bright-eyed and bushy-tailed."

"Good night, Neal." I practically slammed the door behind him and leaned against it, exhausted. "The last thing I want to do is get up and go to work tomorrow," I groaned.

"Honey, I've told you my friend Marjorie's daughter is—"

"Don't worry about it, Mom. I can find a new job if I need to."

"I just thought—"

"I think you've got bigger issues to deal with at the moment."

Her eyes filled with tears. "I'm so sorry I lied to you girls. You probably hate me, and you have every right to."

"I don't hate you."

"Claire, I never meant for . . ."

Dad moved to stand beside her and gently placed his arm around her waist. "None of us hate you, Barbara." He gave her a squeeze. "None of us."

She broke down in sobs and he pulled her into an embrace.

I didn't know whether to stay or go. They obviously needed time to talk, but where?

"Do you guys want to, uh, use my room and I'll sleep out here?" As much as I didn't want to think about them having make-up sex on my bed, I didn't know what else to suggest.

"I booked a room right down the street," Dad said, then whispered to Mom, "Let's go, my girl." My heart lifted a little at his trademark endearment. "We have a lot of talking to do."

I said good night to both of them, once Dad had gathered her things together, and hugged them tightly before they walked to the door.

"Is everything all right with Paul?" Dad asked.

"No."

"Are you going to be okay?"

I was amazed that he could be concerned about me when he had so much to deal with himself. As much as I wanted to cry on his shoulder and tell him that it would be a long time before I'd be okay, I couldn't add to his burden.

"I'm fine, Dad. Don't worry about me."

"We'll see you tomorrow," he said. "Sleep well."

It was an impossible request.

EIGHTEEN

After a night spent rolling from one hip to the other, yanking the covers up to my neck, then throwing them off, only to pull them up again when I awoke with goosebumps, and staring at my ceiling for what seemed like hours on end, the last thing I wanted to do was go to work. I watched the digital numbers on my clock inch closer to alarm time, wishing there was some way to stop the day from arriving. If nothing else, at least it was Friday.

When I did crawl out of bed and into the bathroom, I was disturbed to discover, courtesy of a cracked mirror and a focused squint, that I looked positively gray. My normally rosy cheeks had faded to the shade of baked concrete, which only accentuated the bruised-plum effect of the dark circles around my eyes. My hair was a few steps beyond limp, and I knew, beyond a doubt, that the task of putting myself together far surpassed the contents of my cosmetic drawer. I needed revitalizing conditioner for every cell of my body and mind.

I was grateful for the steaming heat of the shower, and spent longer than necessary basking in the steady stream of hot water coursing over my skin. I scrubbed, loofahed, lathered, and rinsed, hoping the effort would galvanize me for the day to come.

It didn't.

Despite the certainty that I would remain alone forever, I even took the time to shave my legs. Life was bad, but it didn't have to be bristly.

I threw on some clothes and, after some burned (of course) toast and a glass of excessively pulpy orange juice, raced out the door, chased down my departing bus, and barely, just barely, made it to work on time.

"Rough night?" Carol mocked, her ever-present Lifesaver clicking against her teeth.

"Not really." I wasn't about to give her any satisfaction.

"Neal scheduled a meeting at eleven." She paused to shift the candy from one side of her mouth to the other with her tongue. "But I'm sure you already know that."

"Whatever." I shrugged, moving into the office.

I dropped my satchel on my desk and raced to the break room for a cup of coffee, only to discover one of my illustrious coworkers had opted to finish the pot without brewing a new one.

"Son of a bitch," I muttered, lifting the used filter from the machine.

"Behind you," a voice warned, just as I turned and smashed into a hard, male body.

My treacherous cargo was crushed against my chest, and warm, wet grounds quickly saturated my blouse.

"Shit," I moaned.

"Oops," Adam Carello said, with false cheer. "Sorry about that."

I looked up into his eyes, ready to rip him apart, but when I saw the concern housed there, I couldn't complete the mis-

sion. The coffee collision was a simple accident, and everything else? As much as I would have loved to pin blame on
anyone but myself, Adam Carello hadn't technically *done* anything to me. Hell, when it really came down to it, nobody had.
I'd spent the whole night fully aware that every speck of misery I'd experienced concerning Paul and work over the past
week was my own damn fault.

"It's okay," I told him, voice wavering. "It's an old blouse,
anyway." I attempted a smile, but when I felt my face begin to
crumple, I made a hasty exit from the break room.

"Ha!" Carol barked, as she breezed toward me in a blur of
pleather. "Nice look."

"Yeah, rub it in," I murmured, chin wobbling dangerously.

"Will do," she called over her shoulder, once she'd passed
me.

I returned to my cube, grabbing a handful of tissues to
wipe the mess from my shirt.

"My God, Claire," Heather gasped. "What happened to
you?"

"I think it's obvious, don't you?" Sleeplessness had apparently depleted my tact reserve.

"Are those coffee grounds?"

"Uh, yes."

"That's never going to come out." She shook her head,
frizzy hair shifting like an errant cloud.

"I'll make do."

"I'm serious, Claire. That blouse is ruined."

"I heard you."

She placed her hands on her hips. "Why are you so
cranky?"

Not, "What's wrong?" or "Can I help?" but "*Why are you so
cranky?*"

"I have a lot of crap going on right now, okay?"

"Did Neal break up with you?"

"No."

"Well, that's good, isn't it?" She smiled, as though that solved everything.

Jason popped up from behind his cube wall to grin wickedly at the stain. "Shit, most people just drink it, Claire."

"Thanks for the tip." I blotted the fabric, soaking up most of the moisture.

"So?" he asked, raising his eyebrows.

I sighed and began to explain. "I was changing the filter, and—"

"No. I mean, so what happened with Paul?"

"Paul?" Heather asked.

"Let's see." I started to count off the dismal events on my fingers. "I told him I loved him, and—"

"What?" Heather squawked. "What about Neal?"

"What about Neal?" Jason asked, clearly confused.

"That's what *I* want to know," Heather said.

"There is no Neal," I told her.

"I beg to differ," the man himself chimed in as he walked past. "Meeting's not until eleven, people. Let's get on the phones, please."

"I don't understand," Heather whined.

"There is no Claire and Neal," Jason explained. "There never was." He turned to me. "There *was*, however, Claire and Paul. Can we expect an R-rated repeat performance?"

"It's doubtful."

"Why did you tell Paul you love him?" Heather asked. "He cheated on you."

"No, he didn't."

"But you said—"

"I was wrong." Horribly wrong.

"So, what happened?" Jason asked.

"I don't know. Things started out okay, but then everything got screwed up."

"You want him back?" Heather asked.

"Yes. I want him back." Could she be any more obtuse?

"So, where do you stand?" Jason asked.

"In the loser section, waving a fucking banner."

"Come on, just talk to him."

"Now why didn't *I* think of that?" I paused. "Oh, yeah. Because he doesn't want anything to do with me."

"Ooh, I've got it!" Heather shrieked.

I steeled myself for a love recipe from the woman who tried to woo an ex-boyfriend by using whipped cream for sexual purposes, and wound up in the hospital. The woman who had ignored the warning "refrigerate after opening" and discovered that her uterus is a very warm place.

"What?" Jason asked, before I gathered the nerve to hear her master plan.

"It's *perfect*! I can't believe I didn't think of it sooner!" She was practically foaming at the mouth.

"What?" Jason and I snapped in unison.

"Send him a cookie bouquet!"

If only her enthusiasm were contagious.

"Are you insane?" I asked.

"I think it's a great idea. They're really cute, and they come in all flavors. You could even get gingerbread."

"Even gingerbread?" Jason mocked.

"Yeah. All different shapes, too. You could have a theme, like small animals, or hand tools . . ."

"Speaking of tools, Heather," Jason said, "you are one."

"Excuse me?" A stunned expression took over when the smile slipped off her face.

"I'm just kidding." He patted her shoulder in a gesture she correctly perceived as patronizing and she pulled away.

"I don't think you are."

"What? Come on. You know I didn't mean it."

"You don't even *like* me, do you?"

"On the phones, folks." Neal snapped his fingers as he passed us again.

My sparring cubemates dropped into their respective seats, while I sunk into my own and logged on to my computer, relieved to be free of them for the moment.

Our new television survey had arrived, full of the expected insipid questions about prime-time viewing and violence.

Just as I was gearing up for my first call, Carol appeared next to me, carrying a platter of individually bagged popcorn.

"Take one," she grunted, straining under the marginal weight of kernels and air. *For God's sake, eat a pork chop!*

"What's it for?"

"The TV promotion. You know, popcorn . . . TV. It's from Neal." She rolled her eyes. "Can't you just take one, like everybody else?"

I grabbed a bag and set it next to my training manual. A couple of weeks earlier it had been jumbo muffins; before that, bottled juice. Not only was I trapped in a cube, but food was actually being delivered to me.

I'd already felt like a peon and a robot, but suddenly, I felt like *veal*. A calf in her own little stall, forced to fatten up on buttery popcorn before being slaughtered and served.

Bleak. The mood was bleak.

I concentrated on the task at hand and made it through six questionnaires, with only one hang-up. I was just hitting my stride when the system dialed again.

"Hello?" A male voice answered.

"Hello, Mr. . . ." I glanced at my screen for the high-lighted name.

Oh, shit. The odds were a million to one.

"Hello?"

"Hi, Paul . . . it's Claire." How on *earth* did it happen? I had never found a familiar voice at the other end of the line. It was impossible!

"Claire." He sighed with agitation.

Oh, God. Did he think I was *stalking* him?

"This is the weirdest thing," I rushed to explain. "I'm at work . . . doing surveys, you know, and can you believe my computer dialed your number?"

"No, I can't."

Under the circumstances, I didn't believe it myself.

"Oh . . . well . . . it did, and now I'm supposed to ask you a bunch of questions about car crashes and showing naked butts on screen, and—"

"Claire . . ."

"It's a TV survey, about how programming affects people and whether it should be—"

"Claire."

"There's only nineteen questions, but if you don't have time, I understand. I mean, I hate telemarketers myself—"

"Just hold on a second," he interrupted. "If you want to talk to me, you have to let me get a word in."

"Sorry, I just—"

"Maybe more than one word, if you don't mind."

I started to apologize again, but held my tongue.

"It's bizarre that you called. I was just thinking about you."

Dear God, there was hope! "Really?"

"Well, cursing you, actually."

Shit. One step forward, seventeen back.

"You know, I've thought a lot about our relationship over the past few months, and even more over the past few days," he said, and my heart skipped a beat.

Our relationship.

"Things have been really screwed up between us."

"Tell me about it," I murmured.

"I want to be able to trust you."

"You can," I assured him. "Nothing happened with Neal . . . or Adam."

"Yeah, I know. Once I'd cooled off last night, I have to admit, I believed you."

"Thank you, Paul. I know that—"

"Hold on. You're jumping the gun. The fact that I believe you doesn't mean that everything's changed."

"It doesn't?" My fingernails dug into my palms.

"I think we have a lot to talk about, don't you?"

"Well, yes, but—"

"We don't communicate very well."

"True . . ."

"But, amazingly enough, after all that you've put me through, I still care about you."

Jackpot!

"I care about you, too."

"My friends think I'm crazy. Jared says I'm making a huge mistake by even considering this."

Don't listen to the drunken boobs you call friends!

Jared thought that if he was caught in a runaway elevator, jumping into the air right before impact would soften the blow. Jared was a complete idiot.

"Don't you think it's up to us?" I asked.

"Yes."

"So do I."

"But we need to straighten some things out."

"When?"

"Slow down, Claire. I don't want to rush into anything. Let's just ride out the next week, and plan a dinner for next weekend."

A whole week?

"The weekend is fine with me," I told him. Maybe knowing the glow at the end of the tunnel was candlelight would be enough to get me through the upcoming days.

"Let's go out on Saturday."

"Not Napoli." As if management would let any member of my family back in.

"Right." He laughed. "Not Napoli. I'll pick you up next Saturday at seven, okay?"

"That's perfect."

He paused for a moment. "I can't make you happy, Claire. It's up to you, you know."

"I know."

"I'm not saying I'm any better. I've got to make some changes too."

I didn't know whether the time was right, and it probably wasn't, but I jumped in anyway. It couldn't hurt to take a chance.

"Paul?"

"Yeah?"

"I love you." I bit my lip and waited far too long, my heart ricocheting against all of my other organs, for him to respond.

"I don't want you to take this the wrong way, but I'm not ready to say the same right now."

"Uh . . . okay." Painful but okay. There was no point holding back my feelings in fear.

"We have a lot to sort through."

"I know."

When I hung up the phone, Jason raced around the cube wall and raised one hand for a high-five.

"Woo-hoo!" His hand slapped mine. "You told him you love him!"

"He didn't say it back."

"He didn't?" Jason's hand dropped to his side.

"We're going out next weekend. To talk things over."

"So, there's a chance?"

"Yes." Despite Paul's hesitation to say the words, I knew, deep down, that we had a chance. We were both willing to work at a relationship, and that was more than half the battle. My smile was tentative, but a smile nonetheless.

I returned to my surveys until it was time for Neal's big meeting, when I filed into the conference room with the rest of the livestock.

He began with the usual overblown propaganda, followed closely by some self-indulgent horn-blowing and back-patting as he took all of the credit for a month of fantastic call statistics.

Eventually, his ego threatened to burst, and he had to move on to the real point of the meeting.

"We're going to be making some changes around the office," he said, rubbing his hands together.

"Here we go again," Jason murmured.

"Weekly potlucks?" Amy asked.

"Uh, no," Neal replied, obviously thinking of the ham salad botulism incident eleven of us experienced the last time we tried to get festive. "I'm talking about structural changes. Staffing changes."

"Fuck, a bunch of new hires," Jason whispered. "If they try to make me do the training again, I'm walking out."

"Streamlining is the word of the day," Neal continued.

"Does this mean layoffs?" I asked Jason.

"If it does, it won't be us. We've been here too long."

"I've got some handouts for you folks," Neal said, brandishing a stack of yellow paper for all of us to see.

"Sorry to interrupt, Neal," Carol called from the doorway. "Claire has a phone call."

Was it Paul, calling to say he couldn't wait all week to see me?

"We're in the middle of a meeting," Neal said.

"I know, but—"

"Can you take a message?" Neal asked.

"Yes," she sneered, "I can take yet another message for Claire. You know, with the number of personal calls she gets, I'm beginning to think she needs her own assistant."

"Well, I'm beginning to think you need . . ." I suddenly realized that all eyes and ears were focused on me. "Just tell whoever it is that I'll call them back."

The yellow sheets eventually reached me, and I took one, passing the stack on to Jason. At first glance, I couldn't comprehend the diagram in my hands.

"What is this?" I muttered.

"New office structure," Jason said. "It looks like we're splitting up into teams."

I searched for my name and found it at the bottom of one list, with no mention of my auditing position. No asterisk. No bold print. No parenthesis.

As if that weren't unnerving enough, Neal blew us all away with one sentence.

"The member of each team with the lowest call stats in a given month goes on probation."

The collective gasp could have been heard for blocks.

"If the same person ranks lowest three months in a row, they're gone. It's three strikes and you're out, folks."

"You can't do that," Heather said.

"Can and will," Neal told her.

"But if we're meeting our goals . . ."

"The rules have changed."

"But . . ."

"That's all I've got to say at the moment. Now, let's get back to the phones."

As my coworkers left the room, cursing and grumbling, I moved toward Neal.

"For the record, have I been demoted?"

"Uh . . . I wouldn't call it a demotion. You're just going back to your old job."

"That's a *demotion*, Neal," I snapped. "You promised me last night that I could keep my position as auditor."

"Nothing was set in stone."

"You said it was a 'deal.'"

"Listen, Claire, I had a phone conversation with Gord this morning and it was really rough going. Nothing is certain right now."

"But you told me—"

"He's coming in to meet with me today."

"This has nothing to do with—"

"It's every man for himself. Welcome to corporate America," he said, and walked out of the room.

I returned to my desk and found a pink memo on my keyboard. It was a message to call Laurie Mitchell.

Who in the hell was Laurie Mitchell?

I dialed the number and was both surprised and confused when a woman answered, "Tolan-Bernstein. How may I direct your call?"

Tolan-Bernstein was one of the largest advertising agencies in the city. Why on earth were they calling me?

I asked for Laurie and was told she was in a lunch meeting, so I left a message with my name and number, wondering what exactly was going on.

More concerned with the new stat situation in the office, I returned to the TV questionnaire and managed to get eleven finished before I needed a bathroom break. On my return through the reception area, Carol hissed, "Gord's here."

"Already?"

She looked angry that I'd cheated her out of the thrill of new gossip. "You knew he was coming?"

"Just one of the innumerable perks of sleeping with the boss," I snapped.

As soon as I rounded the corner, I ran directly into Gord's elbow.

"Claire?"

"Gord!" My heart pounded. "Nice to see you!"

Had he heard me?

"Claire." His bushy white eyebrows gathered.

Yes, he had.

"Uh, in case you happened to—"

"May I speak to you in private?"

"Sure." I tried to smile as he led me to the neglected corner office. The scene of my spinach debacle.

"How are things going?" he asked, once we were seated.

"Fine, thanks," I lied.

"I've been hearing quite a bit about you lately."

"Oh, good," I said. Maybe my auditing efforts wouldn't go unrewarded after all.

"Not so good, actually." He cleared his throat.

"Oh." My palms began to sweat.

"I understand your personal life has started to interfere with your work."

"My personal life?"

"In addition to what I'd already been told by Neal, I just overheard you tell Carol that—"

"I was joking."

"Hardly appropriate, if it was indeed a joke. Claire," he sighed, "Neal said that—"

"Gord, he—"

"He said your work has been suffering due to problems at home, and issues with your coworkers."

That little twerp had turned Gord against me! Well, I wasn't going without a fight.

"He's just trying to protect his job."

"From what?"

"Disappearing. He knows that he can't run this place by himself. He just demoted me from an auditing position to make himself look good."

"There are rumors circulating that you and he had a bit of a . . . *tryst*." Gord winced. "And, from what Neal has explained to me, you're having a hard time dealing with the demise of the relationship."

I couldn't speak. I thought the rage would boil right through my skin.

"This is precisely the reason Alta Media frowns upon intraoffice romance."

"Gord," I croaked.

"I'm going to do my best to come up with a solution to this problem. Naturally, I'd be pleased if you both continued to work for me, but I'm afraid I have to put the business first when I consider our options."

"But . . ." Was I being *fired?*

"We'll work all of this out."

"Does that mean—"

Gord checked his watch. "Oh, I've got to run. Neal and I are meeting with some new clients for lunch." He stood and shook my hand. "I hope you'll think about what I've said."

I nodded. I wouldn't be able to think about anything else.

After Gord left, I sat for a few minutes, trying to collect myself. He hadn't even given me a chance to explain about Neal! What kind of a boss would only listen to one side of the story? And Neal's new plan of probation, then termination? It was ridiculous! We already had to deal with call monitoring, stats, and low pay. What more did they want? The longer I thought about it, the more certain I was that I had to get out of Alta Media. I'd heard our rival, Torch Enterprises, was hiring, but did I want to just leap from one telemarketing hole to another?

I sighed and stalked out of the room, only to be flagged down by Carol, who was pointing at her phone receiver.

"She's on her way over," she said. "Just a moment."

"What?" I asked, moving toward her.

"Phone call, you moron," she snarled, lifting her hand from the mouthpiece and passing it to me.

"Hello?"

"Hi, Claire. This is Laurie Mitchell."

"Oh, hi."

Carol sat and watched me, making no attempt to hide her interest.

"I'm sorry it took so long to get in touch. It's been an incredible week."

"That's okay." Who was she?

"I got your résumé right before I left on a business trip to Dallas and I just didn't have time to call."

"Oh." My *résumé*?

Carol rolled her eyes, apparently bored, and stalked off to the break room.

"I don't usually go in for this favoritism bit, but we've been using these temps that just aren't working out, and when we advertise we get swamped with applicants. I simply don't have time to deal with picking through all of that mail. Anyway, it's an entry-level position, and sometimes Mother really does know best, so I thought we should talk."

"Mother knows best?" It was like listening to another language. What was she talking about?

"My mother. Marjorie Walden."

The name sounded awfully familiar.

"When your mom contacted her, it was like a sprint down memory lane, and the two of them talked for a couple of hours. I met your mother at dinner the other night, and she's a riot! I can't believe all of the craziness those two got up to in nursing school."

"Me neither," I mumbled. Oh, yeah. Marjorie Walden.

"Your mom mentioned how unhappy you are at work, mine told her how difficult it is for me to find decent people to hire, and here we are."

"Yes. Here we are." Lost in another dimension.

"I see you don't have any advertising experience, but it looks like you've done a lot of customer service work. The position I'm trying to fill is sort of a receptionist-slash-gofer slot, so there's a lot of customer and employee contact, which seems like it would be up your alley. I know this is fast, but our current receptionist is moving to Los Angeles and just gave her notice. I'm beyond desperate. Is there a possibility of meeting today?"

"Today?"

"Maybe on your lunch hour?"

I felt like God had just reached down from the heavens and kissed my forehead. In a matter of seconds I agreed to meet her and copied the address onto a scrap of paper.

I hung up the phone, grinning like a madwoman, until I glanced down at my blouse and raced back to my cube.

"Heather," I gasped, as I peered at her over the wall. "I need a favor."

"What kind of a favor?"

"I need to borrow your shirt."

"My what?"

"Look, you've got a T-shirt on under it. Can I just borrow your blouse for my lunch hour?"

"What for?"

"I don't really want to go into it."

She pouted. "Well, I don't really want to loan it out."

"Just give it to her," Jason said, from his seat.

"Not until she tells me what it's for."

"It's a job interview, okay?"

"Oh," she gasped. "Where?"

"I'll . . . uh, tell you about it when I get back."

She reluctantly shed her lavender blouse and I ran to the rest room to change my shirt, and hopefully more.

EPILOGUE

After much discussion, encouragement, and coercion, Mom returned to Omaha on the arm of my father. They are seeing a marriage counselor and working through issues on a day-by-day basis. I have high hopes for the survival of their relationship, and I think they do too. It hasn't been easy for them, as the Don Estes affair was a very hot topic in their tight-knit suburb, and it was hard for Mom to look anyone in the eye in those first, tenuous weeks. Luckily, Mavis Carter was recently the victim of a botched boob job, and the gossip spotlight has moved on to a new target (or two).

It took a few days for Steph to come around on the Mom and Dad issue, but with a little nudging from Alison, she did patch things up with them, and even threw in an apology for her behavior. During a long heart-to-heart session, Steph admitted she'd only gone into nursing to please Mom, and she quit her job at the retirement home. She and Alison pooled their resources to start a gay and lesbian newspaper. There's no entertainment or living section, no sports, travel, or employment. They only cover serious issues, the "straight news," as it were.

I heard through the grapevine that Heather and Adam Carello dated for a couple of months before the romance fizzled out. She's currently seeing an Amway salesman from Gresham and he's dating a hairdresser from an expensive salon in Lake Oswego, so neither Heather or Adam has to talk much. I think it's best that they're both playing "listener" roles in their respective relationships.

Jason informs me that Carol is smiling on a regular basis, now that she's seeing a restaurant manager. She's back on the meat track after an ambitious sausage breakfast on their second date. She's still into pleather, but Jason caught her wearing suede shoes last Wednesday.

Gord observed a few of Neal's staff meetings, watched him work, and sent him to some kind of middle-management camp in Boise to work out the kinks. Danielle finally dumped him and he says he's taking a break from dating until Steph relinquishes her lesbian lifestyle.

It's going to be a long wait, and women of the free world thank him for holding out, I'm sure.

Jason is marrying a rather high-maintenance anarchist next summer. The plan is no white dress, no church ceremony, no wedding bands, and, judging by the brown bag lunches he's been taking to work since he annihilated his bank account pursuing her, no money.

I love my job at Tolan-Bernstein a good seventy-five percent of the week. The rest of the time, I just like it. It's a lot of work, but there's enough variety in my day that I never feel worn out on the bus ride home. There's a junior copyeditor job opening up, due to a transfer, and I might just apply. I may not stand a chance of getting it, but I'm learning that sometimes it pays to try new things.

I have my mother to thank for my new career, and I've

done so at least a thousand times. Who knew that her middle-aged networking could be so successful? I know now that I should have listened to her more often, that her endless suggestions weren't meant to be criticisms, and she truly was trying to help me the only way she knew how.

My dinner with Paul ended with breakfast, thanks to a lot of talking and more than a few sparks between us. We are thinking about moving in together, but we're not quite ready yet. He's working on his electrician's apprenticeship right now and fears his study time would be compromised if we shared living space.

I'm very happy with him, and with our life together, but, as I told Mom, we're handling the relationship in baby steps.

Of course, she deliberately misunderstood and mailed me a box filled with tiny knitted booties.

I love her very dearly, but subtle she is not.